Praise for Tim Maleeny

GREASING THE PIÑATA
The Third Cape Weathers Mystery

2009 Winner of the Lefty Award, Best Humorous Mystery

"Maleeny is the kind of writer that makes you want to jump in the passenger seat and go for the ride—okay, maybe with eyes jammed shut and your hands gripping the armrest—but then you want to go again."

—Don Winslow, #1 *New York Times* bestselling author

"Tim Maleeny nails it with this new installment from Cape Weathers. It's an intriguing murder mystery crossed with a fast-paced political thriller. The whole thing is tied together with a witty protagonist and a finely tuned sense of humor. In Greasing the Piñata, just as in Mexico, anything can happen, and most of it does."

—Bill Fitzhugh, award-winning author of *Pest Control*

"Maleeny smoothly mixes wry humor and a serious plot without sacrificing either in his third Cape Weathers mystery...an appealing hero, well-crafted villains, snappy dialogue and an energetic plot."

—*Publishers Weekly*

"A cracking good mystery definitely not for the faint of heart but just right for readers who like a gritty crime novel with a labyrinth of plot twists."

—*Library Journal*

"The Cape Weathers novels are smart, snappily written, energetic mysteries starring an engaging hero."

—*Booklist*

BEATING THE BABUSHKA
The Second Cape Weathers Mystery

"The snappy writing and a parallel plot of drug-dealing Italian and Chinese mobsters keeps the pace lively and will resonate with Elmore Leonard fans."

—Publishers Weekly

"Maleeny does a nice job of showing us the cutthroat side of the movie industry. Keep 'em coming."

—Booklist

STEALING THE DRAGON
The First Cape Weathers Mystery

2008 IPPY Award Bronze Medal Winner
2008 Macavity Award Finalist, Best First Novel
2008 Nominee of the Rocky Award by LCC
2008 Nominee of the Arty Award by LCC
IMBA Killer Book of the Month

"Tough, original, compelling—a perfect thriller debut."

—Lee Child, New York Times bestselling author

"Readers will want to see more of Cape and Sally."

—Library Journal

BOXING THE OCTOPUS

Also by Tim Maleeny

Jump

The Cape Weathers Investigations
Greasing the Piñata
Stealing the Dragon
Beating the Babushka

BOXING THE OCTOPUS

A CAPE WEATHERS MYSTERY

TIM MALEENY

Poisoned Pen
PRESS

Published by Poisoned Pen Press, an imprint of Sourcebooks
P.O. Box 4410, Naperville, Illinois 60567-4410
(630) 961-3900
sourcebooks.com

Library of Congress Cataloging-in-Publication Data
Names: Maleeny, Tim-author.
Title: Boxing the octopus / Tim Maleeny.
Description: Naperville, IL : Poisoned Pen Press, [2019] | Series: A Cape Weathers
investigation
Identifiers: LCCN 2019021335 | (hardcover : acid-free paper)
Subjects: | GSAFD: Mystery fiction.
Classification: LCC PS3613.A4353 B69 2019 | DDC 813/.6—dc23 LC record avail-
able at https://lccn.loc.gov/2019021335

Printed and bound in the United States of America.
SB 10 9 8 7 6 5 4 3 2 1

For Phil Zinn
Driving a 1966 Thunderbird

"The development of San Francisco's underworld in all likelihood would have proceeded according to the traditional pattern and would have been indistinguishable from that of any other large American city.

"Instead, owing almost entirely to the influx of gold-seekers and the horde of gamblers, thieves, harlots, politicians and other felonious parasites who battened upon them, there arose a unique criminal district that was the scene of more viciousness and depravity, but which at the same time possessed more glamour, than any other area of vice and iniquity on the American continent."

—Herbert Asbury
*The Barbary Coast: An Informal History
of San Francisco's Underworld*

1

As he suspected, the village was full of misery, fear, and blood.

The Doctor adjusted his headphones, cranking the volume. After visiting the first two villages, he couldn't get the sounds of dying out of his head.

Nothing a little Katy Perry or Ariana Grande couldn't fix.

It wasn't his fault these people were born on the ass end of the planet. One thing he'd learned in medical school is life is cheap, and not everybody gets to live in the first world. Or even in the same century.

There were over a hundred cities in China with populations in excess of a million people, but this wasn't one of them. After a three-hour drive from the urban sprawl and pollution of Beijing, the Doctor crested a mountain range at the border of Hebei province. The Toyota Land Cruiser barely fit on the dirt track running to the village from the main road, the terrain as inhospitable as the surface of Mars. Some of the homes were only accessible by foot.

The Doctor stepped gingerly into the temporary structure erected on the outskirts of the village. The cots were full, most of them occupied by young children and their grandparents. As cities grew and jobs disappeared from rural China, many teenagers and able-bodied adults left family behind in the villages and headed to the nearest city, in hopes of bringing prosperity back home one day. The Doctor knew that day would never come.

These people were dead before they were born.

One of the nurses handed him a clipboard, but the Doctor already knew what it would reveal. He didn't have to take off the headphones or listen to her nervous voice explain that everyone who took the placebo was doing fine, but over twenty percent of the patients who took the new drug were writhing in agony, blood seeping from their ears, eyes, and nose.

Three weeks to the day since the drug was ingested. Just like the trials in Tunisia and Angola.

Two more sewers where years of work and millions of dollars got flushed down the drain.

The Doctor thumbed the controls on his phone and skipped over Beyoncé to find a better tune. He needed a new playlist. Beyoncé was overrated, and he desperately needed to cheer the fuck up.

He stepped outside onto the barren earth and stood under the unforgiving sun. The Doctor didn't want forgiveness, and the irony that this place was hot as Hell wasn't lost on him.

As his SUV bounced along the rutted road and the village shrank in his rearview mirror, he passed the convoy of mercenaries coming from the opposite direction. They were late, and he wasn't going to wait around to give them instructions. This was the third village, and they knew the drill. After Tunisia, the Doctor made sure they brought enough propane to keep the burn pit going for days.

…you just gotta ignite the light, and let it shine…

It was almost as if Katy Perry had written that song just for this moment. The Doctor hummed along as he grabbed the satellite phone from the passenger seat. The song would be over soon, and he needed to make a phone call. He kept his eyes on the road ahead as he dialed, not sparing another glance in the rearview mirror.

He had witnessed enough death for one day.

2

No one should witness his own murder.

The thought didn't occur to Hank because he had other things on his mind.

His partner was fifteen minutes late. Not the end of the world if you're giving someone a ride to the airport, but a very big deal when you have five million dollars in your vehicle.

Time to go, Lou.

The armored car squatted on the pier, its fat tires clutching the broken asphalt. San Francisco Bay sloshed lazily in his side mirror, and the engine vibrations threatened to rock Hank to sleep. Coffee wasn't an option unless he felt like pissing in a bottle, and his aim wasn't what it used to be.

Hank fingered the cross around his neck and considered asking God to find his partner or grant him the divine power of telepathy so he could summon the dipshit from the other side of the pier.

Where the fuck are you?

Lou didn't answer. Neither did God.

The backside of Pier 39 was almost deserted, only restaurant employees cutting behind the buildings where they worked. Although this access road was quiet, Hank knew the main thoroughfare of the pier was buzzing this time of day, clogged with families from a dozen countries navigating an obstacle course of souvenir shops and chain restaurants on their quest to find the sea lions swimming at the end of the pier.

Visited over ten million times a year, Pier 39 had become San Francisco's leading tourist attraction, and none of the locals could understand why.

For Hank the pier was simply a job. It was also proof that even a natural beauty like San Francisco could look like a tramp if you dressed her like one.

He had parked along a narrow strip of asphalt running behind the pier, in the shadow of a crooked line of buildings on the east side. This was the last stop before the pier opened onto the street and he drove to the bank.

To his right, the rear entrances of the merchants, and on his left, a wooden railing to protect drunken tourists from falling into the adjacent marina. Sailboats, motorboats, and skiffs bobbed gently in the current from the bay. Hank caught the smell of dead fish every time he breathed through his nose, even though he couldn't roll down the windows in the armored car.

Hank twisted in his seat and looked to the uppermost level, almost directly above him. A lone window, curtains open, but no sign of movement.

She's minding the store. Doesn't have time to wave at you, dumbass.

Hank smiled and felt himself relax. Maybe Lou had found himself a girlfriend on the pier, too. There was a reason Hank preferred making the pickups instead of waiting in the car, but today was his turn to drive.

He glanced at the sloping driveway at the front of the pier, scanning traffic like he was trained to do. Taxis and cars drifted past, a monotonous blur of color.

A forklift emerged from the back of an eighteen-wheeler parked on the shoulder of the main road. The semi was too heavy for the pier, so the forklift turned off the street, boxes stacked high, and headed down the ramp. Hank had parked closer to the marina railing than the stores, so there would be plenty of room for the narrow forklift to pass. His only job was to sit tight.

Hank watched the forklift bounce and shimmy toward him.

A UPS truck followed a moment later, just narrow enough to fit on the ramp. The driver angled to avoid scraping the under-carriage, and Hank got a clear view of the man behind the wheel.

It was Lou.

It took a second to register a familiar face in a confusing context. By the time it clicked, there was nothing Hank could do.

The forklift spun violently against Hank's front bumper, the steel arms sliding beneath the armored car. The boxes were empty, collapsing and temporarily obscuring Hank's view. A metallic scream rose with the arms of the forklift. Hank's world swooned as his front wheels left the surface of the road.

As the broken boxes fell to the ground, the forklift driver leapt from the cab and ran toward the main road. His work was done.

Hank locked eyes with Lou as the UPS truck slammed mer-cilessly into the back of the forklift, driving it under the armored car like a wedge. The car reared backwards, balancing on its rear wheels for a sickening instant before flipping onto its roof.

The day wasn't supposed to go down like this.

Sparks flew as the car skidded across the asphalt and crashed through the wooden railing at the end of the pier. Free fall, and then the armored car struck the water. Hank bit through his tongue, the blood tasting like an unpaid debt.

He was upside down and sinking, and he couldn't roll down the window. Boats sloshed into view through the windshield. He threw his weight against the door but only a small gap appeared. Water poured in, drowning any hope of escape.

He tried to take a deep breath, but the frigid water had other ideas. Reflexively, Hank reached for the gun on his hip, but the small part of his brain still working remembered the glass was bulletproof.

The car hit bottom twenty feet down, the water green and murky.

Dashboard lights reflected off the windows, transforming them into mirrors. The only thing Hank could see was himself. He stared at his reflection as the water rose, a lone witness to his own fear.

By the time the water crested above his chin, it was a face he barely recognized, wearing an expression he'd never seen before.

He looked like a man who didn't want to die.

3

Cape Weathers looked like a man who wanted to kill someone.

He glanced at his desk and wondered if he could use his stapler as a bludgeon. The client sitting across from him followed his gaze but kept talking.

A self-important and bellicose man, Roger Simmons was a San Francisco divorce lawyer known for big settlements and famous clients. His cuff links cost more than Cape's car, and his droning voice could make Lady Justice wish she were deaf as well as blind.

The stapler wasn't going to work. Cape scanned the cluttered desk, wondering where he'd put his letter opener.

"Distracted?" Roger's voice rose an octave.

"Disgusted." Cape abandoned his search and looked his client square in the eyes.

"Excuse me?"

"You hired me because you were worried about your wife."

"No." Roger sat up straighter and pulled his gut away from the edge of the desk. "I hired you because I thought my wife was cheating."

"You implied she was missing," said Cape.

"I said she'd run out," said Roger. "What's the difference?"

Cape set his elbows on the desk and rubbed his temples, his

blue eyes almost gray in the subdued light of the office. The unexpected detour along the bridge of his nose spoke of past conflicts that didn't get resolved from behind a desk.

"I find people," said Cape. "That's what I'm good at. It's why people hire me."

"So?" said Roger. "You found her."

"She wasn't really missing."

Roger pointed across the desk, his index finger both judge and jury. "What else did you find?"

"I found that you were already cheating on her," said Cape. "With two different women, one of whom is also married."

Roger's mouth opened and closed a few times before the words became small enough to emerge. "You...followed...*me?*"

"You hired me to investigate." Cape shrugged. "So I investigated."

"But I'm the one paying you."

"I'm paying you back." Cape took a check from his drawer and placed it on the desk in front of Roger. Cape felt stress flow out of him.

Who needs yoga when you can fire your client?

Roger's face turned purple. "Are you banging my wife?"

"I've never met her," said Cape. "But now that you mention it, she is very attractive." He shuffled some papers out of the way. "Have you seen my letter opener?"

Roger came halfway out of his chair. "You're supposed to be a private investigator!"

"This is a private matter," said Cape. "And it should stay that way."

"I thought private dicks helped people get divorced."

"I'm not a dick, Roger, you are," said Cape. "And that's not my job description." He sighed. "But I'm the idiot who took your case. Sorry I wasted your time."

Roger blinked like a broken traffic light. "What?"

"Go home, talk to your wife," said Cape. "And try to stop being an asshole."

"I hired *you*," said Roger. "You can't fire *me*."

"Maybe your conscience hired me and forgot to tell you."

Before Roger could reply, Cape held up a hand, stepped away from his desk, and walked to the open window. He needed some fresh air.

The office was longer than it was wide, the furniture as well-worn as a comfortable shoe. To the right of the desk was a leather couch that looked like it sometimes doubled as a bed, the middle cushion visibly lower than the other two. A cluttered bookcase covered the opposite wall, worn paperback novels stacked alongside legal volumes and local directories. Cape ran his fingers along the spines of the books as he crossed the room.

Roger stood abruptly, his chair falling over backwards. Cape heard the crash but didn't turn around as his ex-client stomped to the door. When he reached the threshold, Roger turned and muttered loud enough for Cape to hear.

"*I'm going trash you on Yelp!*"

Then he slammed the door.

Cape almost smiled. He'd been punched, stabbed, strangled, and shot, and more than a few times, he'd found people that others believed were lost forever. Most of his business came from referrals—people talking to people in the analog world. Yet now his reputation depended on some loser with a laptop.

He wasn't sure if he'd chosen the wrong profession or was born in the wrong century. Probably both. This wasn't the first client Cape had fired, and it probably wouldn't be the last, but it was starting to feel like a pattern. Or a sign.

Cape looked toward the bay, hoping to catch a glimpse of some sailboats. He had a narrow view across the Embarcadero, the sloping boulevard that encircled the city. The view would be worth every penny of his rent, if he paid any. Keeping a landlord's son out of jail can do wonders for the terms of your lease.

The neighborhood was spotty, too close to tourist traps for most residents and too far from downtown for most businesses, but still beyond his means. One day his landlord would knock on the door and apologetically inform Cape that a new, paying tenant was moving in, and that Cape had to move out.

Until then, Cape spent more time at the window than at his desk.

The only blemish on the face of his view was Pier 39, a cold sore caused by millions of tourists kissing their money goodbye. Like most locals, Cape only went near the pier to visit the hot dog stand. It stood as a lone sentry at the pier entrance, like a Beefeater guard made of actual beef. Today it was flanked by a fire truck and two police cruisers.

A crane loomed in the near distance, its impossibly long arm visible over a crowd forming on the driveway that ran behind the pier. Tourists weren't standing near the stores or any of the main attractions, so Cape wondered what all the commotion was about.

He thought it strange that so many people were holding umbrellas, even though there wasn't a cloud in the sky.

4

A false rain fell on the pier as the armored car spun clockwise overhead.

Suspended from the crane, it twirled like a drunken spider as brackish water spilled from the chassis, spraying gawkers on all sides.

Police divers had broken the side windows and jimmied the doors, looking for corpses and cash. They had surfaced empty-handed.

It took over an hour to borrow a crane from a construction site on Columbus Avenue, then position it adjacent to the marina. Divers rigged a cable around the four-ton vehicle, and the crane did what cranes do.

The car was still spitting water in random bursts as the crane lowered it onto the pier in agonizingly slow increments.

"You might wanna *move*."

Inspector Beauregard Jones waved at his partner, but Vincent Mango wasn't quick on his feet. A deluge of seawater, algae, and sea lions' piss sluiced over the detective's shoes.

A stream of invective poured from Vincent's mouth as the water ran along the cracks of the pier, leaving him soggy and stained. A woman standing beyond the yellow police tape covered her daughter's ears, but the little girl pushed her mother's hands away and leaned forward with eyes wide, taking mental notes on all the awesome new curse words she could hurl at her brother.

"Those were *Ferragamos*." Vincent looked miserably at his feet, which made loud squishing noises as he stepped away from the expanding shadow of the descending car.

"I like how you're already using the past tense," said Beau. "For a cop, you spend too much on clothes. It's never a good idea to dress better than the guys in Internal Affairs."

"Coming from a man whose idea of looking sharp is high-tops." Vincent unbuttoned his jacket as he walked over to Beau, his olive skin flushed with annoyance. His shoes made a *squish, squish, squishing* sound every step of the way.

Beau was a full head taller and almost eighty pounds heavier than his partner. Today he was wearing jeans and a black T-shirt, stretched tight around his ebony arms, which is what he wore every day. Vincent couldn't fault his sticking with a plainclothes look—buying a bespoke suit for that frame would cost more than either detective made in a month.

"Any prospects?" Beau kept his eyes on the armored car as Vincent casually scanned the crowd.

A pair of uniformed officers kept the circle of onlookers behind the yellow tape, while another cop stood next to the crane operator. A fourth lingered at the perimeter, waiting to assist the detectives in gathering evidence and interviewing any witnesses. But right now, all eyes except Vincent's were on the car.

The goal was to find someone who stuck around because they actually saw something. Find a real witness in a haystack of rubberneckers taking selfies in front of a crime scene. Facebook not only wrecked the news, it was ruining law enforcement.

Vincent reached ten o'clock on the circle when he spotted his first candidate. A woman in her forties strained against the yellow tape like a sprinter at the finish line, not conscious of the tension in her own body. She had grabbed Vincent earlier, as soon as he

"Some people forward their office phones to their cell phones."

"Didn't know you could do that."

"Jesus. Maybe you should try *old-fashioned* investigations. You could buy a fedora."

"Slow day at the precinct?"

"You happen to look out your window this morning?"

"Didn't have to, it's gone viral." Cape let his eyes drift back to his computer screen and the image of an armored car hoisted above the pier. "You were in the neighborhood and didn't come visit?"

"Me and Beau," said Vincent. "We were busy."

"But you're calling me now," said Cape.

"I'm helping you," said Vincent. "Your name dropped, and I wanted to give you a heads-up."

"Who dropped it?"

"Me."

Cape waited.

"We interviewed people on the scene," explained Vincent. "And a woman approached me—you might say she was distraught."

"And?"

"She's connected to a person of interest."

"How interesting is this person?"

"He's one of the drivers of the armored car."

Cape opened a new window on his computer. "Some rumors are circulating online."

"The bit about the diving gear is bona fide," said Vincent. "Found a fin, a strap used to secure a diving tank, and a broken mask." Cape heard Vinnie rustle some papers. "Woman's name is Vera—*Vera Young*—says her boyfriend is innocent. Driver's name is Hank Ryan. He and his partner are both missing."

"Missing?" Cape squinted against the glare from the windows, tried to visualize an armored car driving on the pier. "Doesn't look good for the boyfriend."

"She doesn't want to hear it."

"What do you think?"

"I think she knows I'm paid to hunt her man down," said Vincent. "She's not stupid—knew we'd get to her eventually and wants to steer us away from her guy. She's not bullshitting, if that's what you're asking. Definitely believes he's innocent."

"You think she's in denial."

"Aren't we all?" asked Vincent.

"If SFPD is on the case, I'm just an appendix."

"She wants a third party." Vincent's breath drifted across the phone line. "I gave her your name."

"Thanks," Cape replied without enthusiasm. "So, I'm a hand to hold."

"Nothing personal."

"Maybe my business cards should say *the placebo detective*."

"Catchy."

"You learn anything, you'll let me know?"

"Not necessarily."

Cape exhaled loudly. "Anything else?"

"It's not her fault the boyfriend's a fuckup."

"Never is."

Vincent said goodbye and Cape set the receiver down slowly, as if it had grown heavier during the call. He restarted the video on his laptop and watched the car spin hypnotically over the pier.

A sudden feeling of vertigo came over him, as if his world were about to be turned upside down.

6

Sally hung upside down and wondered if she was about to witness a rape.

She grasped the rope in both hands, body inverted, legs spread to balance her weight and make it easier to swing upright at a moment's notice. It was looking as if that moment had finally arrived.

The guy was in his late twenties. The woman looked younger. Sally guessed his height around six-two, the girl a head shorter. He probably outweighed her by fifty pounds.

Sally had followed them from the club, having sequestered herself on the rooftop across the street. Two women had been raped in as many weeks, but it hadn't hit the papers yet. In a tourist-conscious city like San Francisco, it typically took three serial assaults before newspaper editors risked annoying their drinking buddies in City Hall.

To the casual reader of *The Chronicle,* this was a picturesque city of cable cars, rolling fog, and the cloying smell of sourdough bread. You didn't notice the underlying stench unless you opened your eyes and read the police blotter.

Sally watched the man cajole the girl into the alley. She laughed nervously and stumbled, but he caught her by the arm and said something Sally couldn't catch. The woman was clearly drunk, her dress so short that Sally's own ass was getting cold looking at her.

Sally recalled the last time she'd worn a dress like that and closed her eyes, waiting for the memory to pass through her. She tasted bile and swallowed, grateful for the bitterness.

Things got ugly even faster than Sally expected.

The woman stopped laughing as she realized there wasn't an exit, just a dead-end alley and a rusting dumpster. A she turned around in confusion, the man punched her in the face.

She went down hard, banging her head on the pavement. He landed on top, knocking the wind out of her, and got one hand around the back of her neck. His other hand yanked her skirt up. The woman's eyes rolled back in terror, but she was too shocked to cry out, her mouth already slick with blood.

Sally spun backwards and released, a spider leaping from its web. She landed silently next to the dumpster, a few paces behind the man.

The woman's eyes almost crossed as she tried to focus on Sally, but her pupils were dilated by panic and booze.

She must think she's hallucinating.

Sally was dressed entirely in black, face smeared with lamp-black, long hair an ebony rope braided tightly. Even the shadows couldn't tell if she was real.

The man was unbuckling his belt when he noticed a change in expression on the woman's face, or maybe he sensed movement. As he twisted his head to look over his shoulder, Sally shattered his nose with the heel of her hand.

Cartilage collapsed into his nasal cavity, crumpling like rice paper. To Sally's ears, it was the sound of a thousand broken promises from her childhood.

The man squealed and fell backwards, clutching his face and tripping over the woman's legs. Blood flowed between his fingers, and his eyes were streaming tears.

Nothing like a broken nose to knock an asshole right on his ass.

Sally could have easily extended her arm during the strike, driving cartilage and bone fragments into the brain, but tonight she wanted to make a point. She wanted someone to spread the word.

As the man struggled to stand, Sally punched him in the right kidney, a short jab from her waist that lifted him off the ground. His knees buckled but Sally pivoted and caught him on the left side before he collapsed.

Symmetry in violence was important. She wanted him to piss blood in the morning.

A scarlet reminder of what a yellow bastard you are.

The woman could barely stand, but Sally got her upright and held her by the shoulders until both eyes came back into focus. Sally knew the woman needed a hug, but Sally didn't have one to give.

"Go back to the club and call the police." Sally softened her voice. "Send them here…and tell them *everything.*"

The woman nodded, arms wrapped around herself to stop the shaking as she left the alley behind. Sally crouched next to the prostrate predator, who was still conscious and moaning. Sally grabbed him by the hair and whispered in his ear like a lover.

"Every girl you'll ever meet might be just like me."

Then she slammed his head against the pavement, knocking him out cold.

Sally vaulted onto the dumpster and leapt straight up, grabbing the knotted end of her rope and swinging once, twice, and a third time before hooking a leg over the edge of the roof. She clambered onto her feet and coiled the rope around her arm before slinging it across her back.

Fog flowed across the roof and eddied around her feet. She watched it ooze sluggishly down the walls, spreading faster as it reached the warmer ground below. A cold blanket of comfort for anyone wandering the streets.

Sally decided she was done for the night. Cape had called to say there was a new investigation, which meant she might be working daylight hours for a change.

She disappeared into the fog, heading home, where memories from her childhood waited anxiously for her return.

7

Cape waited anxiously for the call and answered on the first ring.

"Mister Weathers?"

"Vera Young?" Cape heard a slight intake of breath, a moment's indecision. "Vincent...Inspector Mango said you might..."

"Of course." Her voice was strong but strained. "Would you be willing to come to the pier? I'm not sure I can do this over the phone."

"It's a pretty big pier," said Cape. "Where will I find you?"

"I run a store on the second level," she replied. "Walk past the Hard Rock and take the first staircase. At the top, look to the right and you'll see a children's clothing store. That's me."

The walk should have taken less than five minutes, but Cape strolled along the Embarcadero toward the marina where the armored car took a dive. Police had installed a plastic barricade where the wooden railing used to be, and most of the slips were empty. The boats were probably cruising the bay or temporarily docked elsewhere, while their owners made plans to sue the armored car company, the city, and anyone else they could.

No clues were hiding in plain sight.

As Cape moved closer to the pier, his feet got heavier with every step. Investigations like this always ended in tears, but his conscience said there wasn't a good reason to turn it down. Someone had to deliver bad news. If he didn't want to be that guy, then he had no business being in this business.

This wasn't the first time Cape thought about walking away, but now the notion seemed to be swimming just below the surface, a shark of discontent waiting for its next meal.

At the head of the pier, tourists and retail junkies were emerging from cabs, stepping off trolleys, or migrating on foot from Fisherman's Wharf. Cape merged with the crowd as it swept past the hot dog stand, topped by a three-dimensional placard of its famous wiener. A phallic signpost marking an invisible barrier that most locals never deigned to cross.

Straight ahead was a small stage where local acts performed, only a handful of stragglers pausing to watch. Cape sometimes heard echoes of the entertainers in his office. Any given night there might be a lone singer with a boom box, a soloist with a saxophone, a high school chorus, or a juggling act. Today it was an Elvis impersonator who clearly studied method acting, forty pounds overweight and high as a kite. The sequined prophet drew a sweaty hand across his forehead and launched into a herniated rendition of "A Little Less Conversation."

Cape veered to his right, looking for the secret staircase.

A trampoline nestled in a corner of the pier, a teenage girl bouncing giddily as nervous parents counted out the twenty minutes that cost them thirty dollars. Past the trampoline was the stairway.

Adjacent to the stairs was a small booth, its sides covered in aerial shots of San Francisco, the Golden Gate Bridge, and Alcatraz. A man in his twenties was calling out to passersby.

"Ever take a ride in a float plane?" The guy looked more surfer than pilot.

Cape spotted the plane tethered in the marina behind the pier, bright yellow and white, a single engine two-seater. "Do you fly the plane?"

"Fuck, no." The guy held up his hands. "Gerry's the pilot, went home for the day."

"How come you're still here?"

"A lot of people book the night before, come back the next day."

"How many?"

"Ten to fifteen a day, this time of year. High season we can turn twenty a day, easy."

"How much?"

"Hundred bucks for thirty minutes, one-seventy-five an hour. That's per person, but couples get a twenty percent discount."

Cape's eyebrows rose as he did the math.

"Interested?"

"Fascinated." Cape turned slowly, scanning the myriad shops in his immediate vicinity. He lost count before his head turned ninety degrees.

The pier was an optical illusion.

At first glance it seemed to be a cluster of colorful stores and restaurants, but a few steps, twists, and turns revealed side alleys with smaller shops, open performance spaces, and free-standing carts.

By the time tourists reached the marina on the west side of the pier where the sea lions swam, they had passed through an endless gauntlet of temptation. It reminded Cape of the floor plan in a Vegas hotel, forcing guests to walk through the casino on their way to the elevators.

Cape studied the foot traffic and thought about armored cars. Even on a slow day, this place was a gold mine. Like the pier he was standing on, there was much more to this case than he first thought.

Cape took the stairs two at a time.

8

Anastasia arranged the children two at a time, until they were all standing in a perfectly straight line. Then she tore their heads off, one by one.

She was careful not to break a nail as she pried her fingers into their necks. It was delicate work, and their little bodies were fragile. She laid the heads next to the torsos, adjusting their positions so she could stare into their unblinking, lifeless eyes.

The nesting dolls were hand-painted, the largest as big as her open palm, the smallest no bigger than a thimble. These *matryoshki* were imported from Russia by her uncle, who owned the store. Her older cousin managed a similar store in Los Angeles, and her two siblings, Sergey and Eva, handled deliveries and distribution.

Anastasia managed the San Francisco store on the pier. She was also responsible for quality control.

Every nesting doll had to be taken apart and examined. Many were given to children as gifts, so if a single doll had two halves stuck together, it might ruin the magic. That fragile moment of wonder when a child discovered another doll inside the first, and the second, until the tiniest of dolls was revealed.

Each *matryoshka* in front of her was painted to resemble a

Russian child in traditional dress, alternating *girl-boy-girl-boy* as they diminished in size. Anastasia stared at their eyes and smiled, thinking of the layers of clothes she wore as a young girl, remembering the braids in her hair.

The bell over the door chimed, breaking her reverie.

Anastasia scowled but kept her gaze on the dolls, fixing her place in memory. She took a breath, annoyed she hadn't locked the door. She rarely had visitors this late, but spring and summer brought so many tourists to San Francisco that people sometimes stumbled in after closing.

Anastasia looked up and found Sergey and Eva staring back at her, amused expressions on their faces.

"How are your children, Nastya?" Eva always called her sister by her nickname, less from affection than because it sounded like *nasty* in English. "Have you given the new dolls names?"

"Will you read them a story before you put them to sleep?" Sergey, always trying to sound clever, never quite pulling it off. "How will the little ones breathe when you put them back together?"

Anastasia stuck out her tongue. "You clowns are back early. Did you learn anything?"

Sergey looked at his feet as Eva took a sudden interest in the *matroyshki* lining the shelves. It was Eva who finally spoke.

"Neither driver has been found. The *politsiya* don't know anything."

"You know this?" Anastasia felt her jaw tighten.

Sergey nodded. "Our contact at the precinct swears to their ignorance."

"*Chush' sobach'ya!*" Anastasia resisted the urge to sweep the nesting dolls from the counter. "The armored car company is not responsible for the money?"

"We have the receipt from the driver," replied Eva. "From his pickup—but until the investigation is finished, insurance will not pay."

"Money was stolen, what more do they need to know?"

Eva shrugged. "Until the drivers are found, nobody knows if they were in on it, so the car company can't trust the receipts."

Sergey nodded. "It's a big circle of doubt."

"We will get our money." Eva held up her hands in appeasement. "Eventually."

"This was not *our* money," Anastasia snapped.

Sergey looked perplexed. "Of course not, Nastya, it was uncle's money—we know you like to be responsible, but try being patient."

"You don't know, do you?" Anastasia looked into the biggest doll's eyes as if they might hold the answer. "This last deposit, *it wasn't Uncle's money.*"

"But it came through the store," said Eva. "Didn't it?"

"It came from—" Anastasia started to say something but changed her mind. "It came from our new investors."

"Like a loan?"

"Yes, Eva," said Anastasia. "Exactly like a loan—a small business loan. So we can expand to new markets."

"And these investors aren't patient?"

"They are used to getting paid on time." Anastasia switched her gaze back to Sergey, who suddenly looked like a scared little boy. "You see the problem now, *govniuk*?"

Sergey winced at the verbal castration. "What do you want us to do, Nastya?"

"Find the drivers." Anastasia looked wistfully at her wooden children, each face alongside a matching body. On this counter, the world was still an orderly place. "Bring them here so I can tear their heads off."

Sergey and Eva left without another word, the door chime signaling their flight.

Anastasia's gaze drifted around the store. Hundreds of nesting dolls stared back in mute sympathy. She looked at their perfect braids and ran her fingers through her own hair, trying to remember the precise moment when her childhood was taken away.

Anastasia shook her head, turning her attention back to the disassembled figures on the counter. There was work to be done, and she was the responsible one.

She took a deep breath, flexed her fingers, and started putting the pieces back together.

9

Sally flexed her fingers and watched the pieces of dried blood crack and fall from her hands.

After the rusted flakes of the rapist's DNA had fallen into the sink, Sally studied them as if reading her fortune in tea leaves. Then she opened the tap until the water turned into a pink tornado and disappeared down the drain.

She scrubbed her hands twice before soaking a washcloth in hot water and holding it against her face. The lampblack came off in ebony streaks. A look in the mirror confirmed she still looked like a chimney sweep. It was several minutes before she was clean enough to take a bath.

Sally took off her clothes and examined herself for injury. She lacked any western sense of vanity but liked what she saw, a nearly perfect physique marred only by a constellation of scar tissue. Smooth lines and taut muscle were punctuated by an occasional bruise here and there.

It was a body forged over a lifetime for a single purpose. After a wasted childhood she was finally putting it to good use.

In the Japanese tradition, the water was a few degrees above the temperature of blood, which always felt hotter when it was outside the body. Sally let herself slip underwater and closed her eyes, holding her breath until her past swam forward to the present.

Sally five years old, sits in the backseat, her parents driving.

Sally counted under the water. After a minute she opened her eyes but stayed beneath the surface, watching the bubbles escape from her nose.

Headlights fill the windshield as the sound of a truck's horn fills her ears.

Sally let her buoyancy change as air fled her lungs. For a moment she hung suspended, weightless between the world of the living and the world below.

Orphaned, Sally travels to Hong Kong with her nanny, Li Mei.

She stayed perfectly still and kept counting. Two minutes is a lifetime when you can't breathe.

Sally is enrolled in a school that teaches young girls how to defend themselves.

Images of friends flashed before her eyes as spots appeared at the edges of her vision. All ghosts, only their memories alive.

A school where girls learn how to kill with their hands but without remorse.

As Sally sank to the bottom of the tub, the room slipped away, and she saw the faces she'd been waiting for—her mother and father—telling her to wait just a little while longer.

A school run by the Chinese Triads.

Sally broke the surface and sucked a lungful of air, an involuntary smile breaking across her face. If your childhood friend was Death, there is nothing as nostalgic as drowning.

Sally, the star pupil, flees to America, the land of her father's birth.

Sally grasped both sides of the tub and stood, feeling clearheaded and calm. Drying herself, she walked naked to her bedroom, a small chamber behind the *dojo* where she taught her students how to defend themselves. Her bed was a simple mattress on tatami mats.

Sally held the image of her parents as she closed her eyes, hoping for sweet dreams of a childhood that ended too soon.

10

Never was a childhood as magical as the window of a toy store.

Giraffe's Best Friend was the second shop on the elevated walkway. Tiny mannequins frolicked alongside giant stuffed animals in a cardboard jungle, the eponymous giraffe front and center. The clothes on the plastic kids were playful and stylish, Baby Gap as reimagined by Willy Wonka and Donna Karan.

A sign flipped to *Closed* hung inside the glass door. Cape knocked and waited, idly wishing he could dress as well as a five-year-old.

Vera Young wasn't as old as her telephone voice suggested. As she unlocked the door, Cape guessed she was about his age, old enough to know better but still young enough to make bad choices. Auburn hair and a figure somewhere between comfortable and distracting. As she stepped aside to let him in, Cape got a good look at her eyes, dark brown and impossibly sad.

"Mister Weathers?"

"Cape." He shook her hand and forced a smile, which she returned with some effort.

"Vera."

She relocked the door behind him. A cash register sat on a counter to the left, floor-to-ceiling clothing racks ran along each wall. In the center of the store, a sense of wonder was palpable even with no kids around.

Low tables and chairs covered with wooden blocks, puzzles, and games, too small for anyone over the age of six. Standing sentry around the table was a ring of stuffed animals, each one taller than any toddler by at least a foot. They looked noble but well-used, grateful recipients of daily hugs. Cape visualized parents trying in vain to get their kids to leave the store.

"Let's go in back." Vera led the way through a maze of clothing and toys. "I don't want anyone to think we're open."

At the back of the store was a patchwork curtain, pulled aside to reveal a door. The back room was barely four by ten, just wide enough for a desk on the left and a small cot on the right. A single window overlooked the service road and marina below. Directly opposite, at eye level, was the outsized edifice of the aquarium.

Vera took the desk chair and gestured to the cot.

Cape sat down slowly. "You sleep here?"

"Not often." She looked out the window. "Naps occasionally, after a long day when I know I'll have to do paperwork later. I don't like to work at home."

"Where's that?"

"Burlingame."

"That's quite a commute."

"Forty minutes on a good day, but this is the best location for my store to turn a profit, though it's barely a living since my rent increased." Vera shrugged. "I get to make clothes, something I wanted to do since I was a kid."

"You design these clothes yourself?"

"About half of what I sell in the store," said Vera, with no small about of pride. "I work with a woman on the peninsula who does the manufacturing."

'That's impressive," said Cape, and it was. He was sitting across from a woman who ran a business and could make clothes, while the only thing he knew how to make was trouble. "You have kids of your own?"

"I had a daughter." Vera's face clouded and cleared in an instant.

Cape replayed her answer in his head to make sure he'd heard the tense correctly, then cursed himself for asking the wrong question. Small talk was meant to get clients relaxed before he transformed into an intrusive bastard.

"I don't have kids," said Cape.

"That's too bad, they change everything."

"I imagine they like coming to your store." It was the best recovery he could manage. "But you called me about something else."

Vera smiled, maybe at the compliment, more likely at finally cutting through the bullshit. She took a breath before letting the words rush across the room.

"Hank is innocent."

Cape waited.

"Inspector Mango, and his partner—"

"Beau," said Cape. "Inspector Jones, he's also with the Personal Crimes Division. On bigger cases they often work together."

"They were both very nice, but..." Her voice trailed off before regaining its pitch. "They don't know a damn thing."

"They only know what they know." Cape chose his next words carefully. "That means what they can prove, not what someone tells them."

"I told them Hank didn't do anything wrong."

"Does Hank own scuba gear?"

"I know how it looks." She turned back toward the window. "He's out there somewhere. They just haven't found him."

"They're looking."

"I don't mean out there, hiding," she said. "I mean out *there*, in the water."

Cape studied her reflection in the window, distorted by imperfections in the glass. She had aged a thousand years since he'd arrived.

"What do you want me to do?"

"Find Hank," she said. "Prove he's innocent."

"What if he's not?"

"The police said you were good."

"I'm competent."

"*A good man.* That's what they said."

"Maybe." Cape paused. "That's why I asked a question you chose not to answer."

"You know these officers."

"For many years," said Cape. "If that's a problem, I could recommend another private invest—"

"No," said Vera. "I like that—I liked *them*. This isn't personal, I just need someone who can talk to them, someone they might respect. Someone who isn't me." She tried again. "They have their job to do—"

"—and their job is to put someone in jail."

"*Yes.*" Vera almost lunged out of her chair. "And Hank isn't a criminal."

"But he is a suspect." It sounded harsh, but a delusional client was just a lawsuit waiting to happen. "I may not be able to help you."

"You sound like you don't want to help me."

"I doubt I can," said Cape. "Hank is missing, and even if you don't believe everything you've seen on *CSI*, the police have more resources than I do."

"How much do you charge?"

Cape considered inflating his day rate to discourage her, but Vinnie warned she wouldn't take no for an answer. He quoted a number. She didn't flinch.

"When can you start?"

Cape didn't answer at first. He stood and looked out the window at the marina, a lone sailboat bobbing in the water, silver masts reflecting lights from the pier in a constantly shifting, drunken constellation. He thought of armored cars and millions in cash, ancient shipwrecks and lost gold, and wondered if mermaids played poker with the treasure they found on the sea floor.

He tried to think of anything other than the words he was about to say.

"I'll get started right away."

11

"Get started right away."

The Doctor waited for the inevitable stream of expletives before saying anything else.

It came in a torrent of Cantonese that he struggled to follow, but the Doctor kept himself calm by counting from *yat* to *sup* before it came to a halt. He adjusted the phone against his ear and plowed ahead in English, in part to assert control over the conversation but also to annoy the bureaucrat on the other end of the line.

"I gave you the modifications," the Doctor said blandly. "And we already picked the next village, so what's the problem?"

He squinted through the windshield, traffic growing dense in both directions. Miles ahead, the road would expand like a snake eating a rabbit, fifty lanes wide by the time he reached Beijing.

His brow furrowed as he tried to do the math. "Okay, so how much can you make?" In the near distance, a cluster of skyscrapers cloaked in brown haze dominated an otherwise flat horizon. The closer he got to the city, the harder it would be to breathe.

But in another three hours he'd be on a private jet with an open bar.

"Then wait," the Doctor said. "I said wait—*deng hou.*" He took his foot off the gas, realizing he'd been accelerating every time he raised his voice. "Say again?"

He pulled to the side of the road as a truck rumbled past. The shoulder was too narrow but driving distracted in this country was tantamount to suicide. Traffic accidents caused more deaths in China than cancer or any disease the Doctor had ever diagnosed. In countries around the world, cancer was the great equalizer, but in China it was the automobile.

"How could anyone hold you responsible for something that never happened?" He paused to let that sink in. "Just fucking *deng hou*. We'll be getting more of the compound soon, and I want to supervise the modifications personally."

The voice on the other end sounded mollified, but the Doctor knew anger often decays into fear. "I'm coming to the island."

He hung up and checked the mirror, searching for an opening in an unbroken line of cars that stretched as far as the eye could see. He needed to get back on the road if he wanted to arrive at the airstrip before dark.

Then the Doctor would tell the pilot to fly over the horizon and land in the middle of the ocean.

12

The bacon landed in the middle of the plate, and Cape felt his heart skip a beat.

The waiter tossed the extra side of bacon on top of the pancakes with a carelessness that bordered on rude, but Cape didn't take it personally. The waiter was probably jealous.

Cape's only concern was that the thrill of seeing bacon, eggs, and pancakes together on one plate had triggered a massive coronary and he was already in heaven. Or that other place. He took a quick bite before the Devil could steal his fork.

Inspector Beauregard Jones succumbed to one of the seven deadly sins and studied the meal with envy. He glanced at his own small bowl of fruit with open disdain.

"You could've ordered the pancakes," said Beau. "I was prepared for that."

"I did."

"I mean *just* the pancakes," said Beau. "Like, breakfast for one, instead of picking up the slack for both of us." He speared a strawberry and swallowed it whole.

"I ordered first," replied Cape. "Didn't realize you were on a diet."

"Twenty years a cop," said Beau, "and the biggest threat to

my survival is scrambled eggs. My doctor thinks cholesterol is going to kill me."

"Tragic." Cape ladled syrup onto the pancakes.

"You're a dick."

"I break my leg, you plan to start using crutches?"

"A little empathy would be nice."

"There's too much cholesterol in empathy." Cape took a slice of bacon between his thumb and forefinger and studied it like an art student painting his first nude.

Beau's arm shot across the table like a cobra. He snatched the bacon and, before Cape could react, it had vanished behind Beau's grinning teeth. "Beats taking a bullet." He raised his hand to signal the waiter. "You're buying."

"No problem," said Cape. "I'm on an expense account."

Beau nodded, glanced over the railing to his right and wrinkled his nose. "Should've sat inside."

The Eagle Cafe was on the second level of the pier. Its balcony overlooked the north marina, where a motley assortment of smaller boats surrounded a floating dock. The far end of the dock was the tourist magnet that pulled all the visitors across the pier like so many iron filings. That was where the sea lions played.

Over fifty sea lions regularly jostled for position on the floating dock. Each weighed at least two hundred pounds, and at this time of day they were sleeping on top of each other. Every few minutes a restless sea lion would shimmy its oblong body into a better position, until it had enough leverage to force its neighbors back into the water.

The displaced sea lion would swim around the marina, gathering momentum until it could vault onto the pier. Its impact was met by angry barking from the snoozing sea lions, who could be heard as far away as Alcatraz.

You could smell them from where Cape and Beau were sitting.

"I wanted to meet on the pier," said Cape.

Beau nodded. "Impressions of your new client?"

"Anxious…smart…worried…cautious." Cape paused before adding, "vulnerable…attractive."

"Watch out for those last two, Achilles."

"I traded my white horse in for a Mustang convertible," said Cape. "Just making an observation."

Beau held up his hands. "Not that I'm in a position to give advice."

"Yeah, how was LA?"

"A day trip that lasted a lifetime," said Beau. The waiter swung by with a meal matching Cape's and set it down. "Denyce is graduating this year, so my ex-wife and I had to talk college."

"Expensive?"

"Outrageous," said Beau. "But we saved. Problem isn't money, for a change. It's getting Denyce and her mother to agree on *where* she's going to school. Or agree on anything."

"Like what day it is?"

"*Where should we eat? Is the sky blue? Who killed JFK?*" Beau rolled his head as if his neck muscles had suddenly tightened. "Pick something, *anything*, and please, God almighty, don't stick me in the middle." Beau massaged the back of his neck with both hands. "Janine's got custody, and my life being what it is, I'm fine with it."

"Doesn't sound like it."

"I'm a better cop than I was a husband," said Beau. "But Janine and Denyce always butted heads, even when D was little. Janine's a control freak, and my D is stubborn beyond her years."

"Wonder where she gets that."

"You're just full of helpful observations today," said Beau. "It's like having breakfast with the Buddha."

"Have some more bacon," said Cape. "It's the key to inner peace."

"Now you're talking." Beau took a strip off his plate and bit it in half. "So what do you want?"

"To discuss why you and Vinnie are setting me up."

"So *that's* why you're grumpy." Beau feigned sorrow, but his expression looked more stern than sad. "Got you a job...you're welcome."

"I'm partial to cases I can actually solve."

"She needs someone to tilt at windmills," said Beau. "And you're the only honest guy we know."

"That's because you spend too much time with criminals."

"A cop's dilemma," said Beau.

Cape blew out his cheeks but didn't say anything.

"I think you're pissed because you want to help but know you can't," said Beau. "You ask me, your white horse is still hiding in your garage, taking a dump in that convertible even as we speak."

"Did I ask you?"

"Yes," said Beau, smiling as he cut into his pancakes. "You most certainly did."

Cape took another bite of bacon. Then another, worried he was becoming immune to the chemical euphoria induced by breakfast. Beau watched from across the table, bemused.

"Here." Beau reached into his jacket and produced a small rectangle, which he set on the table. A color photograph of a heavyset man in his forties. Blond hair going gray, hazel eyes, strong jaw. Wearing a blue uniform and white shirt.

"Hank?"

"Yup, the guy driving on the day." Beau produced a matching rectangle, this photograph a younger man. Wiry, dark hair and darker eyes. "Here you have the partner, Lou, the one handling collections."

"Both are suspects or you just want them for questioning?"

Beau shrugged. "Some witnesses claim there was a man in the truck when it sank, others aren't so sure. All we know is both men are missing."

"Not good."

"We'll find them." Beau pressed his hands together. "We always do. Cell phones, credit cards, the usual shit. Give it another day— nobody can disappear anymore."

"Unless they had help."

Beau cracked his knuckles. "In which case they are most definitely suspects."

"So that's a waste of my time."

"I'd say so." Beau shifted in his chair and aimed his fork at the eggs.

Cape studied the sea lions before turning back to his friend. "I was thinking I'd work the pier."

"Makes sense," said Beau. "But probably a dead end. *If* the drivers had help, crime stats suggest it was some asshole buddy from their past—a known felon, or someone inside the armored car company. And SFPD is all over the company."

"All the store owners got ripped off," said Cape. "Maybe they know something."

"Maybe you're gonna win the lottery."

Cape made a face. "I'm going to work the pier."

"At least you won't get in my way."

"You're not going to interview the merchants?"

"Already took statements from anyone who came forward," said Beau. "But me and Vinnie, we'll get more mileage from the usual suspects. Known criminals and fuckups in the vicinity."

"Too many stores, not enough cops."

"Exactly." Beau half smiled. "*Unless* you have insider information."

"You could ask my client—"

"—and she wouldn't tell me shit. *This* we both know."

"She approached you and Vinnie."

"To cover her boyfriend's ass."

"So you find the drivers, I find the angle."

"You are an optimist." Beau rested his hands on the table. "But that's what I would do." A sea lion started barking in the distance. "Just know that you're probably wasting your time."

"That's what I get paid for."

"Your job sucks."

Cape signaled the waiter for the check.

"Tell me something I don't already know."

13

"Tell me something I don't already know about the pier."

Cape was trying to get the interview underway but deeply regretted not bringing a gun.

"You seem tense." Vera's voice pulled his attention away from the seagull.

"I don't like bullies," said Cape.

Sitting outside on a balcony seemed like a good idea until the waitress brought a basket of chips and the seagull took notice. It stayed airborne until Cape spotted a finch sitting hopefully on the railing and tossed a chip at the tiny bird.

Before the finch could break off a single crumb, the seagull swooped in and knocked the smaller bird off the railing. Then it swooped onto their table, snagged another chip and flew off before Cape or Vera could shoo it away. The seagull was the size of a pterodactyl.

They turned back to their meal but heard a yell from two tables away. The seagull had snagged a hot dog off a young girl's plate. The girl's mother lunged heroically but the bird was too fast. It swallowed the hot dog before landing just out of reach on the railing. Now it shifted from one foot to another, waiting for an opening.

"I should've known having two meals on the pier in one day was a bad idea," said Cape.

"Maybe bullies who die in this life are reincarnated as seagulls in the next." Vera took a bite of her burrito while it was still in her possession.

"Nice idea," said Cape. "I think the restaurant should add seagull tacos to the menu."

Vera smiled, an unexpected sight. Cape was glad he'd insisted on meeting outside the store. There was a palpable sadness in the back room of her shop. He glanced across the patio to their left, where an athletic-looking woman with a baseball cap over a ponytail sat alone, nibbling on a taco salad as she flipped the pages of a novel.

Vera asked, "You sure you don't want some lunch?"

"I should probably stick with the chips." Cape turned back to his client as he collected his thoughts. "I had an enormous breakfast, talking to the police."

"Oh," said Vera.

"I wanted to ask you," said Cape. "The girl minding your store—"

"Sharon."

"Your only employee?"

"Sharon and another girl named Natalie work part-time. Both students, but it's enough hours so I can coordinate my schedule around theirs."

"This must be a busy time of year."

"Pier traffic is fairly constant," said Vera. "That's why I'm here. But everybody's rent has soared since the tech companies decided San Francisco was a better place to work and live than Silicon Valley." She looked across the bay toward Alcatraz. "Nothing's ever as easy as we imagine, is it?"

Cape followed her gaze. "Ever been to Alcatraz?"

"The Rock?" Vera shook her head. "Guess I'm the typical local who's never been where the tourists go."

"They say the hardest thing for the prisoners wasn't the tough guards or the brutal cold. It was the acoustics. Convicts could hear laughter floating across the bay from balconies in downtown San Francisco."

"That's awful," said Vera.

"Haunting," said Cape. "Their imaginations became their punishment." He waited until her gaze shifted back to him. "Did Sharon and Natalie both know Hank?"

"Of course." Vera put her burrito down. "Why?"

"No reason," said Cape. "Just asking dumb questions till I can think of a few smart ones. I talk to anyone willing to talk to me, until I find a pattern."

"You said you talked to the police."

"They're confident that they'll find Hank or his partner."

"Lou?" Vera's face darkened.

"You don't like him."

"It's not that." Vera took a halfhearted bite and thought a minute. "He's fond of himself, but that's never bothered me. He was Hank's partner, but they weren't friends, if that's what you're asking."

"Let me ask it another way," said Cape. "Does it surprise you that he's a suspect in a robbery?"

"Not really...but nothing surprises me anymore." Vera shook her head as if to clear it. "What else did the police say?"

"That I was wasting my time."

"What do you think?"

"That I'm wasting your money."

"You're quitting?"

"I don't think—"

"—that Hank is innocent," said Vera, eyes flashing.

"I think maybe—"

"—that I'm naive."

"Maybe."

"And you don't want to break my heart with more bad news."

Cape studied the woman across from him, the certainty in her eyes, the set of her jaw. She looked as confident as he wanted to feel.

"Look at this." Vera reached into her purse and removed a photograph, then pushed it across the table. It was a color snapshot of Vera and Hank, trimmed to fit a wallet. Snowcapped mountains in the background. Vera, relaxed and smiling, hair pulled back. Hank looking tan, his collar open. Around his neck was a silver cross.

"I gave him that cross," said Vera. "Hank was a lapsed Catholic, like me." An edge crept back into her voice. "I told him it would keep him safe."

Cape handed her memory back but didn't say anything.

"That's the face of an innocent man," said Vera. "But whatever you find out, I want to know the truth."

Cape nodded. "Where was that taken?"

"Up in Oregon," replied Vera. "After an eight-hour drive, you escape to a different world of mountains, lakes, trees..."

"Any seagulls?"

"Not a one." Vera smiled, the lines around her eyes sudden rays of hope. "So you'll help me?"

Cape sighed. "If you'll help me."

"Anything."

"I won't find your friend faster than the police," said Cape. "I want to ask around the pier, find out if someone saw something—or if anyone knew about the robbery."

"Where will you start?"

"I was hoping you'd tell me."

Vera's mouth turned down at the corners. "That's why you asked about the girls in my store."

"Yes," said Cape. "If I could interview everyone who works on the pier and interrogate every tourist from the day of the robbery, that would obviously be ideal. But that's hundreds, maybe thousands of people, and we don't have much time."

"I see." Vera looked down at her hands. "Harkness." When she looked up, her eyes were calm. "I'd start with John Harkness."

"Where do I find him?"

"You haven't seen the store?"

Cape shook his head.

"The Left Hand of Harkness." Vera held up her left hand and wiggled the fingers. "Sells anything designed for lefties—golf clubs, guitars, everything imaginable."

"Why him?"

"He's paranoid," Vera said without sarcasm. "Came by my store twice last year, asking merchants to sign a petition against the restaurant owners. Something about a tax scam that he wanted the city council to investigate. He was on a rant from the minute he came into my store and didn't shut up until I asked him to leave. Then he stopped by again a few months later, and it was the same thing all over again, as if we'd never met."

"As least I know he's willing to have a conversation."

"He'll talk to anyone who will listen." Vera looked at her watch. "I'm really sorry, I have to get back to the store."

"Go ahead." Cape stood. "I'll get the check."

"Thank you." Vera forced a smile.

"Don't thank me yet."

She looked as if she might say something else, but then simply turned and walked to the exit. Cape waited until Vera was out of sight, then sat down and looked over the bay.

After a few minutes, the athletic woman on his left stood and walked over, then sat down facing him. She took off her baseball cap and pulled the elastic band from her ponytail. Her hair was black as onyx, her eyes green, features Asian with a splash of freckles across her nose.

"What do you think?" asked Cape.

"I think she's in denial," said Sally.

"Give it time," said Cape. "We all lie to ourselves."

"Not all of us."

"You never lie?"

"Not to myself."

"Are you a good liar?"

Sally's jade eyes twinkled. "Very."

"Then how would you know?

14

Eva never lied to herself but routinely kept secrets from her idiot brother.

She stared openly as he fidgeted on the front seat of the car, his right hand thrust in his jacket pocket. Eva sometimes wondered if he'd been left as a baby on their family's doorstep by a vindictive oligarch.

Sergey was oblivious, eyes on the apartment building across the street. He fingered the ice pick in his pocket and thought about blow jobs.

The ice pick was very sharp. Sergey had punctured an expensive jacket and stabbed himself twice before he decided to cap the tip with a cork from a wine bottle. The spike was tempered steel, the handle a hardened plastic with a rubber grip which fit nicely in his palm, like his cock. It was almost eight inches long.

The ice pick, not his cock. That was considerably smaller.

"This is making me horny."

Eva lurched as if the front seat was electrified. "*Zadrota*, what are you talking about?"

"This stakeout." Sergey jerked his chin toward the windshield. "The last time I got laid was in this apartment building."

Maybe this brother sitting next to her was an alien, switched with her real brother at birth. Some vile creature from the outer reaches of space, an agent from Planet Porno, a little-known celestial body located somewhere beyond Uranus.

"You're serious?" Eva asked, leaning closer to the driver-side door to maximize the space between them. "What was her name?"

Sergey hesitated. "Marta...Martha...no, Margaret—"

"Ha!" Eva sneered. "*Zasranees*, her name was Margot. You introduced me. Did she give you a blow job?"

"Oh yes."

"*Opesdal*." Eva shook her head sadly.

"What?"

"Men never remember a girl's name, but they never forget a good suck."

"What do you know?" Sergey said defensively. "You're only twenty-one."

"Twenty-two." Eva removed a raspberry Tootsie Pop from her jacket pocket. "But why should you remember my birthday?" She unwrapped the lollipop and popped it in her mouth. "Unless some girl went down on you the day I was born."

"Sadly, no." Sergey's voice dropped to a whisper. "Look...we have company."

He slouched in the seat, and Eva followed his gaze across the street.

A man approached the entrance to the apartment building. He had curly black hair which fell across the collar of a leather jacket. Eva couldn't see his face, but his clothes and gait suggested a young man.

The night was cold, the temperature a good twenty degrees cooler than during the day. In this part of the Sunset District, fog was so constant that rents were cheaper than higher elevations in the city.

Brother and sister watched as the man opened the front door to the building. A minute later he reappeared on the open balcony of the second floor and made his way along the row of apartments.

He stopped at the second door from the left, then turned and looked in their direction. Sergey ducked beneath the dashboard, but Eva didn't stir, trusting her stillness would keep her invisible. The man leaned into the weak light of the balcony and studied his open palm like a fortune teller.

"That's the driver?" Eva's brow furrowed in memory. "Or the other one?"

"It's supposed to be the one named Lou." Sergey narrowed his eyes as he peeked above the dash. "But it's not."

"So?" Eva watched the man turn away from the light toward the apartment door. "Must be his neighbor."

Sergey frowned. "But it *is* his apartment."

The man went inside and shut the door. The front window of the apartment remained dark.

"We wait?"

Sergey twisted in his seat and scanned the street. "If cops are watching, they'll show themselves soon."

"Unless they're already inside the apartment."

"We wait until he comes out."

It didn't take long. Less than ten minutes later, the man emerged onto the balcony. By the time he descended the stairs and exited the front door, Eva was waiting on the sidewalk, sucking on her lollipop.

The man stopped short but recovered smoothly, doing his best to look like a tenant leaving his apartment. He smiled and stepped aside to let Eva pass.

She moved laterally and blocked his way.

"*Excuse me.*" Eva slurped the lollipop loudly.

He smiled awkwardly and shifted his right leg to step around her.

Eva stepped into the gap and kicked him in the balls. The man dropped to his knees, gasping as Sergey appeared from the shadows.

That's when things went horribly wrong.

Sergey's plan was to thumb the cork off the ice pick, lean in close and press the tip against the man's neck—all in one smooth motion. He might even whisper fiercely into the man's ear, paralyzing him with fear.

Sergey tripped instead.

Sergey leaned forward, but the man kicked out his right leg, either in a vain instinct for self-defense or a spastic attempt to stand up. The move sent an electric shock through the man's tender testicles, causing him to fall forward onto his face. His right leg shot backwards and caught Sergey's right ankle like a trip wire.

Sergey tumbled forward, his right arm lunging to stop his fall. As gravity had its way with him, Sergey realized his fingers were still clenched around the ice pick. In sickening slow motion, his forward momentum became a death sentence for the man with the bruised balls.

The tip of the ice pick penetrated the soft spot behind the man's right ear, sliding up through the base of his skull into the brain. He died on his knees without a prayer on his lips.

Eva stopped sucking her lollipop and stared in disbelief.

Sergey rolled onto his side and looked at his sister ruefully.

"*Oops,*" he said.

Eva blinked, then spat at him.

"*Hey!*" Sergey scuttled sideways to avoid the pool of blood that was spreading like an oil leak. "It was an accident."

Eva glowered. "We were *supposed* to bring him to Nastya so she could ask him questions."

Sergey got to his knees, stood, and walked to the end of the drive. He looked up and down the street, listened for a long minute, then popped the trunk on their car.

"Grab his legs."

"Excuse me?" Eva clenched her hands into fists and set them firmly on her hips. It was a posture she'd used with her brother since she was five. "He's dead, fucknut."

"*His legs.*"

Eva sighed and lifted her end of the corpse. Sergey grunted as they shuffled sideways to the car.

"*Raz, dva...*" Sergey hissed through his teeth as they made the final swing. The body landed with a meaty *thunk*.

Sergey checked the street again and closed the trunk. From somewhere far to the south, a siren was heading toward them. Sergey climbed into the passenger seat.

Eva opened her door and slid behind the wheel, a sullen look on her face. "What are we doing?"

"Do not worry, *sestra*." Sergey patted her knee. "Just because he is dead doesn't mean he can't tell us anything."

15

"Dead men tell no tales."

"Yeah, I heard that one before." Lou watched the chum flow over the ship's rail like champagne at a vampire's banquet.

"The Devil's Teeth, have you heard that one?"

Lou ignored the lunatic on his left and stared at the red water. It wasn't long before a triangular dorsal fin broke the surface like a slice of pizza from Hell. An extra-large pizza. After a few minutes another lopsided triangle emerged, then a third and a fourth.

Lou fought the urge to be seasick but the rocking of the boat was getting worse. He gripped the rail and looked east, toward San Francisco and dry land.

All he could see was fog and whitecaps, and all he could smell was death.

"You're lookin' the wrong way. The Devil's Teeth are portside."

Lou felt the calloused hand on his shoulder. The captain of the boat squeezed once and released him. The physical contact brought his name back to Lou, who couldn't stop thinking of him as Ahab, or Quint from *Jaws*. A hint of an accent, but Lou had no clue where this madman was from—for all he knew, the man was born and raised at sea.

The guy's name was Cragg, a perfect moniker for a seafaring

whack job. He was tall, with a craggy face like the name implied, a tangle of black hair going gray, and a Gregory Peck gleam in his eyes.

You'd have to be crazy, coming out here for a living.

"Say what?" Lou forced himself to let go of the rail and stand upright. Since the heist, he'd been moved around like a pawn in a game of chess. Now he was on this carrion cruiser for no reason except it was the last place on earth the cops might come looking. He spat into the ocean and ran the back of his hand across his mouth.

"These islands." Cragg made a sweeping gesture. "Sailors call them The Devil's Teeth."

"Guess a dental plan isn't one of the perks for being Prince of Darkness." Lou looked toward the jagged rocks and had to admit the Farallon Islands were arguably the spookiest place he had ever been.

The day was pitched to him as a pleasant cruise—sail under the Golden Gate Bridge and leave trouble behind—get Lou out of town while they planned their next move. But instead of touring the headlands, they sailed twenty-seven nautical miles due west, until talons of rock broke the water like giant claws reaching for any passing boat. You could barely call them islands, the largest not much bigger than a soccer field. Volcanic shards thrust angrily into the air.

"You see how the island moves?" Cragg asked.

"What do you mean, it moves?" Lou squinted across the water. The biggest island held the only evidence of habitation, a lighthouse that had seen better days. A wan light pulsed from the tower, barely penetrating the fog.

Cragg wasn't lying. The island seemed to pulse with each pass of the light, as if the rock were breathing. A leviathan flexing its muscles.

Lou started to pick out distinct shapes. Seals so black they looked like boulders in the surf. Dark brown sea lions jostling for space above them. The clouds dissipated enough for the sun to shred the fog, and Lou gasped. Higher still, encircling the lighthouse and cliffs beyond, thousands, no, *tens of thousands* of birds. Seagulls, puffins, and a hundred other species huddled together for warmth. Lou hadn't seen so many varieties of bird since the drive-thru at KFC.

"Almost two hundred different species on one island," said Cragg. "Some call them America's Galapagos."

"Devil's Teeth has a better ring to it."

"I agree." Cragg smiled grimly.

Two sailors with the buckets dumped another bloody banquet overboard. Lou tried to not think about what was in those buckets. He knew his blood was just as red as the cocktail frothing the waves. A steel cable ran from a winch overhead and disappeared into the water below.

Cragg held the rail lightly, like a man admiring the view from his balcony. Lou studied the scars across the captain's knuckles, like scrimshaw, skin pale and thick from a lifetime of abrasions and salt water. The fingers were unnaturally wide, flattened from years of clenching, tying, and tearing. Lou made a mental note to never thumb-wrestle this guy.

Cragg's eyes had that unfocused, faraway look so characteristic of the stoned or the truly mad. "The first European here was Sir Francis Drake in 1579, to collect seal meat and eggs. He's remembered as a famous explorer, but do you know what he really was?" The captain didn't wait for an answer. "*A pirate.*"

"Like Johnny Depp."

"Queen Elizabeth gave him a commission during the war with Spain," said Cragg. "Keep all the loot you can carry, as long as you fuck with the Spanish navy."

"Not bad."

"He was knighted after the war. And rich."

Lou asked what seemed like a logical question. "If he was already rich, why the fuck would he come here?"

"He was an explorer!" Cragg spat over the railing. "Circumnavigated the globe, stumbled upon these rocks, and the rest is history."

"I usually fell asleep in history."

"Died of dysentery while trying to invade Puerto Rico."

"Should have gone to the Bahamas," said Lou. "Gambling is legal and the beaches are nicer."

"An ignoble death for a great man," muttered Cragg. "Any other time, Drake would have been branded a criminal—he was in the eyes of Spain. If captured, he would have swung from the gallows."

"Is it true you get a hard-on when they hang you?"

"I think you're missin' the point."

"What is the point?"

"Was he pirate or patriot? A great man or villain?" Cragg nodded at some inner voice. "All depends on whose side you're on."

"If you say so."

Cragg's gaze hardened. "So tell me, Lou, whose side are *you* on?"

Lou's answer was cut short as the ship shuddered from a sudden impact below the waterline. Something had slammed against the hull. Even the captain almost lost his footing.

Lou dared himself to look over the railing. Dorsal fins slipped in and out of sight.

"You've tried this before?"

Cragg nodded. "These islands have the biggest concentration of great whites in the world. That's why cage diving is so popular, despite the cold. You almost always see a big one."

"How big?"

Cragg studied the fins. "These are probably males. Females get as big as an SUV, but these are probably no larger than a compact car."

"We talking a MINI Cooper or a Corolla?"

Cragg shrugged. "Maybe a Prius."

"You're insane."

Cragg's eyes went flat as another thud rattled the gunwale.

The water roiled as Lou traced the cable into the water, trying to visualize a cage suspended twenty feet below. The cable groaned, followed by a shudder across the deck and a piercing electronic whine from the cabin.

"What the hell?" Lou felt the blood drain from his face. "Are we fucking sinking?"

"Calm yourself," said Cragg. "That's a signal, not an alarm."

Lou felt his sense of humor fall overboard and drown.

"You actually—?"

"Yep." Cragg removed his hands from the railing and rubbed them together, then gestured at the sailors handling the winch. "I think we have a new pet."

Lou gripped the rail until his knuckles hurt. The cable screamed as the winch hoisted the cage out of the water. He wished Scotty could beam him off this ship of insanity, but instead of Captain Kirk at his side, there stood Cragg. Lou turned toward San Francisco, but it was still an ocean away.

Lou had risked everything to get his hands on a pile of cash, but right now he'd give it all away for a chance to walk on dry land.

16

Cape knew he was walking on dry land but felt like a drunken sailor as he strode across the uneven planks of the pier. An ebbing tide of tourists made it impossible to walk in a straight line.

The first thing Cape noticed upon reaching the store was that the front door was hinged on the left. The handle was bronze and shaped like an extended left hand, which Cape gripped firmly and pulled.

He stepped inside. As his eyes adjusted to the shade, the man behind the counter looked at him expectantly. "May I help you?"

"You Harkness?" asked Cape.

"Indeed, I am." Harkness was tall and wiry, with olive skin and black hair that couldn't decide which way to fall. He wore faded jeans and a T-shirt that proclaimed *Lefties do it Right*.

Papers were splayed across the counter. A calculator sat near his left hand, a pen with a gnawed end clutched in his right. Cape looked from the hand holding the pen to the eyes of the man behind the counter.

"You're right-handed."

Harkness dropped the pen as if it were a spider. "Maybe I'm ambidextrous."

"Are you?"

"Actually, no." Harkness looked around to see if there were any other customers, but they were alone in the store. "Why should you care?"

"I don't."

"I'm providing a service to an underserved minority." Harkness had a defiant edge to his voice. "Emancipating my left-handed brothers."

"Okay."

"Just like the southern whites who led the civil rights movement."

"Aren't you forgetting about Martin Luther King?"

"Was he left-handed?"

"I'll have to check *Wikipedia*." Cape glanced around the store. "I didn't realize left-handers were so subject to discrimination."

Harkness looked like he'd been slapped. "What about polo?"

"I assume you mean the sport," said Cape. "And not the short-sleeved shirts."

"Did you know it's against the rules for polo players to compete left-handed?"

"Not exactly the back of the bus, is it?"

"You try riding a horse and swinging a mallet with your weak hand," Harness replied. "Then come back and tell me which side you're on."

"Well, clearly you're on the left side."

"Damn right."

"Well said." Cape walked to the door and flipped the *Closed* sign to face the pier. Harkness eyed him warily.

"I could tell you weren't just another customer," said Harkness, a slow smile forming. "You must have gotten my letter." He pushed some papers out of the way and set his elbows on the counter. "Are you from the state attorney's office?"

Cape was glad he'd tucked in his shirt for a change. He summoned his most noncommittal voice and replied, "I am an investigator."

"A *special* investigator?" Harkness leaned forward.

"I like to think so," said Cape. "Let's start at the beginning, why did you send the letter?"

Harkness waved his arm toward some shelves. "What do you see?"

Cape looked around the store. T-shirts, place mats, mouse pads, door mats, baseball caps, coffee mugs. Every imaginable form of *tchotchke* emblazoned with a pro-left-handed slogan. A poster featured images of Da Vinci, Marie Curie, Aristotle, Napoleon, Jimi Hendrix, and Bill Gates. Specialty items abounded, from left-handed golf clubs to guitars strung upside down, cooking implements, and left-handed scissors.

Harkness impatiently answered his own question. "You see stuff. *Things.* Physical inventory. Tangible items. Products with bar codes." He moved around the counter, pointing an accusing finger out the window at the pier. "Now…what do you see out there?"

Directly across the pier was a restaurant with a surfing theme, a longboard mounted over the entrance and tiki torches illuminating outdoor seating. Cape ventured a guess.

"Food?"

"Exactly!" Harkness stomped behind the counter. "Disposables…intangibles. Food and service."

"So?"

"A *cash-fucking-business*," said Harkness. "Sure, they take credit cards, but almost half the patrons pay cash for their meals. And how much food do they *really* serve? How much produce goes bad or is never delivered?"

Cape shrugged. "I don't know."

"Nobody knows!" Harkness paced around his store like a lion in a cage. "If you're the IRS, how can you track that shit?" He stopped near the register and slapped his left hand on the counter. "You'd have to eat at every restaurant on the pier, every day for a year, then estimate the annual foot traffic and do the math. It's the equivalent of auditing every pizza parlor in New York, just to nail the one that *might* be owned by the mob."

"You think all the restaurants are underpaying on their taxes?" Harkness practically lunged. "Wouldn't you?"

Cape wanted to ask about the armored car but knew the best way to lead a conversation was to follow it. "This is all a bit vague."

"You want specifics."

"It usually helps." Cape forced a smile. "In an investigation."

"What if I'm afraid of reprisals?" Harkness glanced outside, as if his imaginary tormentors had their faces pressed against the window.

"Give me a hint."

"Maybe you feel like a donut."

I feel like an idiot, thought Cape. "Maybe you feel like not jerking me off."

"There's a place that sells donuts." Harkness raised his eyebrows conspiratorially. "Dave's Donuts—you passed it coming here."

Cape waited for the rest.

He waited a beat longer but nothing came.

Harkness smiled hopefully. "Who doesn't like donuts?"

Cape considered the question and had to admit he didn't know anyone.

17

Cape didn't know anyone who liked standing on line, but the donuts were worth the wait.

The line stretched through the crowd like a ravenous snake, extending all the way back to the main entrance. It took Cape twenty minutes to reach the front of the line. Dave's Donuts was just a triangular hut in the middle of the pier with a walk-up window.

Inside, a conveyor belt moved jerkily beneath a giant funnel that spat dough into measured rings. The belt curved inward, sending the uncooked donuts into a vat of boiling oil, where they were rescued by another conveyor after frying, finally passing under a funnel filled with powdered sugar before being bagged. It was ingenious and simple, the kind of mechanical wizardry that first appeared in factories at the turn of the last century.

Cape guessed it would cost fifty cents worth of dough and sugar to make a dozen donuts, which they sold for five dollars. Not a bad margin, even after rent. He counted the number of people in line and did the math, then compared it to his own annual income and hoped the sugar high he would get from the donuts would counteract his sudden feeling of depression.

At the window he ordered a half dozen, paid in cash, and was handed a bag by a teenaged boy with more braces than teeth. Cape retreated to a nearby bench and studied the conga line closely. Most of the people waiting looked like tourists, often two or more chatting together, sometimes a lone parent standing patiently while kids and other relatives stopped by to say hi, then leaving to check out the stores nearby until the donuts were ready.

Cape popped one of the donuts into his mouth and almost swooned. The simple dough and sugar concoction was weaponized. A sudden image popped into his head of a snake in a tree, tempting Adam and Eve with a mini-donut. Cape deeply regretted not ordering a full dozen but looked at the line and stayed where he was.

Though he didn't know what he was looking for, Cape didn't try the direct approach. Harkness was an anomaly, a whistle-blower with an agenda. He might be onto something, but Cape couldn't assume everyone on the pier was so candid or crazy.

He was on his fourth donut when he noticed someone in line who didn't look like a tourist. The guy was in his early twenties, longish brown hair and a week's worth of stubble covering a crap complexion. Long-sleeved flannel shirt over arms that darted nervously in and out of the pockets of his jeans. His eyes jumped around as if wasps were swarming around him. By the time Cape swallowed the fifth donut, the man in flannel was at the window.

Cape noticed three things simultaneously. Even from a distance, the wad of bills the man thrust quickly across the counter seemed fat, unless he was buying donuts for the entire pier. The kid at the window handed the money to someone standing behind him, in the shadows, then reached under the counter and grabbed a bag of donuts, which he handed to the flannel man. When Cape had bought his donuts, all the bags of six or twelve were arranged on top of the counter, so he wondered what was so special about the bags underneath.

The third thing was the most interesting. As the exchange occurred, Cape saw a man in uniform walk around the corner of the donut shack. At first he thought it was a uniformed cop strolling the pier, but the stocky man with the dark cap and sunglasses was private security, a Pier 39 logo emblazoned on the left pocket of his shirt. He had a wire in his ear and stun gun on his hip.

The guard had a disinterested look on his face as he watched the flannel man buy his donuts. He scanned the rest of the line and saw only tourists, then turned and walked around to the other side of the shack.

Flannel Man moved upstream toward the pier entrance and street beyond. Cape reluctantly abandoned his last donut and tossed the bag into a nearby trash bin. He'd consumed enough sugar for a lifetime, and he desperately wanted to know what was in that guy's bag.

18

"I'm telling you, it's in the bag."

Anastasia looked at her idiot brother in disbelief. A stern glance at her younger sister couldn't get Eva to look her in the eyes, so Anastasia knew Sergey was bullshitting her.

"It's not in the bag, *mudak*," snapped Anastasia. "Do you even know what that idiom means?"

"Idiom?"

"Idiot." Anastasia gestured at the car, squeezed into the back of her uncle's warehouse. Rows of metal shelves were stacked with boxes of nesting dolls. The inventory moved quickly so the warehouse was small, barely large enough for the three of them and the car. "From what Eva just said, it's not in the bag, it's in the fucking trunk." Anastasia kicked the car's fender angrily. "You brought me a dead body?"

"Nastya, calm yourself." Sergey held up both hands, belatedly realizing that telling a furious person to *stay calm* was like reheating napalm in a microwave. "We had no choice."

Eva shuffled her feet and took a sudden interest in the ceiling fixtures.

"That's what I meant to say," Sergey continued, "it's under control. Nobody saw us, but he might have seen us, so we…" He paused and glanced at Eva, whose jawline made it clear he was on his own. "...that is, I...I took the initiative."

Anastasia stared at him for a full minute. Sergey thought she might explode if her nostrils ever stopped flaring.

Then without warning, Anastasia burst out laughing.

The sound echoed around the warehouse like a pinball with a drinking problem. By the time Anastasia caught her breath, tears were running down her cheeks, but she was still smiling.

"Sergey, if all men think with their dicks, your *xyй* must be very small indeed." Anastasia looked at Eva, who was suppressing a giggle. "Okay, you nincompoops, let's open the trunk and see what kind of mess we're in."

Sergey almost defended his manhood but decided to hand Anastasia the keys while she was still smiling.

The man in the trunk wasn't laughing. His body had rolled during the drive, so his head was higher than his feet, as if sitting up in the trunk. His mouth was open and he was staring right at them.

Anastasia stopped smiling.

"I know this man," she said quietly.

Eva started. "Are you sure, *sestra*?"

"Just look." Anastasia gestured at the slack face, the dead eyes more sad than angry. "He works on the pier."

Sergey leaned in close. "He does look familiar, now that you mention it, but I didn't recognize him." He turned to look at Eva. "Did you?"

Eva shook her head.

"That's because he's not wearing his uniform," said Anastasia.

Eva started nodding. "You're right! He is one of the security men. I've seen him walking near the store."

Sergey frowned. "This is really bad, Nastya."

"No, it's not." Anastasia stared into the eyes of the dead man. "It might turn out to be really good."

19

"I'm telling you, this is really bad."

The pilot was nervous, but the Doctor knew better.

"Relax, I've been out here before." The Doctor downed the rest of his cocktail and gestured at the windscreen with his glass, ice rattling in rhythm to his speech. He liked that, having a backbeat to everything he said. Made him feel like a rapper. An original gangster. *Maybe I could call myself Doctor Ice—*

"—are you fucking deaf?" The pilot quailed. "How many of those have you had?"

"These?" The ice stopped rattling as the Doctor's brow furrowed. "Two...no, four...*maybe* three?"

"Bullshit." The pilot's knuckles were white on the yoke of the plane. "I told you an hour ago, we're past the point of no return. Even if we wanted to fly back to mainland China, we'd never make it. I need to radio for help *now*." He tried to get the Doctor to make eye contact. "Now, as in right fucking *right now*, before we crash into the ocean."

"It's a sea," said the Doctor nonchalantly. "The South China Sea. You should know that, you're a pilot." He plucked an ice cube from his glass and started chewing. "You follow the coordinates I gave you?"

"Yes, but I told you—"

"—then don't worry about it."

The Doctor had hoped the pilot would be cooler, but when you promise a guy a hundred thousand dollars to file a bogus flight plan before flying to the middle of nowhere, you can't be picky. This guy was sweaty, despite the air conditioning in the cockpit. His shirt was pitted out and his thinning hair was pasted to his forehead. The Doctor suspected there was too much gluten in the pilot's diet but kept that little tidbit to himself.

"I checked the charts," said the pilot. "There's nothing out here except a bunch of crappy little islands and submerged reefs." He turned on the Doctor, his eyes a jumpy pair of brown rabbits. "Nothing, and I mean, nothing you could land a plane on."

The Doctor never had much of a bedside manner, so he just shrugged. "Then where did that come from?" He gestured to the left of the aircraft, where a small tactical fighter had appeared out of thin air and was now flying alongside them.

It looked like a Shenyang J-11, what NATO referred to as a Flanker, a rip-off of the old Soviet Sukhoi Su-27. The Doctor's eyes weren't as good as they used to be, so he couldn't be sure. He once knew a lot about planes, but lately he just didn't give a shit.

"The hell did he come from?" The pilot gawked at the fighter.

"Up ahead, I'll wager." The Doctor waved at the Flanker pilot before pointing at the water below.

Five hundred miles from the mainland, the sea was as blue as a baby's eyes. Straight ahead was a cluster of islands so small they looked more like piles of sand that could wash away any minute.

"Spratlys," said the Doctor. "And it looks like they're making a new one."

"A new…island?" The pilot followed his line of sight toward the stunted archipelago.

"Follow our new friend off your left wing," said the Doctor. "He's our escort."

"You *knew*," sputtered the pilot. "Why didn't—?"

"Slipped my mind." The Doctor held up his empty glass. "We'll probably do a fly-over, then circle back and approach Cuarteron Reef or maybe Fiery Cross." He pointed with the middle finger of his hand holding the glass. "That reef right...over...*there*."

"You mean that island."

"It was a reef only a year ago," said the Doctor. "Submerged just below the surface, a coral shelf, home to cute little fish, an occasional ray, maybe a docile shark or two—all that *Finding Nemo* shit. Until the Chinese government decided to bring in barges, dredge up the ocean floor, and make themselves some new islands." The Doctor shook his head in mock sadness. "Then it's goodbye Nemo, fuck you Dory, and hello airstrip!"

"My God."

"He's got nothing to do it," replied the Doctor. "The last good island He made was Hawaii."

The fighter cut in front of the private jet and wobbled its wings, then banked into position for an approach. The pilot of the small plane couldn't believe what he was seeing. The vestiges of a coral reef were still visible from the air. Subtle curves and trailing wisps of rock just below the breaking waves, the geometry too fractal to be anything man-made. But the reef itself was merely a ledge now, like an old tree stump used for a coffee table. Millions of tons of white sand mixed with gray concrete had been dumped, shaped, and cemented into straight lines and hard rectangles balanced on top of the reef.

Positioned at strategic points around the island, five barges were dredging sand from the ocean floor, impossibly long hoses spitting a sand-concrete mixture to reinforce the fragile coastline.

"It's like a Bond movie," said the Doctor. "Only it's real."

The Doctor took note of the new structures. A radar installation. A hanger. Even a solar array, that was definitely new. And just beyond the runway, a massive building that had intelligence agencies around the world puzzling over satellite imagery.

Conspiracy theories ran the gamut from weapons manufacturing, army barracks, a prison, even a lab where evil scientists concocted plans to take over the world.

How about all of the above? thought the Doctor.

The pilot was saying something, but the Doctor closed his eyes and turned the nervous chatter into background noise. He didn't enjoy landings and had already spent too much time talking to this guy. The Doctor didn't like him but didn't dislike him either, and even ambivalence came at a cost.

It was always a bad idea to get attached to any of your patients. The same rule could apply to pilots, especially when you know something they don't.

The Doctor would step onto the tarmac and soldiers would escort him to his lab. Then the pilot would disembark from the plane and they would shoot him in the head. Loose ends were always a bad idea, and there was too much at stake to be sentimental. Still, the Doctor felt a twinge in his gut as the wheels touched down, and he didn't think it was motion sickness.

The feeling passed like a wave crashing against a reef, and as they taxied down the runway, the Doctor felt relieved to finally reach his destination.

20

When they finally reached their destination, Cape felt nauseous.

If he'd known that following Flannel Man meant riding a city bus, he might have taken the direct approach and accosted the guy at the donut shack. Maybe he could have bribed the security guard.

Feeling queasy was a common reaction to public transportation in San Francisco, but this particular driver repeatedly stomped on the brake pedal like a crazed exterminator trying to kill the last cockroach on earth. By the time they made the transfer and arrived at Golden Gate Park, half the passengers looked annoyed and the other half looked green.

San Francisco was the birthplace of Uber, Lyft, and every other ride-sharing service for a reason. The number of taxis per capita was less than one-twentieth of any major city, so rates were astronomical, assuming you could find a cab in the first place. Vintage trollies were undeniably quaint but claustrophobic, the conductors refusing to move until each car was standing room only. And city buses offered all the charm and convenience of a rusted chastity belt on a honeymoon.

Flannel Man exited through the front door of the bus, and Cape slid through the accordion doors in the middle. Fresh air greeted him like an old friend as he stepped onto the grass. They were on the northeast corner of the park, near the intersection of Fulton and Stanyan.

The park wasn't crowded this time of day, but it wasn't empty either. People taking a break from work, families with small children strolling or playing on the lawn. Cape let Flannel Man get a healthy lead before following at a distance.

Cape admired the man's willpower. There was no way Cape could've traveled this distance and not consumed every last donut in the bag.

They headed south. On the right was the Conservatory of Flowers, a crystal palace with surrounding gardens that could make Louis XIV jealous.

As they crossed John F. Kennedy Boulevard, a Segway tour made an otherwise placid landscape look surreal. The tourists looked anxious, as if the Segways might become sentient at any moment and veer into oncoming traffic or right off a cliff. Cape dodged one of the stragglers and shook his head in wonder. Not safe for the roads and illegal on the sidewalks, never had so much technology been developed for no discernible purpose.

Flannel Man ignored them and kept walking in no particular hurry. After a sloping patch of lawn, a castle came into view.

Cape knew the park well enough to recognize the Sharon Building from any angle. Built as an elaborate playhouse to accompany the playground, it was almost destroyed by the 1906 earthquake and two fires in the years since. Now it was an art school, but it still resembled the estate of a medieval lord, with heavy stone walls, iron gates, and an octagonal tower.

Flannel Man headed to a small hill overlooking the playground. Locals knew it as Hippie Hill, a notorious gathering place in the sixties when the city had a fleeting cultural relevance beyond its own borders. Cape lingered near the playground as he realized what he was about to witness.

After enduring the bus and nearly getting squashed by a Segway, it seemed terribly anticlimactic.

The man in flannel sat on the hill, opened the bag, and took out a donut. While he chewed, he reached back into the bag and removed a small packet that look like a bag of tea. Tearing along its long edge, he held the packet sideways in his left hand while fishing something from his breast pocket with his right. It looked like a fountain pen, but Cape knew it was an e-cigarette, a *vape* pen.

Cape watched as the man sprinkled the contents of the packet into a small compartment on the side of the pen, then snapped it closed. Placing the pen between his lips, he took a long drag and closed his eyes.

Watching someone get stoned is about as entertaining as watching a mime with your eyes closed.

Cape was still a long way from finding the missing driver of the armored car, but he had found yet another reason to question his career choice. Flannel Man idly watched the kids on the playground as he inhaled. A boy around ten was on the swings, laughing and yelling as his mother pushed him higher, higher, *higher.*

Flannel Man's left leg kicked involuntarily, and he gave it a sharp glance, then shook his foot as if an ant had crawled inside his shoe. He leaned back, both hands behind him on the grass, and took a deep breath like a man breaking the surface of a pool. His leg stopped wiggling. He lay still for a full five minutes, eyes open but unseeing, until his eyelids started to flutter, blinking long and slow, a semaphore signal that he was shutting down. The vape pen fell from his grasp as he closed his eyes.

Cape waited another minute before strolling nonchalantly up the hill, passing within a foot of the sleeping stoner. The man lay unmoving. The sun was out, the hillside was warm, and Flannel Man was fully baked.

Cape plucked the empty packet from the grass and snatched the bag of donuts without breaking stride. A glance inside the bag revealed two more packets, five more donuts, and a small vial about the size of a bottle of eyedrops.

Cape was ten paces away when a sudden pang of guilt made him turn around. He gingerly removed the packets and vial, slipped them into his pants pocket. Then he returned the bag of donuts to its spot alongside the sleeping man. Cape couldn't deny he was a thief but didn't want anyone to say he was inconsiderate.

As he walked down the hill past the playground, Cape wondered what he had in his pocket, and why it was worth so much.

21

Some things are priceless because of all the lives they cost.

Sally moved through the crowd like a ghost, completing her second circuit of the pier without bumping into anyone or having to change her course, despite the number of people looking at their phones instead of their feet.

She marveled at the money flowing through people's fingers, wondering what they would be doing next year with the things they bought today, or if they'd even remember buying them. Her own possessions, not counting the weapons, could fit inside the small trunk she kept at the foot of her bed.

She considered one or two items to be priceless. The rest she could leave behind in a heartbeat if she had to disappear, as she had before.

Cape had possessions, but Sally doubted he knew where half of them were. She almost smiled, always surprised to be working with a man with whom she had nothing in common. A man who didn't consider this world so strange.

But he was also a man who had never lied to her, which was as foreign a concept as the pier beneath her feet.

The pier was the cultural antithesis of everything she learned growing up—not that she considered her childhood a template for normalcy. Most stores had someone cajoling tourists with *take a look, just step inside and enjoy the air conditioning, try a free sample or have your photo taken, step in front of this mirror and see how it looks on you!*

As she glided over the wooden planks and pretended to browse the stores, Sally caught snatches of French, Russian, Japanese, Spanish, and Chinese, both Mandarin and Cantonese. She understood them all, some more fluently than others, but none of the conversations were anything but mundane.

A few shops warranted more attention, less because of their clientele than for their absence of customers. The proprietors seemed disinterested in the endless flow of foot traffic just outside their doors.

Sally found the security personnel most interesting of all. All private, not a beat cop in sight, and most of them in better shape and younger than typical security guards. A few moved as if they'd had training, a subtle set to the shoulders and hips that Sally recognized. She watched one guard make his rounds and decided his training wasn't very good, his level of awareness marginal, but in a physical encounter he probably knew how to fight.

Taking a last look down the length of the pier, she walked across the Embarcadero and headed south. Before she headed home, Sally wanted to view something truly priceless.

Despite the hills in San Francisco, Sally preferred to travel by foot whenever possible, only took mass transit reluctantly and never drove, so it took her half an hour to reach The Asian Art Museum.

The museum had moved from Golden Gate Park to the former main library near City Hall, a structure dating back to 1917. A hundred years was old by San Francisco standards, but now treasures spanning six thousand years resided inside its walls.

The museum was only moderately crowded. Couples on culture dates, parents with kids, and one middle school field trip.

The Japanese art was on the second floor. Sally took the stairs.

The exhibit was popular. Sally moved around the perimeter of the crowd until she found an opening and angled toward the center of the chamber. On the far side of a long glass case, a tour guide was describing the various artifacts to the schoolchildren, her voice clear and melodic.

"In twelfth-century Japan it was a great honor to be *samurai*," said the guide. "But did you know that one of the greatest samurais of all time was a *woman*?"

Murmurs among the children—skeptical muttering from the boys and a chorus of cheers from the girls.

"It's true," said the guide. "Her name was Tomoe Gozen, and during the Genpei War, she was a retainer for the great warlord Yoshinaka."

"I have a retainer," said one of the schoolgirls.

"So do I!" said a boy next to her. "My teeth are all crooked."

"Does it bother you when you sleep?" asked another girl.

"No, not *that* kind of retainer," said the guide good-naturedly. "A retainer was a warrior on horseback. Now pay attention, children, because I think you'll find this fascinating. Before we look inside the case…no, no peeking…look at me, so I can read to you from *The Tale of the Heike*."

Sally had seen countless horrors in her life and a few things of real beauty, but the object in the display case took her breath away.

The children quieted and the guide began. "'Tomoe was especially beautiful, with long hair and charming features. She was also a remarkably strong archer, and as a swordswoman she was a warrior worth a thousand, ready to confront a demon or a god, mounted or on foot. She handled unbroken horses with superb skill; she rode unscathed down perilous descents. Whenever a battle was imminent, Yoshinaka sent her out as his first captain, equipped with strong armor, an oversized sword, and a mighty bow; and she performed more deeds of valor than any of his other warriors.'"

Inside the case, resting on a simple wooden stand, was a sword.

"Now children, come forward and look at Tomoe's weapon of choice."

Sally learned how to judge a blade by the time she was seven and mastered *kenjutsu* before she was twelve. This was a *naginata*, a long sword that resembled a spear, the hilt almost as long as the blade. It was the third type of bladed weapon Sally had mastered, after the *katana* of traditional sword-fighting and the *tanto* knife for close-quarters defense.

Her instructors in Hong Kong borrowed techniques from every martial art across the centuries for her curriculum. Styles of combat from China, Southeast Asia, Korea, and Japan. She even studied Krav Maga, a hybrid form designed by Israel military to master deadly force in a matter of weeks, not years. Every fighting technique from each culture offered certain advantages, but her Chinese teacher once grudgingly admitted that the Japanese were unmatched in swordsmanship.

Since she was half-Japanese herself, Sally felt a small hint of pride, suitably self-aware to admit that the line between ego and identity thinned over time. This weapon spoke to Sally like an echo from a past life.

The *naginata* was a cavalry weapon, its long reach a threat to any oncoming horse and devastating if used from the saddle. Sally recalled the unbridled joy of riding a horse the first time. Reflecting on a childhood focused predominantly on the killing arts, she was always surprised by any memory of girlish delight.

The metal had been folded hundreds of times, ripples of black and silver flowing along the edge of the blade. A current in an endless stream.

A sword like this should not be in a glass case.

Sally knew that what the museum guide failed to mention was Tomoe Gozen was the sole survivor of an epic battle. When her clan finally met defeat on the battlefield, the warlord ordered Tomoe to protect her honor as a woman and flee before the enemy could overwhelm their position. She reluctantly complied, but the opposing army's greatest rider tried to intercept her.

Without breaking stride, wielding the *naginata* from her saddle, Tomoe decapitated him with a single stroke of the blade.

Paintings of Tomoe invariably show her galloping away, severed head in one hand and long sword in the other. Arguably too gruesome for a class tour of the museum, but when Sally read *The Tale of the Heike* as a student, it was the first time she had encountered an historical figure with whom she could identify. So Sally knew everything about Tomoe Gozen.

She knew that Tomoe disappeared after that battle, and after the war resurfaced as a nun at a Buddhist shrine. Some historians claimed that during this period, Tomoe opened a school for girls.

Sally tried to leave her past in Hong Kong when she turned away from the Triads, but her connection to history was a tougher cord to cut. A sword like this needed to breathe.

The school tour was wrapping up. Sally stepped around the case to view the sword from the opposite side. The guide gestured for the children to line up behind her, then turned toward Sally and began walking.

Sally froze.

The woman was Chinese and very beautiful, long black hair and lustrous eyes. But it was the way she moved that got Sally's attention. Like judging a blade, one of the first things Sally learned was how to evaluate a human weapon.

The tour guide didn't make eye contact with Sally, her attention seemingly on the children. She moved like a dancer, but Sally doubted that she had studied ballet. Torso perfectly balanced, hips flowing from side to side like water in a glass. Her feet landed soundlessly on the marble floor.

It took years to move like that, muscle memory formed by thousands of hours of training. Sally felt like she was looking into a mirror.

The woman walking toward her was a trained killer.

22

"You might be looking at a killer."

Cape leaned over the microscope and adjusted the focus, but the substance under the lens looked about as dangerous as oregano. "I thought it looked like marijuana."

"*Synthetic* marijuana." Dumont Frazer shook his head like a disapproving headmaster. He wore a meticulous white lab coat over a polo shirt and jeans, his black hair tousled and graying at the edges. Glasses on the bridge of his nose reflected the overhead halogens like a signal mirror. "Calling it marijuana, pot, weed... all misnomers. It's entirely different, chemically."

"Looks like rosemary," said Cape. "Or thyme, I always get those two mixed up."

"Well, it is called *spice* on the street," said Dumont. "Or K2."

"That, I've heard of," said Cape. "Just never knew what was in it."

"Neither does anyone else," said Dumont, gesturing at a row of test tubes on an adjacent counter. The first tube was filled with a reddish liquid, the second was bright orange, and the third was black as oil. Behind them was a gas chromatograph, a squat machine that housed three needles zigzagging across graph paper like a seismograph measuring earthquakes. "These are the three samples you brought me, mixed with the same chemical reagents. Notice the three different results."

"You're saying there's not a lot of quality control."

"Practically none," replied Dumont, "but I'm more an engineer than a chemist."

"Sure you are." Cape glanced around the lab. A nondescript warehouse on the seedier side of Market Street, it was practically invisible to casual observers, painted to look like the garage for the building next door. But inside it looked like NASA was having an estate sale to raise money for a children's science museum. Tables were littered with partially assembled electronics, experiments in progress.

An entire corner of the warehouse was filled with remote-controlled vehicles and flying machines of indeterminate purpose, ranging in size from quadcopters over four feet in diameter to minibots as small as a dragonfly.

The last time Cape visited Dumont Frazer's laboratory, the affable scientist was experimenting with sonic grenades and acoustic lasers that weaponized sound waves. One of those grenades had saved Cape's life. He was confident that basic chemistry wasn't beyond Dumont Frazer's realm of expertise.

"I always think of you as a mad scientist."

"I never get mad," said Dumont. "But why come to me with this?"

"SFPD doesn't handle drug testing at their lab anymore," said Cape. "Not since several kilos of cocaine went missing, courtesy of one of the lab techs. Just one of many mishaps that hit the press, so now they outsource all drug testing to private labs in San Mateo."

"And you don't know who owns or controls the private labs."

"But I know you," said Cape.

Dumont smiled. "I did hear they had a cat problem at Hunters Point."

The SFPD had been storing old case files in a warehouse at the Naval shipyards in Hunters Point, but the building was in disrepair and a pack of feral cats moved in and started peeing all over the evidence. Another black eye on a department whose public face was more bruised than a bare-knuckled boxer.

Cape gestured at the test tubes. "So what are we dealing with?"

"Synthetic *cannabinoids* are not cannabis leaves," said Dumont. "It's not a single plant, it's just a bunch of chemicals sprayed onto garden variety herbs. That's why it's called spice."

"What kind of chemicals?"

"I did some more reading," said Dumont. "While I was running my tests."

"Of course you did."

"At last count there were over seven hundred different chemicals being used to make synthetic marijuana."

"Seven *hundred*?" Cape looked at the scientist in disbelief.

"The high people get from marijuana comes from a chemical called THC," said Dumont, "but synthetic pot doesn't contain THC, it's a concoction of chemicals designed to recreate the same effects in the brain. Only the formula varies from one manufacturer to the next. Some of the mixtures are even technically legal because the DEA can't keep up with all the variations."

"Why all the trouble when pot is practically legal for everyone in California?" asked Cape. "Why not just smoke the real thing?"

"This stuff is a lot cheaper," said Dumont. "Made in bulk by labs in China, on the back end of some other chemical production. On the street it's probably a tenth of what an equivalent amount of marijuana would cost. And because of the additives, it's up to a hundred times more potent."

Cape looked over the test tubes. "So these are just variations on a recipe."

"Pretty much," said Dumont. "You said the man's leg twitched before he passed out?"

"Yeah," said Cape. "But maybe he just got a cramp."

"Could be," said Dumont. "But he could be a chronic user.

Some of the stuff in those packets contained traces of the prescription drug phenazepam, a type of benzodiazepine."

"Dumont, we agreed you would always use small words."

"It's an antianxiety drug, but in higher doses it's also an antipsychotic." Dumont gestured toward the black test tube. "The stuff in the vial you took from the bag? That's squeezed over standard tobacco or whatever you're smoking, a few drops to give you an extra kick. Inhale that on a regular basis and you'll start dancing like a marionette, sudden nerve tremors, loss of coordination." Dumont's expression was a weary blend of dismay at the human condition and fascination with the drug's underlying chemistry. "You might not even notice at first, until one day you have a seizure and die."

Cape looked at the black test tube, an oily invitation to oblivion. "Lovely."

"But until you do," continued Dumont, "it's apparently a terrific high." He turned away from the table. "If you're into that sort of thing."

"I'm already addicted to bacon," said Cape. "I don't need another vice."

"What will you tell the police?"

"The truth," said Cape. "But cops won't like hearing that donuts are bad for your health."

"And *when* will you tell them?"

Cape met the scientist's gaze. "I haven't decided yet."

"I see."

"Soon."

"Mm-hmm."

"I just..." Cape let his voice trail off as he looked at the jagged lines on the diagnostic readout. "This drug you mentioned as part of the mixture, it was pharmaceutical?"

"One of several, actually, but that drug has a singular chemical composition. It popped right away." Dumont connected the dots before Cape could interrupt. "You want to know where it's made, don't you?"

Cape shrugged. "If you know the *where*, sometimes you can figure out the why."

"Russia." Dumont answered without hesitation. "That drug is still used in former Soviet Bloc countries. It's like the baking soda of drugs for neurological disorders, it has multiple applications— given to patients before surgery to enhance anesthesia; to office workers to relieve anxiety; to schizophrenics to keep from hearing voices. Like most antidepressants, they have no idea how it works beyond changing the chemical balance in the brain, but since everyone's brain chemistry is unique, its effects vary from one individual to the next."

"Russian roulette in a pill."

"Precisely."

"See?" said Cape. "You're not such a bad chemist after all."

"I suppose not."

"You mentioned Chinese labs."

"That would be my guess for the final product, yes, for the K2," said Dumont. "The ingredient drug is Russian, but the bulk manufacturing, that's got to be Chinese. Nobody else has labs that can mix hundreds of unregulated chemicals at scale. China started breaking bad long before Walter White."

"That's very interesting," said Cape.

"I suppose," Dumont replied. "But you still don't know the why."

"True," said Cape. "But at least I know where to look next."

23

"I want you to look up, okay?"

The man dressed like a pirate gestured toward a dark tunnel, its entrance designed to resemble the gaping mouth of an undersea cavern. The tourists stepped gingerly onto the moving walkway, stealing nervous glances at each other, any traces of boredom wiped from their faces. Return visitors knew this was the main attraction at Aquarium by the Bay, but even they wondered what might be lurking in the shadowy interior.

The underground chamber was a reverse fish tank—people inside and fish swimming outside in the actual bay. Acrylic walls and ceiling filtered the light streaming down from the surface of the water. At twenty-five bucks a head, it was one of Pier 39's pricier attractions, but who could resist a virtual swim with all the undersea creatures of the Pacific.

The conveyor moved at a stately two miles per hour, suspense building as they neared the archway. The pirate crossed the threshold first and pointed his sword at the ceiling. He certainly looked the part. The sword gleamed in the half-light, dark streaks along the blade that could have been dried blood. His face was as pitted as the cutlass, deep crags around his cheeks and eyes, his voice a baritone audible to mermaids ten leagues away. But his whiskers looked about as real as cotton candy, and his tricorn hat was the same cheap felt they sold in the gift shop.

He turned his back on the crowd once the conveyor drew them inside the tunnel, his attention drawn by hundreds of fish swimming through the seaweed on either side. When he heard the first gasps behind him, his leathery face cracked into a smile and he spun on his heel, his voice echoing off the walls like a prophecy of flood.

"Say hello to Oscar," he thundered. "*Oscar G. Octopus* is his full name...the G stands for *Giant*...because he's a giant Pacific octopus, common to these waters."

All eyes turned to the ceiling as the conveyor paused.

A reddish-brown knot of tentacles lurked atop the roof of the tunnel. Bulbous eyes glared at the humans as if studying a lesser species in a zoo. Though Oscar was curled into a dark corner where the ceiling curved against the wall, even in the wavering light it was obvious he wasn't just a giant octopus, he was enormous. His head was a balloon three feet across, and two of his arms draped across the ceiling halfway to the exit.

"Eighteen feet across and over two hundred pounds," sang the pirate. "And a lot smarter than any of you lot."

Some of the tourists looked bemused, wondering if they had just been insulted. The pirate jabbed his sword at a couple near the front, a woman wearing an Iowa sweatshirt and a man sporting a T-shirt with a smoking crab and the name of a local restaurant.

"This your husband?" demanded the pirate.

"Y-yes," said the woman. "You bet."

"Does he have a big heart?"

The woman's mouth did a wave like a crowd at a stadium, her lips deciding whether to land on a smile or a frown. "Sure he does." She wrapped an arm around her husband's waist and pulled him close.

"Well, Oscar has *three* hearts," replied the pirate. Murmurs from the children. "That's right kids, three hearts. Two to pump blood to the gills and a third for the rest of the body. And that's not all!"

The crowd was riveted.

"Your wife, matey." The pirate pointed at the man in the crab shirt. "She have a brain?"

The man hesitated for effect until his wife elbowed him playfully in the ribs. "Yes sir, Cap'n. She's a lot smarter than I am."

"Of that I am sure," said the pirate. "But once again, we humans come up short. *Oscar has nine brains.*" The pirate let the susurrus of the crowd subside. "Nine, can you imagine?"

"That's incredible," said the man in front. "But he's only got eight arms…"

"Says the man with only two," scowled the pirate. "You notice the size of his head, eh? A brain for the head and one in each arm. So each tentacle moves independently, like the krakens of old."

Some of the kids waved their arms up and down, trying to imagine what it would be like to have eight appendages—one to eat dinner, another to do homework, one for video games, one to shop online, another to text their friends, and three more to torture their siblings.

"And he puts those brains to good use," the pirate continued. "Oscar can navigate a maze, open childproof jars, recognize faces, and trick predators by changing color, blending with any background instantly, no matter how many colors or patterns."

Oscar's head swelled as his eyes swept over the crowd. He seemed unimpressed with his monochromatic guests.

"Is it true he squirts black ink?" An earnest voice, a girl who felt compelled to raise her hand. "So he can hide and swim away?"

"Most of his kind do," said the pirate, "but a giant Pacific octopus releases ink that's red." The pirate rested his right hand on the hilt of his sword. "Like blood in the water." The pirate lunged forward, the point of his sword alarmingly close to a man's Adam's apple. "Say I were to cut your throat with my cutlass?"

Nobody moved.

"Would you bleed red like any other man?" Before the man could exhale, the pirate lowered his weapon. "Of course you would."

He sheathed the sword. "Not our Oscar, though." The tourists took their eyes off the belligerent buccaneer and gazed again at the sinister cephalopod. "Cut Oscar and he bleeds blue."

"Blue blood?" A chorus of voices as people tried to visualize the inner workings of the alien life form directly above them.

"Yep, it's being studied by folks almost as smart as Oscar," said the pirate. "Some believe an octopus' blood can help human brains heal. Memories, strokes, seizures, maybe even cure Alzheimer's."

Now the crowd regarded Oscar with a look of shared gratitude. The pirate knew that last piece of trivia would spike sales of stuffed animals at the gift shop. A mere mention of medical miracles could transform a souvenir into a talisman to ward off evil.

The conveyor jerked back to life, startling spectators as the pirate finished his pitch. "Oscar is just one of three Pacific giants here at the aquarium, but he's the biggest. You can see the other two, Ophelia and Sammy, in the big tank upstairs across from the sharks."

A boy toward the back called, "Can we see a Great White?"

"Sadly, no, those beauties don't do well in captivity." The pirate shook his head wistfully. "Some sharks don't care one way or another, as long as you feed 'em, but nobody's kept a Great White alive for long." He paused. "Yet."

"Why not?" asked the boy.

As the conveyor pulled them inexorably toward the exit, the pirate looked into Oscar's eyes as he answered the boy.

"Animals don't like being locked up any more than we do."

24

"I could have you locked up."

"No, you couldn't," Cape replied, giving Beau a knowing look. "I didn't make the drugs, didn't buy the drugs, would absolutely deny that I stole the drugs, and am under no obligation as a private citizen—or as a private detective—to hand over the drugs to my local precinct."

Cape paused to consider the subdued chaos of the Personal Crimes Division of police headquarters. Men and women in plainclothes bustled about, looking more harried than hopeful. A few uniforms shuffled between half-empty desks.

"However, I did bring you and Vinnie some drugs...*after* I had them tested."

Beau's stone visage cracked into a grin. "Now that was thoughtful," he said, "and I would've done the same thing."

"Things still squirrelly in Narcotics?" Cape figured on enough ambient noise so his voice wouldn't carry beyond Beau's desk. After the story broke about the disappearing cocaine, Narcotics-and-Vice had several high-profile resignations.

"I don't work there anymore," said Beau. "I prefer dead people to drug dealers, so homicide suits me fine." He leaned across his desk, the scarred wood groaning as his sequoia-sized arms made contact. "If I was a betting man, I'd say Internal Affairs is just getting started and more heads will roll. Since the SFPD began outsourcing lab work, Narc detectives are expected to do their own initial drug testing, which could make things…" He let his voice trail off.

"Unpredictable?"

"Exactly." Beau flipped though the printouts Cape had brought. "So somebody's selling K2 on the pier." He dropped the report onto his desk and leaned back. "Can't say I'm surprised."

Cape was taken aback. "You knew?"

Beau shook his head. "It's everywhere, that's the problem. And some of this shit is even legal, sold in delis or smoke shops as potpourri, with cute names like Blue Dream, Orange Oh, Black Mambo."

"This stuff does more than make your apartment smell like Haight-Ashbury."

Beau glanced at the lab report. "Last week a street in the Mission was littered with bodies, people having seizures from overcooked Spice."

"You know the source?"

"Don't work vice anymore." Beau drummed his fingers on the desk. "Doubt it's a single source, though. Crackpot chemists are making their own recipes in garages all over town, and stuff keeps getting stronger, a hundred times more than real grass. My guess? Your friends on the pier have their own supplier."

"So you're saying I haven't cracked the case." Cape was mildly crestfallen.

"I'm saying the house is on fire, and you just found termites in the basement."

"You don't think it's connected to the armored car."

"Didn't say that." Beau spread his hands.

"It's connected to money."

"True." Beau gestured at the empty desks adjacent to his own. "But that's a long way around, and we're spread kinda thin around here. Look at it this way—if Narcotics busts the donut guys, you'll never find the source. And if they stage a formal investigation to follow the drugs or the money, it'll take months to make a case."

"And by then…"

"By then we'll have one of the drivers," said Beau.

"Any progress?"

"The guy who was handling the pickups, Lou, might've gone back to his apartment, but he rabbited before we got there."

"*Might* have?" Cape was incredulous. "You weren't watching the apartment?"

"We had it wired," said Beau, a cynical undercurrent in his tone. "Couldn't keep a car there around the clock, and the response time wasn't what you'd call speedy."

"My tax dollars at work."

"Every penny wasted," agreed Beau. "At least we're consistent."

Cape felt a pang of sympathy for his friend. Working for a bureaucracy like the city government was about as satisfying as a tapas bar after a hunger strike.

Beau picked up the lab report and handed it back to Cape. "Either way, if I accept this," he paused, searching for the right word. "This *gift*, then it'll just slow us down."

"By *us* you mean—"

"—you and me both," said Beau. "You'll lose the angle, and I'll have to share."

It was Cape's turn to smile. "And you hate to share."

"Doesn't everybody?"

25

"Does anyone want to share something?"

Captain Cragg pulled the fake whiskers off his face as he slammed the door marked No Admittance. He still wore the pirate costume from his last tour of the aquarium, and with his weathered face and nautical swagger, it wasn't a stretch to believe he dressed like that all the time.

"Anybody?" he asked more loudly, but the only response was a sudden splash and a whimpering cry from somewhere near the rafters. "*Anybody?*"

Directly ahead was an open tank set into the floor, as big as an Olympic swimming pool. Rays of light bounced off the water, chasing the echoes of Cragg's voice around the walls like fairies in a game of tag.

"You still up there, Lou?" Cragg strode along the starboard side of the pool and craned his neck toward the ceiling.

Another muted cry from the overhead beams.

Cragg moved to a control panel with red and green buttons alongside a few metal switches. He slapped a gnarled hand onto the red button and waited for the crying of steel cables to trigger the screaming of his guest.

Lou found his voice as the cage dropped from the shadows

into the watery light. Until then he'd crouched in the dark with his mouth shut and eyes closed, like a child wishing he could make himself invisible.

"I'm here…I'm *fucking-don't-do-this-fuck-me-I-don't-know-shit* here!"

"Glad you're still with us, bucko." Cragg kept his hand over the panel as the machinery turned. "Would've been disappointing if you'd taken a swim without me here to watch."

The shark cage was an aluminum box, but the bars comprising the front panel had been removed to expose its sole occupant. In the early days of shark diving, cages were made from steel, but the weight required a special crane that threatened the stability of a boat. Aluminum cages were stronger and immune to corrosion, but this particular stunt made its lighter weight a liability. A single hook at the end of a steel cable was secured to the center most bar of the cage, so the cage spun drunkenly as the cable wound and unwound with Lou's gyrations.

No matter how much Lou tried to twist and shout, the cage lowered inexorably closer to the pool.

"That'll do." Cragg punched the red button when the cage was a mere ten feet above the water before. "Let's take in the mainsail, shall we?"

The cage jerked to a halt and Lou lurched forward, clutching the bars like a man about to be sucked out of an airplane. He waited until the spinning slowed enough for him to make eye contact with Cragg.

"I did the job," sobbed Lou. "Just like you asked."

"I didn't ask for anything," said Cragg. "But I'm asking you now—"

"C'mon, Cragg, we had an arrangement," said Lou hurriedly. "I mean *Jesus*—"

"—no need to get blasphemous, you fucking barnacle." Cragg spat onto the tile floor.

"Okay…*okay*okay*okaaay!*" Lou was trying not to hyperventilate. "But do you have to talk like a pirate?"

"What did you say to me?" Cragg was taken aback.

"It's freaking me out."

"Me?" Cragg's flinty glare shattered with laughter. "I'm the one freaking you out?" His right hand hovered over the control panel as his left gestured at the pool. As if on cue, a spray of water shot into the air just below the bars of the cage. Lou squawked as a great white shark moved through the water like a junkie on his way to Taco Bell.

It was just a baby, about five years old and eight feet long, but it outweighed Lou by more than five hundred pounds. The dorsal fin broke the water and then vanished as the shark made a languid turn beneath the cage.

Lou's legs buckled and the cage started spinning again. He felt like a drunk stripper doing a cage dance, only in this scenario the asshole in the front row with all the crumpled singles was a known predator with a killer smile. Lou stared at one enormous black eye tracking him as the shark drifted along.

Cragg eyed the shark with a mixture of affection and anxiety. He knew it wouldn't last long in captivity. The great white was an *obligate ram ventilator*, a fish that could only pump water across its gills by swimming relentlessly forward. The tank was too small, like a room without enough oxygen. And even if Cragg set it loose in the communal tank and rang the dinner bell, he couldn't feed it for long. Its movements were sluggish, the powerful tail barely a tremor in the pool.

Cragg turned his attention to his captive audience. "Why was there less cash than you collected? I know you had an explanation, but since it sounded like bilge water I've forgotten what it was. Maybe you've thought of a better one?"

It took Lou a second to respond, his eyes on the shark. "I told you, the cash should've matched the count—"

"—unless you skimmed."

"Or wet suits have big pockets."

"Not likely." Cragg shook his head.

"How can you be sure?"

"That's the best part of being me," said Cragg. "I don't have to be sure...but you do." He rested his hand on the panel but didn't push the button. "So, is that your final answer?"

"We had a deal," said Lou. "We shook hands."

"Maybe you made a new deal," said Cragg. "We both have two hands to shake." The pirate raised his right hand and spread his fingers in a wave before pointing at the shark.

"I knew I'd get my cut." The spinning had almost stopped and Lou shifted his gaze to Cragg.

"Your cut," nodded Cragg, eyes on the shark. "And your partner?"

"Hank?" asked Lou, stunned by the question. "What about him?"

"Did you see him after the truck took a dive?"

"He was at the bottom of the bay with the truck."

"Was he?"

"Wasn't he?"

"I think you're a canvas shy of a full sail, Lou."

"*Godammit!*" Lou practically squeaked. "Would you stop with the *Captain Blood* routine?"

"Errol Flynn's best movie," said Cragg reverently.

Lou stared at the gap between his feet. "Why are you asking about Hank?"

"See, that's the problem." A look of chagrin passed like a wave across Cragg's leathered face. "You keep thinking this is a conversation, instead of me asking questions that you're supposed to answer."

"But—"

Lou's answer got swallowed by a gasp as Cragg's thumb pressed the green button. The ten-foot gap to the water disappeared.

Somewhere in his reptilian brain Lou understood he should

move as little as possible, but when the base of the cage touched the water, he started kicking and screaming like a politician denied a bribe.

The shark had been drifting toward the edge of the pool twenty feet away, but when it sensed the vibrations, it did a slow U-turn and headed toward the cage.

Lou grabbed the top bars and tried to swing onto the top of the cage, but his sweaty hands kept slipping. His legs were already submerged up to the knees when Cragg flicked his index finger against one of the metal switches on the panel.

The steel cable detached and the cage began to sink.

Lou gripped the bars until water covered his face and a stream of bubbles traced the path of his scream. The shark flicked its tail lazily and rolled onto its left side as it closed the gap, jaws opening as the black eye rolled back into its head, as if preparing for a lover's kiss.

The shark moved as if it had all the time in the world.

Lou vaulted out of the cage with unexpected force, but the shark was already too close for a swimming escape, so Lou frantically started kicking. His right foot caught the shark on the nose as it rolled, then his left connected just above the eye.

The shark continued to roll.

Lou continued to kick and kick and kick. He was the Karate Kid on meth.

He managed to shove himself backwards, but the sheer size and momentum of the shark kept it coming, so Lou flailed his arms and tried to swim on his back as the shark continued to roll.

Cragg watched their synchronized swimming with a sense of foreboding.

By the time Lou's kicks faltered, the shark had performed a 180 and was drifting on its back, its white belly exposed. Lou panted and kicked and sobbed until his legs gave out and he, too, floated on his back.

The shark started to sink.

"Shit," said Cragg.

He watched in horror as his prize catch drifted like a turd in a punchbowl, its pectoral fins waving goodbye as the shark sank slowly to the bottom of the pool.

Cragg stared and didn't blink.

The shark sank and didn't move.

Lou started crying and laughing hysterically.

Cragg spat into the pool. "You slipped out of the halter this time, bucko."

Lou, still on his back, regarded Cragg upside down. "The fuck does that mean?"

"It means you'll have to die another day."

Lou flipped over and held onto the side of the pool. He registered the sword on Cragg's hip but was so relieved at not being eaten alive, the prospect of being run through didn't really scare him that much. "You gonna stab me to death?"

"No." Cragg took a long look at his dead shark. "I think I'll buy you a drink."

26

"I could use a drink."

"You just had two." Eva looked at her brother's empty glass skeptically. "And that shit vodka you're drinking is expensive."

"*Khren vam!*" Sergey pushed up on his elbows, realizing that telling his sister to fuck off was like breathing—she wouldn't even notice till he stopped. "How can you say that? Just look at that bottle." He pointed defiantly at an oversized blue bottle behind the bar, a flock of geese in flight painstakingly etched into its gray contours.

"It's French," said Eva.

"So?"

"The French make wine," said Eva simply. "Russians make vodka."

"That's racist," said Sergey.

"That doesn't make it less true." Eva rolled an ice cube around her mouth before spitting it back into her glass. "But it's nice to hear you're so politically correct. Life in America has certainly made you a *samoopravdannyy pizda.*"

Sergey almost fell off his stool. "I am not self-righteous."

"But you are a pussy," replied Eva. "Did I commit a micro-aggression against your bottle?"

"Your mouth is a fountain of bile," said Sergey. "It's not a proper way to talk—"

"—for a girl?"

"Exactly."

"That's sexist," replied Eva. "Didn't we agree this bar was a safe space?" She pouted unconvincingly. "I feel marginalized."

"*Trakhnut' tebya sestra.*"

"Such language," said Eva, tonguing another ice cube free of its neighbors. "Fuck you, too, Brother."

"Why are we here?" Sergey tried for the attention of the bartender, an exceptionally fit-looking woman with hair dyed a vivid blue. Sergey was fairly certain she was a lesbian, simply because she kept ignoring him.

The bartender turned away from a young couple about ten feet down the bar and Eva caught her eye, gesturing for another round. The bartender smiled at Eva before turning to grab the bottles for their drinks.

"I knew it," said Sergey, staring wistfully at the bartender's backside.

Eva gave him a look. "Knock it off."

Sergey shrugged and glanced around the bar. It was filling up with tourists faster than a beer mug under a broken tap. The décor seemed to amplify rather than dampen the ambient noise. Surfboards were suspended from overhead beams, tiki lights stood at crazy angles near tall tables, and The Beach Boys blared from speakers concealed by palm fronds and plastic coconuts. Since the nearest beach for catching a decent wave was two hours along the coast, the bar's presence on Pier 39 made about as much sense as a Western bar in New Jersey.

"This stupid bar—"

"—is next to the guard station."

Sergey shifted on his stool. "I don't see any security guards."

"Sergey, would you wear your uniform when having a drink after work?" When her brother gave her a sullen look, Eva held out her right hand, palm up. "Give me the picture."

Sergey hesitated only an instant before reaching into his back pocket and producing a driver's license. The dead security guard stared at them from a photograph only the DMV could have taken. Sergey thought even the guard would agree that he looked better dead.

Sergey had tried to take a photo of the guard's corpse, using toothpicks to prop his cheeks into a smile, but the dead eyes were creepy, no matter how big the grin. Nastya told him to knock it off in the same tone of voice Eva had used a moment ago. Both his sisters could sound like their mother sometimes.

The bartender finished making their drinks as Eva grabbed the license.

"Excuse me," she said. "My brother found this on the pier outside the front door." Eva set the license on the bar. "And we wanted to return it. I suppose we could mail it to the address on the license, but since we were coming in for a drink anyway, we thought we should ask if you've see—"

"*Marty*," said the bartender, without checking the name on the license. "Marty comes in all the time, after his shift ends." A flicker of a smile appeared as she added, "And sometimes he comes in *before* his shift ends."

"His shift?" asked Sergey.

The bartender laughed at her own joke and said, "He's a guard, a security guard on the pier. A lot of the guys come in here."

Eva nodded once but didn't say anything. A second bartender, a guy with earlobes ravaged by piercings gone awry, was working both sides of the bar while their blue-tinted bartender lingered over the license. The hint of a frown appeared between her eyebrows.

"He didn't come in today, though," she said. "Must've dropped it during one of his rounds."

"Does he work the whole pier?" asked Eva.

"You know," added Sergey, "if we wanted to find him?" Three drinks along, his nonchalance didn't require any acting.

"Sector two. Each guard works a section of the pier, builds

relationships with the merchants. Three guys a sector to handle the shifts." She tapped the license. "Marty is one of ours."

"How big is sector two?" asked Eva.

"This bar, the magic store, the coffee shop, the bakery—the one that serves soup in a bread bowl." The bartender fanned the fingers of her right hand. "Oh, and the 800-pound gorilla across the way."

"Gorilla?" asked Sergey, genuinely confused.

"It's an idiom," said Eva impatiently. "She means the aquarium."

"I should've said octopus instead of gorilla," said the bartender. "Surprised that place doesn't have a guard all their own."

"Maybe they do," Eva said.

"Sorry?"

Eva pushed the license across the bar. "Do you want to hold onto this?"

"In case he comes in," said Sergey, "later—"

"—or tomorrow," added Eva. "You never know."

"Sure thing." The bartender took the license and placed it in an empty glass. "Nice of you to take the trouble." She glanced at Sergey. "Most folks would've stepped right over it and kept walking."

Eva placed a hand on Sergey's shoulder and squeezed. "My brother is very thoughtful."

The bartender gave Sergey an appraising look and smiled warmly. Sergey's mouth started to open as if he wanted to ask a question, but Eva stood abruptly and dropped some cash onto the bar, more than enough to cover their drinks. She hooked an arm through Sergey's elbow to yank him off his stool.

Things had gone well, and she wanted to leave before Sergey asked the bartender if she was a lesbian or said something equally stupid.

Eva knew from experience it was only a matter of time.

27

Cape knew it was only a matter of time before one of the drivers of the armored car turned up.

His client only cared about one of them, and Cape was having a hard time imagining a scenario in which he would deliver good news to the woman sitting next to him.

They were on the cot in the rear of her store, the desk chair having been borrowed by Natalie, the young woman minding the register when he first arrived. Some toddlers' outfits on a high shelf had to be checked for sizes, and the chair doubled as the store's step stool. The removal of the chair left Cape with an awkward choice between standing over his client or sitting so close that their knees brushed against each other.

"Sorry I can't leave the store right now." Vera shifted on the mattress. "Natalie's still getting the hang of things, and Sharon has classes today."

"Nice to see the shop busy."

"It's the weekend," said Vera. "And the fog burned off early." She glanced out the window behind them. The curtains were pulled aside and late morning sun made the cot warm to the touch.

"I'm no closer to finding Hank," said Cape, letting that linger before adding, "but I have some more questions."

When Vera turned to face him, the sunlight cast her face half in light and the other half in shadow. "You're not giving up," she said, not as a question but a simple statement of fact.

"I went to Harkness."

"And how was he?"

"Talkative."

The corners of Vera's mouth moved as if smiling had once come naturally.

"Did Hank know how to scuba dive?" asked Cape abruptly. He watched the lines around her mouth tighten and felt a pang of guilt, but questions asked bluntly got the best answers.

"You don't think—"

"I don't think anything," said Cape. "Because I don't know anything. Remember when I said that I had to ask a lot of people questions?" He held her gaze until the frown lines faded and she nodded once. "One of those people is you."

Vera looked out the window as her eyes drifted out of focus. "We went on vacation in Cabo last December, saved up all year. Did everything together—jet skis, took diving lessons, even went deep sea fishing. Have you ever been to Mexico?"

Cape nodded. "I found a dead man and blew up a pig farm."

"That doesn't sound like much of vacation."

"I was working."

Vera looked at him quizzically.

"That's a story for another time."

"Okay," said Vera. "But if you're asking if Hank had a bumper sticker with a red flag and diagonal white stripe, not even close. You said the police found diving gear, but it just sounds like..." Her voiced faded for an instant. "...like some underwater escape Houdini might try. Maybe ask over at the magic shop how they pulled it off."

"That's on my list," said Cape. "How about drugs?"

"*Hank?*" Vera's legs tensed as if she were going to stand, but Cape reached out and touched her hand. He watched a storm rage behind her eyes until Vera placed a hand on top of his and squeezed. "Sorry, this is—"

"—personal," said Cape. "You don't need to apologize, but I still need to ask."

"I never knew Hank to use drugs," said Vera. "Ever."

"I was thinking selling, not using," said Cape. "He had a regular route, a great cover."

"Absolutely not," said Vera. "I would've known. Hank had a steady job, good benefits. It's not like he was trying to start a business." She looked toward the door as if she had X-ray vision, seeing right through the thin wall that separated the idyllic dream of her store and the grim reality of this claustrophobic room.

"Did he need money?"

"Who doesn't?" asked Vera.

"Dumb question," replied Cape. "I meant any big loans or debt, as far as you knew?"

"He would've said something—Hank listened to me complain often enough." Voices carried from the other room. The store was filling up. Vera's eyes shifted from Cape to the door. "Anything else?"

"No." Cape knew he needed to wrap things up but didn't want to leave, if only because he didn't know where to go next. "I know you're busy."

"I know you're trying," said Vera. "And that means a lot." She touched his hand again, hers as warm as the sun on the window. "Is it okay if I ask you a question?"

"You're paying me, ask whatever you like."

"I'm sorry I got defensive about Hank," said Vera, "but some of your questions sound like you're trying to find out why Hank is guilty, not prove that he's innocent."

"Well, if I can't prove something, the opposite must be true."

Relief washed over her, and Vera lunged forward and hugged him. Cape was too surprised to do anything but catch his breath.

Her hair carried the smell of summer rain, a day's optimism only slightly dampened.

She stood quickly, smoothed her skirt, and crossed to the door. As she gripped the doorknob, she turned and smiled. "For a moment I was worried you had no idea what you were doing."

"Yeah," said Cape. "I get that a lot."

28

"You must get a lot of *kiska.*"

Whenever Sergey thought out loud, Eva considered him a prime example of why ingesting too much Ritalin at a young age turned out badly later in life.

"As a security guard," insisted Sergey. "You must get laid all the time."

Eva ignored him and rummaged through her jacket pockets. Anastasia paced around the warehouse but kept glancing at her brother like a concerned mother checking her son's pupils for dilation.

Sergey sensed his flawless logic was getting lost on his sisters, but he was unwilling to cede his point. "Nastya, you weren't there, but this *lesbiyanka* bartender, she practically swooned when we showed her the guard's picture."

Anastasia looked to Eva for clarity but her kid sister only shrugged, unwrapped a wild cherry Jolly Rancher, and popped it into her mouth.

"She doesn't sound like a girl who prefers girls," said Anastasia. "I think maybe she just prefers a man in uniform to a *bomzh* like you."

"Maybe she was a *zero girl,* a novice," said Sergey defensively. "But you see my point, yes? It must be the uniform."

"We could buy you a uniform," said Eva over the click-clack of hard candy against her teeth. "Over at the costume shop."

"*Novice lesbian,*" scoffed Anastasia. "Have you ever met an actual lesbian, Sergey?"

"How would I know?"

"Idiot," said Eva. "Maybe I'm a lesbian."

Sergey shook his head. "You talk about dicks too much."

"Maybe it's a cover." Eva sucked loudly on her candy.

Anastasia took a step closer. "I'm a lesbian," she said, "and you're an imbecile."

Sergey caught the look in his older sister's eyes and realized she wasn't pulling his leg. He felt momentarily contrite, but since the emotion was new to him, it didn't take hold.

"No kidding?" he said. "I just thought you were acting responsible."

Eva bit her candy in half. "Straight girls aren't responsible?"

"Not the ones who spend time with Sergey," said Anastasia. "Clearly."

"Good point," said Eva with a smirk.

"How come you never told me?"

Eva smacked him on the arm. "How come you never knew?"

"Because it's none of your business," said Anastasia. "And I want my private life to stay private."

"But this is San Francisco." Sergey's brow furrowed. "And besides, lesbians are—"

"—*don't* say it." Eva cut him off, turning to Anastasia. "You see what I have to put up with?"

"Our uncle is a narrow-minded, conservative old man," said Anastasia. "A relic from *mat' Rossiya,* who has difficulty enough allowing a woman to run his business. But he knows that you, Sergey, are not..." She paused, softening her tone. "...ready. Would you agree?"

Sergey opened his mouth and closed it immediately, then nodded. For the first time, Eva considered the possibility that her brother wasn't entirely stupid.

"So I need you to stop acting the fool," continued Anastasia. "And keep your mouth shut. A chatterbox is a gift to his enemies."

"Now you sound like our uncle," said Eva.

Anastasia ignored her and stayed focused on Sergey. "Do you think you can do that, *mladshiy brat*?"

Sergey was so used to being called names by his sisters that being called "little brother" almost brought him to tears. "Of course, Nastya. But why are we having this conversation?"

"One day soon, I will have to take over for uncle, and you will have to take over from me." Anastasia let that sink in for a moment. "And things are about to get messy on the pier." She strode across the warehouse and took a nesting doll from its shipping box, cradling it like a child. "Each one of these, even with the little dolls nested inside, can hold half-a-kilogram of any powdered substance, from baby powder to cocaine."

"We know this," said Eva, unwrapping another candy. "So why all the trouble now?"

"Because some things are worth more than cocaine." Anastasia placed the doll back in the box. "And when the economics of a situation change, it changes the balance of things."

"If there's more money for everybody," said Eva, "why is somebody acting like a *khuligan*?"

"Too much money is like too much sugar." Anastasia looked pointedly at Eva, who was unwrapping a third candy even before she'd finished the second. "Everyone gets a rush, then they get greedy for more."

"You sound like a communist," said Sergey.

"We are definitely not communists," replied Anastasia, "but we are Russian, and we know trouble never comes alone."

Eva lost patience and bit into the hard candy with a *crack* that echoed around the warehouse like a starting pistol. "So what do you want us to do?"

"I want you to cause trouble."

"We can do that," said Sergey confidently.

"How?" asked Eva skeptically.

Anastasia smiled warmly at them both.

"I want you to send somebody a message."

29

Cape got the message but wasn't sure he understood it.

Sally asked to meet in Chinatown, which wasn't surprising since she lived there, but her message said to rendezvous at the Willie Woo Woo Playground.

Cape had been to Sally's home and dojo countless times, so meeting in a playground in the middle of the night was a bit unusual, even for Sally.

Cape crossed Waverly Place, passing by the First Baptist Chinese Church, an imposing structure with extruded stone accents pockmarking its brick exterior at irregular intervals. A medieval fortress with a skin condition.

The playground was locked, but Cape kept walking to Hang Ah Street and hopped over a low wall. To his right was a tennis court, on his left basketball, and straight ahead was a jungle gym constructed over a bed of sand. There was a big slide and a smaller one, a rope bridge, and a climbing tower covered by low trees.

There were no lights in the playground, and the nearest street-light was half a block away. It was too late for families and too early for the local gangs. Cape had the place to himself.

He walked over to the jungle gym and took a seat at the base of the big slide, his shoes in the sand and his eyes on the gate.

Cape's glance drifted toward the basketball court. The playground was named for Willie Wong, a champion basketball player for the University of San Francisco in the late forties. Whenever he scored, the crowd would cheer "Woo Woo!" The nickname stuck the rest of his life. Cape remembered hearing the story when Willie was inducted into the USF Hall of Fame in 2007.

Being in the Hall of Fame was impressive, but having a playground named after you was totally badass.

A car sped by on Waverly, its tires a hoarse whisper that barely reached him. Despite a gentle breeze, the branches overhead didn't rustle, their leaves still green. The only thing Cape could hear was his heart.

"Thanks for coming."

Cape couldn't hear his heart anymore because it had stopped. As soon as his pulse returned, he said, "You could've knocked."

The shadows at the base of the tower shifted, melted across the rope bridge without making it sway, and flowed down the small slide.

Sally emerged from a pool of darkness that made the night look pale.

"There isn't any door."

Cape took a breath. "Bang on the monkey bars, wear squeaky shoes, try developing a cough."

Sally's mouthed twitched, a mere frisson of a smile.

"Why are we here?" asked Cape.

"And not my place?"

"Yeah." Cape tried to read her implacable expression but gave up as she sat cross-legged on the sand.

"I might have a shadow."

"You practically are a shadow," said Cape. "Who could follow you?"

"Someone like me."

Cape started to say there is no one like you, but he knew that wasn't entirely true. Sally was certainly one of a kind, but her training was specialized, not exclusive. The school where she spent her childhood was full of girls who had been orphaned, abandoned, or sold outright by their families to the Triads.

One child too many and not a boy.

Some of the girls became escorts, the rest became weapons.

Cape had met one of Sally's instructors from Hong Kong, and the man's face still appeared in nightmares as unexpectedly as Sally appeared tonight. Cape never wanted to meet anyone from that school ever again.

"You're sure?" asked Cape.

"No." Sally frowned. "Yes."

Cape stayed quiet.

"I left a long time ago," said Sally, "but some things are imprinted on your memory. She could be as she appears, on the surface, and honestly there is no indication that she's not."

"But..."

"The surface is too perfect," said Sally. "Too placid, not a single ripple or wave."

"Nice metaphor."

"She moves like water," said Sally simply.

Cape understood what she meant, even if he didn't understand how it was done. He felt clumsy just looking at Sally.

"If she didn't train at the same school as I did," said Sally, "she trained somewhere else."

"There's more than one?"

"Think of the Triads as a franchise operation," replied Sally. "Global reach, all the way from Hong Kong to the Tong gangs in San Francisco, New York, London, Toronto, Sydney."

"Like McDonald's, only with knives and throwing stars in the Happy Meals?"

Sally nodded. "Any city with a big Asian community."

"Why is she here?"

"That's why we're *here*," said Sally, her right arm encompassing the playground. "I don't want us to be seen together until I know why she's here."

Cape started to say something, but she held up a hand.

"I want to control what she sees," said Sally. "She is here to protect something, protect someone, steal something, or kill someone."

"I vote for the first two."

"We may not have a choice," said Sally. "She's seen me, and I'm known in Chinatown."

"Didn't I say that if you wanted to play vigilante and run across rooftops, you should invest in a bat costume?"

"You watch too many movies."

"That's like saying you eat too many vegetables," said Cape. "Secret identities are important."

"Then why don't you have one?"

"I do," said Cape. "By day, I'm masquerading as a private detective."

"And by night?"

"I'm usually asleep."

"Your secret is safe with me."

A few blocks away a car alarm wailed and died. Sally sat motionless as Cape considered the implications of what she had told him. Another car passed by like a wave at low tide. When the silence returned Cape said, "I learned how to make synthetic marijuana."

"New hobby?" asked Sally. "Or relevant to our situation?"

"You tell me." Cape described his donut discovery and subsequent visit to the lab. Sally was so still, even the playground forgot she was there.

Cape finished his narrative by saying, "Guess where the final product is manufactured."

"China." Sally replied without hesitation.

"It occurred to me that you might know someone with Chinese connections."

"I do," said Sally. "I see her every time I look in the mirror."

30

The Doctor held the mirror steady until his patient caught sight of her reflection and realized the entire surface of her skin was black and blue.

"Okay, Marge," said the Doctor in a soothing voice, "say *calamari*." He tilted the mirror to catch the yellow gleam of the overhead lights, which triggered a rush of blood beneath the surface of her skin. Before the mirror had stopped moving, Marge was looking more sickly than bruised, her flesh mottled green and gray.

"See that?" said the Doctor. "Instantaneous pigment realignment, and not monochromatic either." He gazed in admiration at Marge, who was a fine specimen of *octopus rubescens*, a fresh catch flown to the island that morning. Around twenty centimeters in length, she wasn't very intimidating, but the Doctor knew her eight arms were strong enough to break a glass jar if there was something inside that she wanted. "You know how much neurochemistry that takes?"

"Chromatophores."

"What?" The Doctor turned toward the medical assistant on his left, a petite Chinese woman with a slight British accent, short black hair, and absolutely no sense of humor. She had flown in from Hong Kong only yesterday, after being vetted by his sponsors.

Her name was Joy, which the Doctor found ironic because he'd never seen her smile. He sensed that had something to do with her feelings toward him, but he wasn't introspective enough to give a shit.

"Chromatophores," she repeated. "Specialized skin cells that can expand or contract to change the pattern of reflected light to mimic any surface, predator, or environment."

"Yeah, but before the *chromato-whatever-you-call-em* transform—"

"Chromatophores," said Joy in a lightly accented monotone.

"You said that already."

"I thought you were having trouble saying it."

"Are you always this literal?"

"I thought it was my role to—"

"—that was a rhetorical question." The Doctor held out his hands. "May I finish?"

Joy nodded, her eyes neutral but her mouth a straight line of disapproval.

"Before Marge or any octopus can change color," said the Doctor, "she has to recognize a pattern, identify it as potential threat or prey, then send a signal across her nervous system to replicate the colors down to the most minute detail. That means her eyes are better than ours, and her brains—she has nine, by the way—are faster than ours." He drummed his fingers on the curved surface of the tube that held Marge captive. "Because her underlying blood chemistry is more efficient." The Doctor gazed lovingly at Marge. "She'll never get Alzheimer's or dementia of any kind."

Marge appeared disinterested in her own state of mind, drifting aimlessly inside a tall glass column jutting upwards from the counter. There were ten such containers, each with its own colorful tenant. Second in the row was a female red octopus, followed by a male California Two-Spot, named for iridescent blue rings that looked like the eyes of a much bigger creature. A fish caught unawares would be hypnotized by that false stare just long enough for the tentacles to capture their prey.

The Doctor passed an octopus of almost every conceivable hue as he strode along the counter. Some were smaller than a child's hand, others big enough to reach the top shelf in a mermaid's library.

At the end of the counter, a pair of genome sequencers hummed. Each had a small door through which trays of test tubes could be inserted. As the blood, urine, or saliva was processed, a scrolling sheet of graph paper would emerge alongside a matching digital display, the peaks and valleys revealing the seismic shifts in DNA that define every living organism.

"On the left we have a DNA run from Marge," said the Doctor, "and on the right, we have the corresponding sequence from the, um, pilot." He congratulated himself for not saying *dead* pilot. Though he had hated every minute of it, the Doctor had to admit sensitivity training at his last job really paid off.

He turned to Joy and jabbed a finger at the two readouts. "Your job is to find the gaps. Not the big ones, those will only tell us which one's an octopus and which is *homo sapiens*. Look for the tiny gaps and circle them. All of them."

Joy looked perplexed. "That's it?"

"That's only the beginning." Behind the sequencers a sound-proof window was set into the wall, providing a clear view of the adjoining laboratory. A handful of technicians moved between stations, carrying racks of test tubes and digital clipboards. The Doctor pressed his right index finger against the window. "In the lab, do you see the guy in the lab coat—"

"—they're all wearing lab—"

"Will you let me finish?" asked the Doctor. "The guy in the lab coat with bright red hair?"

"You could have just said the technician with red hair," said Joy. "After all—"

"Holy shit."

"I see him," said Joy sullenly.

"That's Archie," said the Doctor. "Show him the gaps, and he'll know what to do."

"May I ask what we're trying to do?"

"Close the gaps."

Joy looked intrigued but perplexed.

The Doctor loved an audience, even an audience he didn't love. "We can't change someone's DNA, clearly, but we can rewire their body chemistry so it appears as if we have." He pointed toward a far corner of the lab at a wooden shipping crate labelled with Cyrillic letters. "We've had some promising results using phenazepam, but the effects vary across different blood types, for reasons we don't understand yet, and deviate wildly depending on which of our friends…" He gave a quick wave toward octopus row. "Depending on which species is the donor."

"Aren't some of these creatures poisonous?"

The Doctor shrugged. "Whatever doesn't kill you makes you stronger."

"That's not always true," said Joy. "Take cancer, for example. Or tendon damage. Even tooth decay—"

"Is Joy *really* your given name?"

"Why do you ask?"

"No reason." The Doctor studied Joy as if she were floating inside a glass tube. "Just curious."

Joy shifted her gaze to the twin readouts emerging from the machines, the peaks and valleys of creation scrolling along uninterrupted. "This is a very ambitious project."

"You've no idea."

"I'm glad to be a part of it." Joy looked back at him. "And after we close the gaps, Doctor, will you work with regulators to put out a call for volunteers?"

"Volunteers?" The Doctor blinked, as if the word were new to him.

"For the testing," said Joy. "To begin clinical trials on human subjects?"

"Just find the gaps," said the Doctor. "I've got all the volunteers I need."

31

"I need a volunteer."

Cape didn't realize the man behind the counter was addressing him until the blinding sun from the pier shrank to a square of light on the floor. Once his eyes adjusted to the dim interior of the store, Cape saw he was the only one inside Houdini's Magic Shop besides the magician, who smiled and took a step back from the counter. Then he rubbed his hands together and drew them apart, slowly.

The magician held a ball of lightning in his hands.

Cape felt the hairs on his arms rise as the air crackled with the sweet tang of ozone. Bolts of energy jumped with primal urgency between the magician's fingers, sparks twisting and spitting but somehow staying within the confines of an invisible sphere.

Cape's eyebrows and hair shimmied with static, but the magician's hair didn't budge. A black widow's peak pointed downward to an aquiline nose and gray eyes that regarded Cape with a spark of amusement.

The electric storm grew to the size of a beach ball before a wave of the hands made the lightning vanish as suddenly as it appeared. Cape noticed the almost skeletal quality of the hands, silver bands on the ring fingers of both right and left.

"That's quite a trick," said Cape.

"A trick," repeated the magician with just a hint of a smile. "I see you noticed the rings."

Cape met his gaze but didn't say anything.

"You must be curious," said the magician.

"I am," said Cape, "but—"

"There is a thin line between curiosity and impertinence."

"Hadn't thought of it that way," said Cape. "But doesn't it ruin a trick if you know how it's done?"

"Indeed it does." With deliberate slowness the magician pulled the ring off his left hand, then his right, and laid them both delicately on the counter. He flexed his bare fingers, then extended them toward the rings in a welcoming gesture. "Please, examine the rings and see for yourself."

As Cape reached the counter he felt a thickness in the air, a prickly sensation against his skin, and even before he touched the first ring realized they were just dead bands of metal. Misdirection from the real magic.

With the natural grace of a dancer, the magician stepped around the counter and brought his hands together, this time interlocking his fingers. As he pulled them apart, another tropical storm appeared, too bright to scrutinize for very long. As it dissipated, Cape saw spots and blinked for a minute before looking into the magician's pale gray eyes.

"How much does a trick like that cost?" asked Cape.

The magician gave an apologetic smile. "Some things should remain a mystery." He extended his right hand, which was remarkably cold considering it held a bolt of lightning only moments ago. "My name is Davik. Like David, with a K."

"Cape. Like cake with a P."

"Welcome to my store."

"Thanks, I'm—"

"—not here to discuss pyrotechnic prestidigitation."

"You're also a mind reader?"

"Not at all." Davik returned to the far side of the counter and put the rings on. "But you're not dressed like a tourist, and you're too patient to be a policeman—"

"Patient?"

"A policeman never would have let me finish both parts of that demonstration," said Davik. "And he would have introduced himself right away. You have a writing callous on your middle right finger, which might suggest you're a reporter, but the skin isn't red or particularly swollen, which means it's a residual indentation from years past. That could mean you work on a laptop, but reporters typically dress better. No offense."

"None taken."

"Your jeans and running shoes indicate you want to be comfortable enough to move easily, but the sport coat is well made, perhaps so you can appear respectable as you ask prying questions. And you *are* here to ask questions, aren't you?"

"You don't happen to live at 221B Baker Street, do you?"

Davik smiled. "I always wanted to live in Victorian London."

"I hear the rents were atrocious," said Cape.

Davik's grin was as sharp as a letter V. "My earlier observations, along with your age, suggest you are some kind of investigator."

"My age?"

"Most of my customers are under the age of fourteen," said Davik. "Unless they come with children in tow."

"I used to be a reporter." Cape wistfully regarded the gentle slope of the callous on the last knuckle of his middle finger. "And used to think I was pretty observant until I met you."

"A magician who lacks attention to detail will never notice what others might see while he's performing."

"Then there's no more mystery."

"Precisely," said Davik. "Though you must believe mysteries are meant to be solved."

"I was hoping to figure out how a few million dollars could disappear."

"That was quite a trick," replied Davik.

"I thought you might have some ideas."

"May I ask whom you're working for?"

"You can ask."

"Of course." Davik smiled. "May I ask why you're no longer working for a respectable newspaper?"

"Are there any respectable newspapers?"

"You didn't answer my question."

Cape looked around the store. "I thought I was making a difference—"

"—and?"

"It was just an illusion." Cape met the magician's gaze and smiled.

Davik nodded and moved to the front door, removing a set of keys from his pocket with his right hand. With his left he flipped a hanging sign from Open to Closed. "Shall we take a walk?"

"You don't mind leaving the store?"

"It's slow until school lets out." A second sign hung on the door, its face that of a clock. With one of his delicate fingers Davik spun the hands to Be Right Back In 20 Minutes.

Cape was blinded all over again as the sun struck him square in the eyes. Once his pupils contracted, he looked at his new acquaintance more carefully. The man was even paler in sunlight, obsidian hair immobile in the slight breeze coming off the water. He wore a dark suit over a white shirt, the sharp lapels of his collar reminding Cape of sepia photographs he'd seen from a century ago.

The magic shop was mentioned by Vera, and it had caught Sally's attention as well, and there was something mesmerizing about this man. His speech and manner came from some other place, another era.

Without any particular destination in mind, they drifted through the crowd toward a row of benches overlooking the west marina where the sea lions lounged.

"The trick I performed in the store wasn't magic," said Davik. "And in the strict sense of the word, it wasn't really a trick. Magic is merely a combination of science and art."

The sea lions came into view, their barking intermittent. Several were asleep on the floating dock, most in the water.

Davik continued, "Science we don't understand seems like magic, and all magic tricks are merely illusions. The science of optics plus the art of misdirection."

"So, in the case of the armored car, where was the misdirection?"

"I'd say it depends on whom they were playing the trick," said Davik. "Have you heard of the vanishing elephant?"

"Can't say that I have."

"New York in 1918, the Hippodrome Theater," Davik replied. "Harry Houdini."

"You named your store after him."

"The greatest magician in the world, "said Davik. "Almost a century ago, he does something unthinkable. He promises to make an elephant disappear."

Cape indicated an empty bench, and they both sat as Davik waved his arms theatrically.

"The theater is packed." Davik spoke as if he had been there. "People sitting in the audience can watch from every vantage point as Houdini—with the help of twelve men—wheels an enormous cabinet onto the stage. The cabinet is on wheels, so it can be turned to show the audience its interior from every angle. It is empty, the front and back of the cabinet open, merely covered by curtains. When the curtains are pulled back, people sitting in the front seats can look straight through the cabinet to the rigging at the back of the stage."

"Where's the elephant?"

"After Houdini explains the premise of the trick, a five-ton elephant is walked on stage and led into the cabinet by its trainer," said Davik. "The curtains are drawn and the twelve men, with considerable effort, slowly spin the cabinet around in plain view of the audience. Once the pachyderm pirouette is complete, Houdini pulls both front and back curtains aside. And when he does, what do you think the audience sees?"

"The back of the stage?"

Davik nodded. "The elephant has vanished."

"Magic."

"Art *and* science," said Davik. "Where do you think the elephant has gone?"

"That would have to be one big-ass trap door," said Cape. "And elephants aren't known for their ability to fall gracefully."

"So," asked Davik, "where is the elephant?"

"It never left the cabinet."

"Very good!" Davik brought his hands together in a single clap and held them in a position of prayer. "That *is* the only logical conclusion."

"Is that what really happened?"

"After Houdini's death the cabinet was examined, and the elephant trainer revealed the secret. The interior was wider than it appeared, because the opening at the front and back were framed to give the impression you were looking at a perfect rectangle. Houdini knew that even though the cabinet was on stage the entire time, any given seat in the theater only offered a partial view. Inside the cabinet was another curtain, which in the controlled lighting of the theater was invisible."

"Like a false wall."

"During the turn, the trainer simply had to walk the elephant sideways a few feet, behind the secret curtain that ran the length of the cabinet, and keep the elephant calm. Then wait for Houdini to draw the front and back curtains after the turn."

"So the audience could see the back of the theater—"

"—which completed the illusion they expected to see, a missing elephant. But if they had come on stage and peered laterally into the cabinet, they might have noticed the aberrant width and wondered if the interior surface was another curtain and not the wall of the cabinet. But of course nobody asked to come on stage, the entire audience was on its feet applauding wildly."

Cape looked at the sea lions and let the magician's story fill his mind's eye. For several minutes neither of them said anything, until the cry of a gull broke their reverie.

"Why are you helping me?"

"I like puzzles," replied Davik simply. "And whoever they are, they stole from me, too."

"When they pulled the armored car from the bay, the money wasn't there," said Cape. "Unlike your elephant, it truly has vanished."

"So it would appear."

After a long moment, Cape said, "There are only two possibilities."

"Go on."

"The money was stolen *before* the car went into the water."

Davik nodded. "That occurred to me as well."

"Or it was taken after the car sank," said Cape.

"Does it matter?" asked Davik.

Cape turned to the magician. "How do you mean?"

"Houdini's grand illusion," said Davik. "You didn't figure it out by looking into the cabinet. And you didn't have the benefit of finding the elephant trainer, or Houdini himself, and asking them questions."

"True."

"You solved it because you knew something about the elephant," said Davik. "Its size, its weight, its nature. Once you considered the elephant, there was only one explanation."

Cape admired anyone who could make him feel so incredibly stupid. "The money is the elephant."

"Classic misdirection," said Davik. "You and the police have been looking at people—"

"—when we should be looking at the money."

32

Vera looked at the money in the cash register and sighed.

It had been a day with plenty of shoppers but very few buyers. Nonstop from the moment she arrived that morning until closing. She had sent Natalie home and locked the door almost an hour ago, but there was always more to do. Clothes to put on display, inventory to check, paperwork to complete, and receipts to count.

She was used to the random rhythms of the store, frenetic days when everyone browsed but nobody bought, followed by days when customers needed to buy something, *anything*, for a birthday or baby or friend or colleague, and they needed it now. Those were the good days.

The seesaw existence of retail once gave her a thrill, but lately all the highs and lows made her queasy. Sick and tired in a way she couldn't understand until she looked in the mirror and saw a face she barely recognized.

The woman gazing back at her wasn't necessarily older, and she didn't look ill, but parts of her face were missing. The crow's feet that used to appear at the corners of her eyes whenever she smiled were nowhere to be seen. The lines around her mouth had drawn much tighter, scars of regret dragging her lips downward in a losing battle between gravity and hope. Gone was the playful upturn of her lips, a missing detail in a familiar painting that made you realize you were looking at a cheap forgery.

Vera felt the loss of her daughter like a phantom limb, gone but forever part of her. That constant, dull ache was an unforeseen source of strength, a reminder to get up in the morning and face the world. Because there was someone waiting in the next world for whom Vera wanted to be brave.

Not having Hank around was another feeling altogether, a farrago of regret, sadness, and an unexpected splash of relief. This last ingredient floated to the surface on a wave of guilt that only a girl raised in Catholic school could appreciate. Things with Hank had gone from straightforward to complicated, but before they had a chance to work things out, the choice was made for both of them.

Choice is an illusion, and self-pity is a choice. So where does that leave you?

Vera looked around the store and forced a smile, got halfway there and settled for something less than a grimace. She had built this place, and when people came to visit, every single one of them smiled as soon as they crossed the threshold, their troubles left waiting outside. Life sometimes takes more than it gives, but no one could take that away from her.

There are places you live and places where you feel alive.

Vera made a decision and walked to the back of the store. She was going to sleep here tonight.

She kicked her shoes under the desk and sat down on the cot, bunching up the pillows so she could look out the window at the marina. She would get undressed and wash her face later, but for now she just wanted to get off her feet.

From this angle her view of the water was partially obscured by the aquarium. Her gaze moved past the blue awning at its entrance to the mural of a blue whale on the wall directly across from her. The undersea scene was softly illuminated by a combination of moonlight and lights from the pier. As clouds drifted and shadows danced across the wall, the whale looked like it was about to breach.

The leviathan was swimming upwards with a primal sense of urgency, the surface so close, air its only desire. The poor whale had been trapped on that wall for too long.

Vera reluctantly looked toward the east marina. The guardrail was still wrapped in yellow tape where the armored car had broken through, and orange cones were positioned to keep tourists at a safe distance. Vera tracked the rise and fall of the waves, shards of moonlight on the water sending her sympathetic messages in Morse code.

Her vision blurred as the tears came.

Vera let them run without raising a hand to stem their course, feeling a sense of release rather than despair. She sat with arms wrapped around her knees until her blouse was soaked through and the river of regret had run dry. If the human body is ninety percent water, Vera was surprised there was anything left of her.

She took a deep breath and then another, until the reflected moonlight finally signaled it was time to move on. A fragile smile bent the corners of her mouth, a private joke at her own expense. Hank once told her that he'd never seen her cry, and now he was missing the big show.

Hank might as well have been stuck on that wall next to the whale.

Vera wondered how the detective was doing and where his search would lead. She felt a pang of anxiety over what lay ahead as she visualized the man she had hired. Despite herself, another smile swam just below the surface of her grief, trying to breach.

The detective was so different from what she'd anticipated. A man without a plan but with a clear sense of purpose. Less jaded than expected, with the open curiosity of a child she might find in her store. But there was something in his eyes, a restless undercurrent that convinced her she'd made the right choice.

The detective was going to make waves, and that was all she

wanted right now. Sitting still and doing nothing had never been an option for her.

Vera let her thoughts drift to Lou, a lousy friend to Hank. He was out there somewhere, probably not giving her or Hank a moment's thought. Maybe he was dead, but Vera seriously doubted it. She wondered when the police would track him down.

She assumed the detective would report anything serious to the police, but Vera suspected Cape didn't know what he was getting into, and neither did she. She just knew that the people behind all this cared more about money than human life. She didn't doubt the detective's tenacity, but she wondered at his capacity for violence.

Vera knew that when bad things happen to good people, bad people are usually involved.

33

"Sometimes bad people are just good people on the wrong side of history."

Cragg caught the bewildered expressions and wondered if any of these hormonal hooligans were listening. Sixth grade field trips were always a disaster.

"Pirates did dreadful things," he continued unabated. "Raided private vessels, plundered, murdered anyone who got in their way." Cragg shook his head in mock disapproval.

A few students were following his monologue, but most were horsing around, ignoring the pleas of their teacher. It was the first tour of the day, thirty kids and one hapless teacher in her late twenties. Cragg thought the student-teacher ratio would be better in San Francisco, but public schools had gone to shit everywhere. It was criminal.

Another reason he didn't pay taxes.

"So, were they criminals?" His voice was a righteous growl. "Consider Francis Drake, a pirate who was *knighted* by Queen Elizabeth." No matter how many tours he gave, Cragg never tired of talking about Drake. In another life, they would have been shipmates. "Knighted, you say, and for what? For committing acts of piracy against the Spanish Armada and cutting down the

Queen's enemies." Cragg drew his sword in a dramatic flourish, which brought gasps from the kids in front and quieted the others for a moment. "Drake brought piracy to the Americas when he sailed the Pacific—he was even a slaver, but the rogue gets himself a knighthood! So you see, as long as you're on the right side of history, you can do anything you want."

The teacher smiled uncertainly at the moral ambiguity of the lesson. Most of the kids started talking again while several snapped pictures with their phones.

That was another thing that made Cragg want to dance the hempen jig. The damn cell phones. *Who gives an eleven-year-old a smartphone when it's hard enough to get their attention?* A national epidemic of ADHD, millions of prescriptions filled, when the root cause was sitting in the palm of their hands.

No wonder the youngsters lacked any social skills. Hardly their fault, thought Cragg. It was the parents who should be thrown overboard. Cragg might have violated marine animal protection laws and arguably had a hand in several untimely deaths over the years, but at least he could sleep at night knowing he'd never bought a kid a six-hundred-dollar phone.

The group was almost at the gangway leading to the undersea tunnel. Once the students got a glimpse of Oscar, they might stop their palaver and give him their undivided attention. Cragg shifted his focus to the teacher, a fetching brunette of robust proportions. He knew women loved poetry, and he loved an audience.

"Pirates were still considered villains until 1814, when George Gordon, otherwise known as Lord Byron, wrote his poem *The Corsair*. Sold ten thousand copies at a time when only one out of ten people could read. And why?"

The teacher smiled expectantly and shushed her students.

"Byron was a romantic, and so was his pirate. His corsair was an outlaw more akin to Robin Hood than Blackbeard." Cragg had his back to the tunnel but knew the grotto was only seconds away. He decided to end his tour with a flourish. "Would you care to hear a few lines?"

The teacher nodded eagerly, and Cragg didn't wait for the students to dissent.

"'O'er the glad waters of the dark blue sea, our thoughts as boundless, and our souls as free.'" As his feet crossed the threshold of the undersea chamber, Cragg took a breath and belted out the next stanza. "'Far as the breeze can bear, the billows foam, survey our empire and behold our home!'"

Cragg spread his arms and bowed dramatically. He didn't expect applause but was taken aback by the screaming.

A young girl to the left of the teacher, mesmerized by the shifting lights of the glass tunnel, had been the first to see Oscar. His bulbous head and gelatinous eyes might have given her a start, but what Oscar held in his eight arms got her yelling at the top of her lungs.

Oscar's tentacles encircled the bloated corpse of a man.

Cragg recognized him immediately.

Marty the security guard looked very surprised to have visitors, and terribly disappointed to be dead upon their arrival.

Marty's swollen face pressed against the overhead glass, cheeks spotted with red rings from the suckers on Oscar's arms, exploratory kisses from Oscar smelling and tasting his new toy. Oscar preferred his prey alive, so Marty was more of a curiosity than a delicacy. Nonetheless, Oscar didn't look inclined to let go.

Since Marty went missing the same night he visited Lou's apartment, Cragg had assumed he'd surface eventually but didn't expect him to end up *below* the surface of the bay, in plain view of a class of hysterical kids.

Marty was wearing his uniform, the Pier Security patch vaguely ironic under the circumstances. His left eye was loose in the socket, so with every passing wave or flexing of Oscar's arms, it moved as if Marty was captivated by his visitors' panicked attempts to escape their underwater prison.

The exit signs glowed red, but before Cragg could leverage his baritone bark to bring order to the chaos, the teacher lunged past him, dragging two of the nearest kids by the arms and shoving them toward the nearest door. The entire class surged forward when the shouting began, and now they were all crashing into each other, crying and pushing toward their teacher, and stealing horrified glances at Oscar, whose stare followed them impassively. The tips of his tentacles moved up and down with the current, as if Oscar was waving goodbye and sad to see them go.

A burly eleven-year-old boy shouldered a girl out of the way and lurched toward the door, catching Cragg broadside and knocking him onto his back. The boy dropped his backpack onto Cragg's face and sprinted for the exit. Cragg felt the girl's shoe use his stomach as a springboard, and the wind left his lungs as another set of tiny feet leapt from thigh to chest before clipping his jaw on their way to freedom.

Cragg saw stars as the conveyor crawled forward, dragging him along.

Another scramble, a kick and a fading scream, followed by the galloping sound of feet on metal stairs, and Cragg knew the last of them had escaped. He idly wondered how bad the publicity would be, and if the aquarium might get sued every time one of these kids became hysterical when they were served calamari.

He tried to focus as the conveyor inexorably pulled him along. A school of silver fish moved in a looping pattern along the left wall, detouring around Oscar as they headed toward the surface. Green kelp shifted hypnotically on either side of the chamber, daring Cragg to lose consciousness.

He blinked and sat up, his eyes on the corpse.

Marty had gotten himself killed, but he didn't die here. He wasn't Oscar's type, and why would a security guard climb into the tank in the first place? Oscar looked as nonplussed as Cragg.

This was clearly a message, but Cragg didn't know who sent it. And if Oscar knew, he wasn't going to talk.

He might be an octopus, but Oscar wasn't a rat.

34

"Nobody likes rats," said the Doctor. "That's why nobody gives a shit when they die."

The Doctor glanced at his passenger to see if he was paying attention, but the act of turning his head caused the Doctor to swerve wildly into the right lane, so the only reaction he got was a look of blind terror. The man from the pharmaceutical company placed both hands on the dashboard in a gesture of pure supplication.

"Relax, Ken." The Doctor straightened out the car. "I'm just not used to the controls on your little rocket."

Ken grimaced, wondering why he'd allowed this lunatic behind the wheel of his car. His boss told him to pick up the Doctor at the airport, but Ken didn't know what to say when the guy demanded the keys and slipped behind the wheel. Actually, he knew just what to say—but knew he'd be fired if he said it.

"I love driving in the States." The Doctor moved to the inside lane and passed a truck on his left. "What kind of car is this anyway?"

"Yaris," replied Ken, checking to make sure his seatbelt was adjusted at the right height. Get that wrong and get beheaded when the car slammed into that truck. "It's a Toyota…it has good safety features."

"It better, considering how fast it goes. Did they just squeeze the engine from a Camry into this baby? It's like half the car with twice the power." The Doctor adjusted his hands to ten and two o'clock as they bounced over a broken patch of asphalt. "I'm surprised we're not airborne."

I'm surprised we're not getting pulled over, thought Ken. Then he repeated the sentiment, this time as a prayer, but no flashing lights or sirens came to his salvation.

"Rats," muttered Ken.

"What?" asked the Doctor, swerving briefly onto the shoulder. "Oh, yeah, you asked about drug testing."

"Mm-hmm."

"Lab rats are useless for the same reason they were useful," said the Doctor.

"I don't understand."

"Why have rats and mice been used in experiments for hundreds of years?" asked the Doctor. "And, yes, that was a rhetorical question." He accelerated into a turn as Route 101 arced gracefully northward, the bay a mirror in the late afternoon sun. "Four reasons." The Doctor eased off the gas at the top of the crest, letting the car settle into a constant but still supersonic velocity.

"Four?" Ken figured if he could keep the Doctor talking, maybe he'd be less likely to seek distraction by stomping on the accelerator.

"One," said the Doctor, "they have naturally short life spans, so any changes to their metabolism occur very quickly. Two, rats breed like, well—like rats—so getting more rats is as easy as turning your back and playing a little Earth, Wind & Fire long enough for the little fuckers to get it on." The car shimmied to the left, as if the Doctor was about to change lanes but changed his mind instead and forgot to tell one of his hands. "Three, and this is the most important, they lack a gag reflex."

"What?" As someone who thought he was going to puke at any moment, Ken found this hard to believe.

"You don't know this?" The Doctor cut off a school bus as he moved to the center lane. "That's why big pharmaceutical companies like yours love the little pink-eyed bastards. You can force them to ingest anything, and as much of it as you want, and they won't vomit."

"That's horrible."

"That's *useful*," said the Doctor, "if you want to force a lifetime's worth of carcinogens down their throats in one day. And big labs like to prove things cause cancer."

"They do?"

"Cancer is God's last weapon against humanity," said the Doctor, his tone almost reverential. "We've cured most of the big plagues."

"What about Ebola?"

"That's just God telling us to get the fuck out of Africa," said the Doctor. "People don't belong in Eden—we were banished after that original indiscretion with the snake, for which I am eternally grateful. But we didn't listen."

"You've been to Africa?"

"Many times," said the Doctor. "It's a hellhole."

"But you said—"

"The country's beautiful," said the Doctor, "but the people, well, they've made a mess of the place. Humanity took a dump in God's backyard."

"I didn't realize you were religious," said Ken.

"I'm not," said the Doctor. "But that doesn't mean I'm not willing to pitch in."

"Pitch in?"

"For God," said the Doctor. "I mean, *somebody* has to."

The Doctor jerked the wheel to the left and swooped around a station wagon that was stubbornly remaining within the speed limit. As he zoomed along the inside lane, the Doctor flipped off the other driver, a middle-aged mom with two kids in the backseat.

"*Jesus,*" said Ken.

"Exactly," said the Doctor. "Anyway, if you live long enough, cancer always gets you in the end. Might be your lungs if you're a smoker, or your liver if you drink, or your pancreas, even though nobody knows where their pancreas is. If you're a woman, your breasts become your enemies, and if you're a man, your prostate might explode any minute. Point being, in the end your cells run amok until one day—when you least expect it—a UPS truck shows up at your door with a box full of tumors."

"But the rats—"

"—the rats get cancer if you look at them funny," said the Doctor. "Because there's no way you or I could ingest two metric tons of, say, lima beans, could we?"

"Um…"

"Of course not, but a rat could eat an amount equivalent to their body mass and not spit any of it out," said the Doctor. "And you know what? It turns out uncooked lima beans contain high levels of cyanide."

"Poison?"

"You bet," said the Doctor. "And if lima beans were an artificial food, they would've been banned years ago. But since we live in an age when anything natural is considered wholesome, lima beans get a pass. Just rinse them, steam them, clean them up and you'll be fine, because to really kill yourself you'd have to gorge like a rat to ingest enough poison to do any damage. You following, Ken?"

"I'm not—"

"Rats can prove whatever you want them to," said the Doctor, "but they don't tell you shit. Not really. Because they're not human. Hell, they're not even monkeys. I'm not interested in tests, I'm interested in *results.*"

The Doctor shocked Ken by letting the car coast until the speedometer dropped to seventy. They were less than ten minutes away from the overpass that would branch downtown.

"Nobody gives a shit about rats," continued the Doctor. "That's the fourth thing. Sure, they're cute, but they're not dog cute, or cat cute. Lab rats are such an accepted part of science, even most animal lovers give drug companies a pass."

Ken took a breath and forced himself to remember why he'd agreed to pick this man up in the first place. This unhinged NASCAR driver who hijacked his car represented ten years of R&D to his company. "My supervisor mentioned you were ready to start trials."

"We already started trials," replied the Doctor. He kept his eyes on the road as he added, "How long you been in the game, Ken?"

"At the company? Almost three years."

"You must know ninety-two percent of all drug testing is done overseas."

"Sure," said Ken, hoping the tremor in his voice didn't reveal his ignorance. He made a mental note to do some reading over the weekend. *What was it with this guy, one minute Speed Racer and the next a secret shopper, checking up on him?* Doctors were supposed to be looking for expensive dinners, tickets to a show, and maybe a hand job at the strip club—not giving pop quizzes designed to see if the pharma rep was paying attention. "But we still need the FDA to authoriz—"

"Sure." The Doctor laughed harshly. "You ever been to China?"

"No, not yet."

"It's the Wild West out there in the Far East."

"Perhaps," said Ken, "but here in the U.S. it can take years."

Ahead and on their left was a hillside with white brick letters embedded in the ground, visible from miles away: South San Francisco, The Industrial City. The once-proud exclamation looked like an S-O-S from a community lost in time, stranded only miles away from a shining city on a hill, where tech companies fueled a new economy that didn't have any use for manufacturing or industrial traditions.

As the hillside disappeared in the rearview, the Doctor nodded as if considering Ken's counsel. "I like history, especially the history of medicine, but if that's not your thing, you might not know that during the Cold War, our own government tested biological agents on U.S. citizens without their consent."

"You're not serious."

"In 1950, right here in San Francisco," said the Doctor. The highway branched to the right, bringing the first solid glimpse of the city skyline. "Our military brain trust decided the Russians might use biological weapons against cities instead of wasting one of their precious nukes on a civilian population. So the scientists did some homework and determined that the combination of strong wind patterns and thick fog made San Francisco an excellent target. Then they ran some tests."

"Simulations?"

"Nope, field tests," said the Doctor. "It was spring, so the winds were strong when a Navy minesweeper sailed along the coast for six days. Servicemen were ordered to aim giant hoses at the city and spray *Serratia marcescens* all over the city. Ever hear of it?"

Ken shook his head and gripped the door handle as they banked further to the right.

"Interesting little bug," said the Doctor. "Blooms bright red in a petri dish. Like blood. Considered harmless at the time, or fairly innocuous at any rate, but because it flared red, it would be easy to spot when they sampled water, foodstuffs, and of course, people."

"How?" Even though the car had slowed again, Ken felt the need to hold onto something and gripped the handle tighter.

"The plan was to intercept people at random, maybe pick them up in the hospitals if they came in for the flu, get extra saliva or blood samples." The Doctor grinned sardonically. "But as it turns out, the people came to them. Apparently, the red bugger is rough on weakened immune systems, so about a dozen people got sick, and one poor bastard died. Doctors couldn't figure out how bacteria foreign to that climate got into their bloodstream."

"How, how, how," Ken took a breath, tried again. "*How* can this be a secret?"

"It's not," said the Doctor, "just Google it. But people have short memories, and governments have institutional amnesia. Over the next twenty years our government conducted over two hundred biological warfare attacks against its own unsuspecting citizens. They learned a ton. It wasn't until it became public in the seventies and the newspapers got involved that Congress got involved and decided maybe it wasn't such a great idea."

"That's an understatement."

The Doctor squinted against the setting sun and shook his head. "Only thing, Ken, it *was* a great idea."

The Doctor merged with surprising grace as traffic converged on the Sixth Street off-ramp. Below and to their right was the baseball stadium, a modern marvel built to mimic the classic ballparks from the days when baseball was America's pastime— before steroids, blood doping, and players' egos as inflated as their salaries.

"What are you saying?" asked Ken.

The car slowed to a crawl, but Ken felt like he was accelerating out of control. In his mind's eye, he was going to crash through the windshield at any moment, speeding toward a collision with a reality he was desperate to avoid.

"Your supervisor didn't brief you," said the Doctor, "because he asked if I would. Figured I could put things in perspective." The Doctor took his right hand off the wheel and squeezed Ken's shoulder. "You've got a new assignment, and millions, maybe billions of dollars are at stake. Not to mention lives."

"How many lives?"

"I'm talking about quality," said the Doctor. "Not quantity."

"What does that mean?"

"I told you," said the Doctor. "Trials have already begun."

"Here?" Ken took a panicked look through the windshield at his city.

The Doctor smiled like a proud parent.

"Everywhere."

35

Everywhere you look in Chinatown, someone is looking back at you.

Tourist, resident, or just passing through, everyone sends ripples through a crowded pond. The most densely populated urban area west of Manhattan, Chinatown is a watchful community that looks after its own.

Sally strode openly along Stockton Street, though she could have blended in or disappeared at will, a chameleon by nature and ghost by nurture. The street reminded her of Hong Kong, crowded and bustling, the cloying smell of fish emanating from open stalls.

Squeezed between North Beach and Telegraph Hill, Chinatown was both a part of the city and apart from the city, an enclave of outsiders that welcomed visitors as long as they had the good sense to leave at the end of the day.

A third of the families lived below the poverty line, and less than fifteen percent spoke English fluently. Anyone who strayed too far beyond Grant Avenue and the dragon gates would discover that stores dropped any bilingual signage and only *hànzì* characters remained.

Sally was both feared and revered in this neighborhood, as

much a rumor as a resident. No one turned as she passed. Staring would be disrespectful, pointing was unthinkable, and following her, even out of idle curiosity, could be unwise.

Sally moved past Hop Sing Ginseng Company, her eyes tracking everything she passed. The ground floors on Stockton favored groceries and live seafood, with second-story apartments renting more affordably than the larcenous rates common to San Francisco real estate.

Some of the upper floors were occupied by community organizations such as Six Companies, the Chinese Benevolent Association, and Citizens Alliance. Most were founded to provide new immigrants with financial assistance, legal counsel, small business investment, and advocacy for the Chinese community.

Benevolent societies had been an integral part of the neighborhood since the 1800s, and most worked tirelessly for the community, but Sally knew one that worked against it.

Tong was once the term for any such organization, the Chinese word for "gathering place," but like the Italian *mafia*, any group with its arms wrapped around bankers, lawyers, and politicians could squeeze the life out of a community. All it took was money in the wrong hands, a vulnerable immigrant population, and men with souls of tar.

Sally knew that benevolent could turn malevolent simply by mixing up the letters and knocking on the wrong door. Tong gangs were less visible than in years past, but the Triads had their tentacles stretching all the way from Hong Kong into the heart of San Francisco.

Sally and Cape had been working a case in Chinatown when a local councilman who was running for mayor got caught using political connections to help smuggle weapons and drugs into San Francisco. The contraband was hidden in container ships sailing from Hong Kong, and when the Feds seized one of the vessels, they found more than guns and heroin. The containers were also filled with people.

In Sally's experience most criminals were thugs and nitwits, but when crime got organized, innocent people always suffered. She blinked away her memories and came to a stop in front of Luen Sing Fish Market. An old woman with hair as white as snow sat on a folding chair out front. She smiled broadly when she saw Sally, lines on her face forming a latticework of joy.

Sally bowed her head and addressed the woman in Cantonese. "Hello, *ayi*," she said. "What's good today?"

The woman's eyes flitted to the top floor of a nearby building before she gestured at the open tubs of water to her right. Plastic containers eighteen inches across, each filled with something swimming, squirming, or crawling. Sally took in the rows of lobsters, shrimp, fish, eels, even frogs. Further back was a row of tanks holding a small school of squid, a lone baby octopus, and a pair of sea cucumbers.

Sea cucumbers were giant slugs that looked like slimy versions of the vegetable covered with spikes. They drifted as aimlessly as abandoned dreams. Sally never could figure out where their eyes were located, how they swam, or why anyone thought to eat them in the first place.

The woman tilted her head at the tanks, pointing to the one in the middle. "You like octopus?"

"Sometimes," said Sally.

"It just came in." The woman's eyes darted across the street a second time, then came back to Sally. "Fresh from Hong Kong."

"I see."

"You might not like it."

"You know, they eat them live in Korea," said Sally. "*Sannakji.*"

"Barbarians." The old woman shook her head in disgust.

Sally laughed. "The Chinese are no better, Aunty. What about drunken shrimp, or *yin yang* fish?"

"I'm a vegetarian."

"Mm-hmm."

"There's only one." The woman gestured at the tank. "You

can see it now, but look closely or it might change color, even disappear. Then you won't be able to tell if it's something you really want in your kitchen."

"I think I'll come back another time." Sally squatted and rested a hand on the woman's knee. "*Xièxiè.*"

"*Wǒ de róngxìng,* little dragon." The woman placed her right hand on top of Sally's and squeezed. "It is my honor."

Sally smiled at the use of her childhood nickname, now a badge of respect.

She stood and turned without another word and walked north, moving through a dense crowd milling in front of a produce stand before she abruptly cut across the road, dodging a honking tourist in a Hyundai. Then she hopped onto the sidewalk in front of a restaurant.

There was a red trellis over a green door, with paper lanterns hung at regular intervals, but Sally moved past the main entrance and stepped through a side door leading to the kitchen.

Moments later she was on the roof of the building opposite her apartment, gazing across the street at the windows and contemplating her next move. The old woman had described the catch of the day very deliberately, and in the process told Sally everything—and everyone—that she had seen.

Sally had a visitor. Someone was inside her apartment waiting for her to walk through the front door.

36

Cape walked through the front door and spotted them right away.

The two inspectors were sitting outside, Beau too tall to miss and Vincent overdressed for a bar that served beers six at a time in metal buckets filled with ice.

Pier 23 was several blocks south of Pier 39, and unlike its more touristy cousin, this short pier was home to an outdoor bar as popular with locals as with out-of-towners. Cape navigated a maze of tables squeezed too close together, dodging a waitress carrying a tray on one arm and two buckets on the other.

"You're late." Beau squinted into the sun as Cape took a seat across from him, Vincent on his right. "I told Vinnie you were buying."

"No comment." Vincent hid behind sunglasses with flecks of green in the frames that matched his suit.

"So that's how it is." Cape fished his own sunglasses from his jacket pocket and gestured at the table. "I see you didn't wait to order."

"Done for the day," replied Beau. "And time off is not to be squandered."

"Want some?" Vincent pushed a basket of fried calamari across the table.

"Disgusting," said Beau to his partner.

Cape noticed the basket was half empty, but Beau's plate was clean. "I thought you liked fried food."

"Not after the morgue," said Beau, "where the M.E. was explaining the finer points of postmortem tentacle scarring."

Cape felt empathy and hunger wrestle for control as he eyed the calamari. "Does seem kind of insensitive."

"It's squid," said Vincent. "Not octopus."

"Still," said Beau.

"Think of it as revenge food," said Vincent. "Humans strike back."

"That doesn't even make any sense." Beau drained his beer and took another from the metal pail. "The octopus in the aquarium didn't kill the guy."

"What did?" asked Cape.

"Cerebral hemorrhage." Vincent plucked a tangle of fried squid from the basket.

"Natural causes?" Cape plucked a bottle from the rapidly melting ice. "Then how did he get in the tank?"

Beau turned to Vincent. "He's got you there."

"Maybe he goes for a swim in the tank when nobody's looking, to cool off after work." Vincent shrugged. "But the water's freezing and he has a stroke."

Cape snorted. "You believe that?"

"Hell, no." Vincent snatched the last morsel, the center piece, tiny suckers visible beneath the batter. "Just saying it's possible."

"Also possible there was a puncture wound behind the ear," said Beau.

"Possible?"

"Tissue degradation from prolonged exposure to salt water," said Vincent, adjusting his voice in imitation of the medical examiner. "*Causes a degree of ambiguity.*"

"Meaning—"

"Meaning it might be a hole," said Beau.

"Or he might've cut himself shaving," said Vincent.

"You shave behind your ear?" asked Cape.

"Only before I go on a date."

"You can ignore him," Beau said to Cape. "Vinnie and I got dragged through this shit for over an hour."

"Never heard so many bullshit words," said Vincent.

"The M.E. is just covering his ass," said Beau, turning to Cape, "And Vinnie's just busting your balls."

"So it's inconclusive."

Vincent set his bottle down. "When the mafia was at full strength, say twenty years ago, North Beach had a sudden epidemic of guys turning up dead in their cars—"

"—dead in their bathtubs," said Beau.

"Dead at the dinner table—"

"—slumped over their linguine," added Beau.

"That's a stereotype," snapped Vincent.

"I meant *rotelli*," said Beau, smiling. "Or maybe *fusilli*, I get those two mixed up."

"*Ti metto un remo in culo e ti sventolo per l'aria.*"

"Vinnie, that sounded nasty—"

"I think he said something about the oar from a boat," Cape offered. "And your ass."

Vincent smiled at Cape approvingly. "Not bad."

"I dated an Italian girl once," said Cape. "Her father didn't like me."

"He probably liked you just fine," said Beau. "But not as much as he loved his daughter."

"On that we can agree," said Vincent. "Point being, all these bodies were piling up. And every one of the victims died from a cerebral hemorrhage."

"Only they didn't?" Cape set his empty bottle on the table.

Beau took the bottle and thrust it into the metal pail upside down, using it to stir the slushy contents around. "Ice pick murders."

"Ouch."

"Small entrance wound, skin begins to heal as the blood coagulates." Vincent ran a hand through his hair. "Became a favorite technique for thugs on a budget. And if you get the angle right and penetrate the skull above the hairline, not easy to detect."

"Unless you're looking for it," said Cape.

Beau stopped stirring and wiped his hands on a paper napkin. "Cops finally nabbed a wiseguy with an ice pick in his possession and connected the dots. Ever since, medical examiners are supposed to flag any hemorrhages that occur under suspicious circumstances."

"And this one is definitely fishy," said Vincent.

"Was that an aquarium joke?" asked Cape.

"Only if you thought it was funny."

"What's funny is a dead security guard," said Cape, "the same week as an armored car heist."

"And you haven't even heard the best part." Beau jutted his chin toward Vincent. "Tell him about the keys."

Vincent lowered his sunglasses along the bridge of his nose. Cape obliged by pushing his own sunglasses onto his head so they could make eye contact. Vincent was making it clear *this is off the record*, without actually saying it out loud and insulting Cape.

"Security guard's name was Marty." Vincent pushed his sunglasses back into place. "And Marty still had stuff in his pockets. Including his keys."

"Only they weren't his keys," said Beau.

Cape arched an eyebrow but didn't say anything.

"His keys were still in his locker," said Vincent. "These were keys to someone else's apartment."

Beau watched Cape as he worked the problem.

"*Lou*," said Cape. "The second driver, the guy you said returned to his apartment that night—"

"Unless it wasn't Lou." Beau popped the cap off another bottle and handed it to Cape, who was still thinking out loud.

"Marty goes to the apartment to make it look like Lou's still on the scene, to get you two chasing your tails, which could mean—"

"—that Lou's dead," said Vincent.

"Unless he's not," said Beau.

Cape nodded. "Because Marty is."

"*Very*," said Vincent. "And somebody killed him."

"If you kill a security guard," asked Cape, "why put his body in the most visible spot on the pier?"

Beau shrugged. "Send a message."

"That's the only explanation, isn't it?"

"There's more," said Vincent. "Remember the armored car got flipped by a forklift that was rammed by a UPS truck?"

Beau drummed his fingers. "Eyewitness accounts suggest Marty might have been the forklift driver."

Cape looked beyond the pier at the water, gulls darting in the distance.

"Who does Marty work for?"

"The pier," said Beau.

"The aquarium," said Vincent.

"Which?" asked Cape.

"That's why we're buying you drinks," replied Beau.

"You told me I was buying."

Beau nodded. "I lied."

"First, you set me up with an unsolvable case, now you want me to do…what?"

"The nonprofit that runs the aquarium has a board of directors," said Vincent. "Some big shots on the board also hold a stake in the company that owns the pier. Other board members have their hands in some of the stores and restaurants."

Cape started to see where this was going and felt himself getting seasick. "So, for all practical purposes, if you work on the pier, you work for these people." His gaze shifted from the bay back to the table, but the sight of calamari crumbs made him feel worse. "And who are these people?"

"Important people," said Vincent.

"Kind of people who don't like being asked questions," said Beau. "Without probable cause."

"The general gentility." Vincent fanned the fingers of his right hand. "Business leaders, political donors, real estate developers, two tech entrepreneurs, one state senator, a Superior Court judge, and a former assistant to the mayor."

"No shit?" Cape looked at Beau, whom he'd known the longest.

"You see the problem."

Cape took a deep breath and blew out his cheeks. "You haven't found the drivers." He looked at his half-empty second beer. "So, no visible progress on the case, therefore no probable cause for interrogating a group of highly connected people with vested interests in protecting their pristine reputations."

"And the reputation of the pier," added Vincent.

"But you have a dead body."

"Who might've had a stroke," said Beau.

Cape said, "So you want me to make trouble—"

"—isn't that what you do for a living?" asked Vincent.

Cape sighed. "Yeah, I guess it is."

37

"I guess it's too much to ask if we have a plan."

Sergey glared indignantly at his little sister. "Of course we have a plan, Eva."

Eva chewed her gum loudly and blew a bubble the size of a softball. When it finally popped, she asked, "Is it a secret plan?"

"What do you mean?"

"I was just wondering." Eva swung her legs back and forth over the edge of the roof. They had climbed the service ladder from the walkway behind their family store to the roof, knowing the security guards rarely paid attention to the back of the pier. From this vantage they overlooked a huge swath of the bay, the seductive undulations of the water a welcome contrast to the cacophony of the pier below. "I thought Nastya was keeping it a secret, since telling us to cause trouble didn't sound like much of a plan."

"We put a dead man in a fish tank," said Sergey. "That took quite a bit of planning."

"That only took me distracting a security guard while you wheeled an industrial garbage can up a ramp." Eva smacked her lips together.

"I never asked what you did to distract him."

"I offered to give him a blow job."

"*Охуеmь!*" Sergey lurched forward as if stung by a wasp. "You didn't!"

"Of course I didn't," said Eva, working her jaw as she positioned her tongue to make another bubble. "There wasn't time." Eva's cheeks swelled as a perfectly pink sphere emerged. "But the subject came up."

Sergey scooted backwards before he fell off the roof. "As your older brother—"

"—you're a hypocrite." Eva popped her bubble loudly.

"Have you not noticed how I've cleaned up my act since Nastya put me in charge?"

"She did not put you in charge." Eva elbowed him in the ribs. "And I noticed you cleaned up your language around Nastya, but I doubt you've cleaned up your act. I read an article that says the average man thinks about sex every other minute."

"What does he think about the rest of the time?"

"Funny," said Eva.

"Besides," said Sergey, "I am above average, in every way." He laid his right hand over his heart. "I'm taking this plan very seriously."

"What plan?" demanded Eva.

"Nastya wants to force a meeting."

A seagull landed nearby. Eva popped another bubble and scared it off. "Wouldn't it be easier to send an email?"

"We have more than one business partner," said Sergey, "so who do you send it to?"

"To *whom* do you send it," corrected Eva. "You really need to work on your English grammar, *starshiy brat.*"

Sergey didn't take the bait and congratulated himself on his self-control. He chalked it up to his masturbatory regimen and made a mental note to jerk off again as soon as his sister left him alone. "Nastya said we don't know who stole from us, so if we approach anyone directly, then we show our ass too soon."

"*Hand,*" said Eva. "We show our hand too soon."

"You can show whatever you want," said Sergey testily. "If we cause enough trouble—"

"—without calling attention to ourselves—"

"—then maybe the *ublyudok* who stole from us will get worried and call a meeting of the partners to settle things down."

"So whoever calls the meeting is the traitor?"

Sergey shrugged. "That's the idea."

"Sounds like a plot point from *The Godfather*." Eva used the thumb and middle finger of her right hand to pull a long string of bubble gum from between her clenched teeth, then she snapped it back and started chewing again. "The person who calls the meeting could be any partner trying to keep the peace."

"True," said Sergey reluctantly. "But either way, we won't be seen as weak for panicking and calling the meeting first."

"Won't that make us seem guilty?"

Sergey held up his hands. "That depends on who calls the meeting, doesn't it?"

"You realize this is a circular argument, Brother?"

"Is that an idiom?"

Eva sighed. "Let's just say it's not a plan."

"All I know," said Sergey, "is that we need to cause more trouble."

Eva looked over the bay. A container ship was passing under the Golden Gate, and only a quarter mile away, a ferry bounced along the waves on its way to Alcatraz. She didn't want to play by the rules, but she also didn't want to go to jail.

It had been Eva's experience that what she wanted and what her family needed were not always the same.

"Okay," she said. "Where will trouble strike next?"

"Let's climb down from this roof," said Sergey. "And I'll show you."

38

Sally climbed down from the roof onto the fire escape and jumped.

The building she used as a springboard was adjacent to her own, the two structures separated by a narrow alley. Each building had its own fire escape, which cut the distance to less than eight feet.

She landed on the opposite fire escape as softly as a cat wearing Converses. Sally waited until her breathing fell beneath the sounds of the night city. Then she padded up the stairs to the roof of her building.

Her loft was on the top floor, divided into an apartment and a dojo, a martial arts school where Sally taught nice young girls how to kill with their hands.

Had Sally entered by the main entrance and climbed the stairs from the street, she would have come to a sliding wooden door that opened onto the dojo, but when locked was virtually impregnable. The skylight was the obvious choice for covert entry, which is why Sally designed booby traps that would deter, maim, or kill the average burglar.

She knew her visitor was anything but average, so Sally walked around the skylight to the base of the water tower. It was a classic wooden structure shaped like a giant barrel, with a curved ladder leading to a conical top. Silhouetted by the moonlight, it resembled a giant ice cream cone.

Water towers were common to rooftops in New York City but rarely seen in San Francisco. This one had been custom built shortly after Sally moved in. The salvaged wood chosen for its weathered exterior made it seem as if the tank had always been part of the building, so nobody questioned its utility, nor did they suspect that it was empty.

Sally knew the importance of having an escape route, and having a back door into her apartment sometimes came in handy. This was definitely one of those times. She climbed the curved ladder, hidden by shadows cast from the overhang of the tower's lid. Halfway up and around, Sally pressed against a cedar shingle that swung open to reveal a metal handle. One pull opened a small door to her left.

Sally slid inside the tower and climbed down to her apartment. The passage terminated inside the wall behind her closet. She listened closely to the sounds of her home before passing through the bedroom into a hallway that led to the large, open chamber of the school.

The skylight was closed, but trip wires controlling spring-loaded guns had been activated. Each wall of the chamber had a wooden dart sticking out of it. The shaft of the darts glistened in the moonlight with a narcotic gleam. In the center of the room, a padded mat was positioned to catch anyone who fell in a tangle of paralysis. Sally would have been disappointed if her visitor let herself get caught that easily.

Like any good host, Sally had disabled the barbed arrows and poison gas.

Her guest sat in the center of the mat, cross-legged and calm, as harmless as a sleeping scorpion. She stood as Sally entered the chamber, rising like a gentle wave, her hands never touching the floor. She bowed respectfully but kept her eyes on Sally.

"*Rènshi nǐ zhēn róngxìng.*" Her Mandarin sounded like music, the inflections polished and smooth. "An honor to meet you, *little dragon*. My name is An."

The corner of Sally's mouth twitched at the name. The Chinese word for peace was not an uncommon girl's name, but the irony wasn't lost on either woman. Sally was tempted to invite An into the other room and serve her tea, as was custom, but under the circumstances it seemed prudent to keep things informal. There was always the chance An might try to kill her, and Sally wanted room to maneuver.

Sally gestured at the mat and sat down, assuming the position An had taken moments before. An flowed back to a cross-legged position ten feet away.

"I was waiting for the door to open," said An, "but you came out of the closet, didn't you?"

"I came out of the closet a long time ago," replied Sally neutrally. "But I suspect you already know that much about me."

An nodded almost imperceptibly, a subtle lowering of her chin. "Your story is not taught at the school, it would be considered…" She took a moment to choose the right word. "…*subversive*. But all the girls know about—"

"—the one that got away?"

"The one who left," replied An.

Sally said nothing but let her eyes share her opinion on the distinction.

"It is a matter of perspective, *ma*?"

"I'd say it depends on whether you're the one in the story," replied Sally, "or the one telling it." Moonlight turned to shadow as a cloud passed overhead, obscuring the expression on An's face. Sally decided she wasn't feeling nostalgic and changed the subject. "Getting a job at the museum was excellent cover."

Another slight nod. "You visit the sword often."

"Yes."

"You're thinking about stealing it."

"It isn't anyone's property," replied Sally, resisting the urge to say: and neither are you. "No one living, at any rate. And it doesn't belong in a cage."

"Security at the museum isn't bad." An looked up at the skylight as the clouds parted, then let her gaze drift to the darts stuck into the wall. "But I've seen better."

Sally grudgingly admitted she was impressed. One of her old instructors used to speak of taking *on* a life before you take a life—the art of studying someone so thoroughly, you could see through their eyes, even anticipate their thoughts. An was making assertions, not asking questions, so there was the very real possibility she had watched Sally long before Sally had noticed her.

"You're here as insurance."

A small smile barely visible, then a reluctant nod as An acknowledged the slip.

"If you came to kill someone," continued Sally, "they would be dead already. If you're meant to be protecting someone, you're leaving them rather exposed by coming here."

"Unless the threat is very specific, *ma*?"

"There are far bigger threats than me in this city."

"I doubt that."

"You should get out more," said Sally. "But that's not it. Something is meant to happen, and you are here to make sure it does."

An didn't flinch. Sally had her answer, but it raised another question.

"This has nothing to do with me," she said. "Why should I care?"

An arched an eyebrow. "That is the one thing the stories never explain, little dragon. Why *do* you care?"

Sally remained impassive. The question was bigger than both of them.

"Do you ever wonder why I left?" she asked.

"It would be rude—"

"Do you even know why you stay?"

"I wanted to meet you," said An, deflecting the question as she rose from the floor. "And pay my respects."

"I'm honored you did." Sally uncurled like a cat and stood. An bowed. "If we meet again…"

"Let us hope that doesn't happen."

An tilted her head to one side, taking the compliment as it was intended. "Thank you."

Sally walked to the main entrance of the dojo, a pocket door made of oak that was half the length of the wall. It was four inches thick and weighed over eight hundred pounds but slid effortlessly once she worked the latch. "This might be easier than the roof."

"The roof wasn't so bad."

"It will be next time."

An smiled and stepped through the door. The two women almost brushed against each other as she passed. Given their backgrounds, this kind of proximity was the equivalent of a goodbye hug that lasted a lifetime, since a true embrace was too dangerous and therefore out of the question.

Sally watched An descend the stairs until she blended with the darkness below, her footfalls silent from the first step. For a long time Sally stood holding the door, listening to sounds from the street below. She didn't want to cut herself off from the world just yet.

A siren broke her reverie, and reluctantly, Sally slid the door shut. As she crossed the dojo floor she noticed a card laying on the mat where An had been sitting. Sally picked it up and turned it over. The back was jade green and the facing side jet black, with silver calligraphy forming two Chinese characters.

Weeping house.

The building that cries.

It was a clue, maybe an invitation. A safe place to meet or an obvious trap. But which? She would puzzle on it later, but for now, Sally couldn't help but wonder if she really cared.

39

Cragg wondered if anyone really cared about the dead.

It was past closing when he stood alone in the undersea tunnel and regarded Oscar, the giant octopus staring back with a disapproving gaze that reminded Cragg of his late mother. Mom could radiate the warmth of the sun, then in the next instant, cut your balls off with a single stare, often with no more warning than a sudden squall at sea.

Cragg often thought his mother would've made a good pirate, like Anne Bonny, who terrorized the Caribbean in the 1700s. When Anne Bonny's pirate husband—Calico Jack Rackham—was taken captive because he was too drunk to fight, she visited him in prison and said, "had you fought like a man, you need not have been hanged like a dog."

Cragg's eyes welled up when he thought of having a woman in his life who would tell him the unvarnished truth like that. That's when he missed Mom the most. But that was just him feeling sorry for himself.

He wasn't really wondering whether Mom would ever make it out of purgatory. He wasn't even sure he believed in any of that bollocks. Memories of the dead were just receptacles of self-pity. And if the dead were past caring, maybe the living should stop caring too.

All the rending of clothes, moaning, and second-guessing, even the guilt, that drama only lasted till the living felt a sense of closure. The only logical thing to do was move forward, leaving behind feelings for anyone who couldn't keep up.

Cragg often thought about the quick and the dead. The dead weren't quick, and the quick had to keep moving.

Oscar wasn't moving. He looked like an orange gargoyle, his flat stare implying he was miffed that a corpse had been dumped in his lap. Cragg didn't blame him, even as he debated whether it was time to add another body to Davy Jones's locker. No matter how he looked at it, Cragg was either going to have to kill Lou or let him go free.

The wily driver was a conundrum, a liability if the cops ever found him, yet Cragg couldn't shake the feeling that Lou was holding something back. The shark attack may have scared the plankton out of his shorts, but the interrupted interrogation only raised more questions.

Then Cragg had gotten him drunk, and that was a mistake.

Go figure, but Lou wasn't much of a talker after surviving a swim with a shark. So once again Cragg ran aground with his questions. Plus, Cragg was a soft touch after half a bottle of rum, and damn if he didn't start liking Lou. By the end of the night they were singing karaoke. Lou knew all the lyrics to every Hall & Oates ditty ever sung—even "Maneater"—and what's not to like about that?

But that was Lou among the living. He was still a guest, staying on Cragg's boat, out of sight and under his control. But as a corpse, would he still be someone Cragg cared about, or just another pile of bones at the bottom of the ocean?

As for the dead guard, Cragg forced the head of public relations for the aquarium—a total nincompoop—to talk to the cops. Cragg merely eavesdropped on the interview. The PR team didn't know their offices were bugged, of course, but it was for their own protection. If credit card companies could monitor calls "for quality assurance," why couldn't Cragg monitor his own employees to make sure he wasn't sold down the river? The PR guy followed the script, answering all the questions earnestly while dropping names of influential board members like gold dust. By the time the interview ended, Cragg was sure the police would check with their superiors before banging on his door again.

But how did that dumbfuck guard get himself killed in the first place? Marty had a simple task—send the police on a wild goose chase and set up Lou to take the fall. Instead, Marty winds up in Oscar's bedroom wearing a tentacle necklace. Cragg glared at Oscar and tried to make a telepathic connection but got nothing.

The problem with conspiracies was all the fucking conspirators. You couldn't trust any of the sneaky bastards. At least pirates had a code. This whole thing made Cragg feel sick to his stomach.

Maybe it was time to visit the doctor.

40

There once was a doctor
  who, behind every locked door,
  took all of his patients to bed.

He thought it was fun,
  till his nurse bought a gun,

and shot the old cad in the head.

Lou stared at the limerick and tried to decipher a hidden meaning.
It was carved on the inside of the ship's hull, above the deck on
the left side if you were facing the front of the boat. Lou knew
that meant port, or starboard, but could never remember which,
and he didn't understand why sailors couldn't tell their left from
their right without making things so fucking complicated.

The poems were ubiquitous, etched into every wooden surface
of the ship with intricate care, like tattoos on a sailor's torso. A
scrimshaw calligraphy that helped Lou pass the time but left him
as clueless as ever. He was hoping a pattern might emerge, each
rhyme a riddle leading to his salvation.

They were sailing in slow circles around Alcatraz, the waves choppy enough to keep Lou off balance. His right knee was swollen from a hard fall earlier, a sore reminder of the importance of holding onto something. The crew had all laughed their asses off.

It was a skeleton crew, only three of Cragg's mooks on board, to man the ship and keep an eye on him. Lou thought he could take one of them, but without a weapon, no way he could take all three. Besides, what good would it do? He couldn't sail a paper boat on a lake, let alone steer this beast into port.

Lou moved closer to the bow and bent down to discover another cryptic lesson scrawled about four feet above the deck.

> *The old scallywag*
> > *liked dressing in drag,*
> > *though all his shipmates found it queer,*
>
> *But they all played along,*
> > *when he wore a sarong*
>
> *and brought the whole crew pints of beer.*

Lou was losing his mind. He knew he was living on borrowed time. Being out on the water again was terrifying, but after that incident in the holding tank, so was taking a bath. He thought about the Great White and tightened his grip on the railing. There was no way Cragg had expected him to climb out of that pool with both legs.

Lou had done the job he was hired to do, and he'd done it with style. He should be lying on a beach with cash in his pocket and a girl in his arms, wasn't that the plan? *So where was his girl, and where the fuck was the cash?* Lou didn't have to think hard about which one he wanted more.

The problem with plans is other people might have plans of their own. Now he was just a pawn in somebody else's game of chess.

Fuck that, I don't even play chess.

Lou moved to the other side of the boat, were Alcatraz was close enough to make him feel incarcerated. Even on a sunny day it seemed grim. He glanced in the opposite direction, toward the city, every whitecap between him and dry land looking like a dorsal fin.

The sailor with the beard, whom Lou named Mook Number Two, left the stern for the bow, where Mook Number One, a fat fuck with bow legs, was helming the ship. Lou studiously ignored them and crossed to the other side of the deck. As he passed the mainmast, another engraving shared its watery wisdom.

The girl from the sea
  was religious, you see,
    so she always would visit the cloisters,

The monks that would meet her
  were sure glad to see her,

even though she smelled faintly of oysters.

He needed to get the hell off this boat.

Like most San Francisco natives, Lou knew the story of Frank Morris and the Anglin brothers, the cons who busted out of Alcatraz and escaped the island in a makeshift raft. Clint Eastwood played Frank Morris in the movie, which ended as the story had in real life, a mystery. The three men were never seen again.

Experts claimed they drowned in the vicious rip currents or died of hypothermia from the frigid water, but that didn't explain why, five decades later, the brothers were still on the FBI's most wanted list.

Lou liked to believe they made it to shore. He had to believe it.

The two sailors were still at the front of the ship, the third below decks. Lou didn't know what went on down there, but the third guy only came on deck once an hour, and his last appearance had been ten minutes ago.

Lou took an interest in a seagull riding in their wake and wandered toward the stern of the boat. He paused to read a cautionary tale chiseled into the boards of the deck.

> *A man all too often,*
> > *winds up in a coffin,*
> > > *from his terrible lust for some gold*
>
> *But if he just walked away,*
> > *he might actually stay*
>
> > *above ground, and one day grow old.*

Finally, a sign. It was time to walk away, even if he had to swim first.

Lou gripped the stern rail with both hands and balanced on his good knee. Checked to make sure the two sailors were preoccupied. Both were smoking, the chubby one laughing at a story the bearded one was telling. Lou hoped it was a long story with a happy ending. He could use a head start.

As he braced himself to jump overboard, Lou silently prayed the water wasn't cold enough to stop his heart.

41

The water was freezing but Cape jumped off the pier anyway.

The bay welcomed him like a spurned lover, with a hard slap and a cold embrace. Cape adjusted his regulator and let the soft undertow of the marina pull him down. It had been years since he'd gone diving, and that was in water as blue as the sky and warm as a bath. In water this cold your buoyancy wasn't the same.

He sank like a stone.

A kick of the fins brought equilibrium as he angled toward the spot where the armored car took a bath. He rotated his right hand to follow the lanyard tied to the Pelican flashlight, gripped the handle and thumbed the switch.

For an instant Cape thought he'd jumped into a dumpster instead of the bay. A marina is a garbage dump, a landfill nobody can see. Cape had lost count of the Greenpeace stickers on the sterns of the boats overhead, but underwater there was no one to snitch when a beer can fell overboard. Sometimes trash was too cumbersome to carry down the dock to garbage cans on the pier, so it miraculously disappeared after the marina lights went out.

Paint cans. Candy wrappers. Shoes too worn for goodwill. Enough cigarette butts to rebuild *Kon Tiki* and sail across the Pacific. Humanity's contribution to the ocean floor.

Less than twenty feet beyond the nearest mooring, the sand of the marina started to clear. Trash segued to mud, silt, and the swirling detritus of decaying sea creatures.

Cape scissored his legs, the sound of his breath through the regulator a raspy rhythm in his head. The water was less than thirty feet deep.

The flashlight cut through the murk surprisingly well. Blowback from the LEDs made his hand glow like a souvenir from Chernobyl. As he neared the bottom, Cape stopped kicking, drifting downward as light conjured detail out of darkness.

A license plate thrown from a nearby cabin cruiser or carried here by the current. *New Mexico, Land of Enchantment.* Mud. Sand. An underwater fern that might one day become seaweed. A dead crab flat on its back, ten arms beseeching the sea gods for a second chance.

More mud. More sand. Broken bits of red and white plastic, pieces of glass. Might be shards from a shattered taillight or headlight, but it could be nothing.

Bingo.

Cape swam in a tight circle until he circumnavigated the impact crater of the truck. Nothing else could have made such a depression. The vague outline of the vehicle was already blurred, in another week it would be erased entirely. He floated idly over the area for several minutes, letting his eyes go in and out of focus, scanning for shapes.

A shoe. Black against the brown of the sand, almost impossible to see unless you caught the contour of the sole, a man-made edge not indigenous to seafloors. Cape grabbed it by the laces and dropped it into the mesh bag on his hip.

Cape sucked on the regulator and choked as his breath caught in his throat. Sudden movement to his right, a shadow bigger than a man, gliding across his peripheral vision.

Shark.

Cape felt a primal fear clutch his heart until the creature was followed by another, this one closer. Cape's subconscious mapped the chubby torpedo shape and released the necessary endorphins for him to start breathing again.

Sea lions were swimming home from the bay, heading to their resting place at the pier. It was sea lion rush hour, and Cape was stuck in traffic.

An undersea roller derby ensued under the pylons as sea lions cut each other off, racing for first dibs on the floating dock and a chance to sleep under the sun. Tourists would be gathering to watch the swimming sausages jostle for position, barking in outrage if shoved back into the cold water of the bay.

Cape swam in the opposite direction, under the larger ships in the marina. He threaded his way past anchor lines toward the adjacent pier, the long cement ramp where cruise ships docked. Cruises heading north to Alaska stopped here, as did ships bearing south for Baja and Puerto Vallarta. Thousands of tourists disembarked daily to stretch their legs and shop on the pier.

Cape was surprised there wasn't more security around the big ships. Then again, maybe there was.

He considered the possibility that Homeland Security or the NSA had underwater cameras tracking his progress with infrared imagery, matching the shape of his earlobes to an Interpol database of known terrorists. Then he recalled his last visit to the DMV and decided it was far more likely the government had a chimpanzee in a wetsuit, hiding in a cage with a disposable camera.

Either way, he wasn't too concerned about setting off alarms.

Banks had alarms, so if something went sideways during a robbery, you were trapped inside. Take down an armored car and you're exposed, out on the street for the sirens to find you, unless you plan your escape routes and work fast. Sink an armored car in thirty feet of water and you've bought yourself quite a bit of time.

Cape knew he should be at a bank now, trying to find an angle on the money. But if he marched into the manager's office and started asking questions, he wouldn't get any answers. He'd be lucky to walk out with a toaster. So he had called his friend Linda, the nosiest reporter he'd ever known, and asked her to work with their mutual friend Sloth, a hacker who couldn't resist a challenge. If Cape couldn't stroll through the front door of the bank, maybe they could find a back door.

Cape was getting distracted, never good when diving. His head was too busy, his eyes no longer registering the geometry of objects passing below. Soon he wouldn't be able to tell the difference between flotsam and jetsam, assuming anyone ever has.

He stopped swimming and let his mind drift with the current. Visualized the armored car crashing, the driver bracing for impact as it hit the water. Cape didn't have to strain his imagination, having once driven his own car off the pier after someone cut the brake lines. His insurance premiums had never been the same.

Cape wondered how different a crash like that would be if you saw it coming. Would you keep your seatbelt on until the last minute, or would you fear getting trapped? Would you try to jump clear of the car before it hit the water?

Cape recalled the swim fin that had fallen out of the truck. If he lost a fin, would he swim with only one or just go barefoot? The water wasn't deep, and it was a short swim under the adjacent piers.

If you wanted to disappear, which way would you swim?

Cape glanced at the junk beneath the boats but saw nothing of interest. He swam past mooring lines, between pilings of the pier that separated small boats from the big ships. The pilings were covered with thousands of barnacles, their Sargasso tongues tasting the ocean and jeering at Cape as he swam past.

Another six yards, nothing. Cape swam below the dock. He swung the flashlight like a drunk pendulum. Bottle caps, rocks, another shoe. He was about to turn and swim the same pattern in the opposite direction when shards of silver shot from the seafloor, as if a star was stuck in the mud.

Cape tentatively extended his hand, turning the flashlight at an oblique angle to see what beckoned. It was a cross. A silver cross on a chain that Cape had seen before, in a photograph he didn't want to borrow at the time.

Cape clutched the chain and pulled it free of the mud. He opened his other palm and hefted the weight of the cross. Even underwater it was heavy.

As heavy as a broken heart.

42

"I don't want to break your heart, but I fucking love calamari."

The Doctor gestured at the cylindrical tank and smiled apologetically at Cragg. A school of squid, each no longer than six inches, swam around frantically. They moved as a single, sentient mass as if trying to generate enough force to shatter the sides of the tank.

Cragg sighed in exasperation. "Calamari is just a fancy word the Italians invented to get squeamish Americans to eat squid without thinking about what they're eating."

"People eat octopus, too, though. Like your friend Oscar. Don't they?"

"You want to eat octopus, you have to order *octopus*."

"Isn't octopus big in Spain?"

"And Italy," replied Cragg. "Here in the city, visit North Beach and you'll find it on plenty of menus, served with pasta."

"Black pasta?"

"That's squid again." Cragg waved a hand dismissively. "Pasta dyed black with squid ink."

"I had that once," said the Doctor. "Didn't taste any different. I've eaten a lot of weird shit, traveling in Asia, but I don't think I've ever had octopus."

"Octopus can be fried, like calamari, or simply cooked in oil." Cragg waited until the Doctor turned away from the tank. The aquarium was closed and deserted, save for the two of them, but the tanks were lit from below. The indirect lighting threw long, squid-shaped shadows onto the walls. "I personally would not recommend eating octopus, but it's considered a good source of B-vitamins and potassium."

"Like bananas."

"I can assure you, octopus tastes nothing like bananas."

"I meant potassium," said the Doctor. "Bananas are a good source of potassium." He turned back to the tank and tried to track one of the squid, maybe make eye contact, but they were moving too fast. "They serve any on the pier?"

"Bananas?"

"Octopus."

"Bananas can also be fried," said Cragg. "They sell them at the far end of the pier, just past the candy store."

"Are you fucking with me?"

"Am I?" Cragg's expression didn't change.

The Doctor gave him a flat stare. "Do…they…serve…octopus… *here*?"

"On the pier?" Cragg frowned. "No…they…do…not."

"How come?"

"Because I won't let them."

The Doctor smiled, impressed. "A fisherman who likes fish. But you don't care about squid?"

"You can eat all the calamari you like," muttered Cragg. "Vicious bastards, squid. They hunt in packs, the jackals of the sea. Tiny hooks on their suckers can strip the flesh from their prey in seconds. If a fisherman falls into a net of frenzied squid, you'll find nothing but the man's bones by the time you haul the catch onto the deck."

The Doctor made a mental note to chew his calamari thoroughly next time, wondering what those little suckers would do to his small intestine if he didn't. "An octopus is different?"

"They are solitary creatures," said Cragg. "Mind their own business, unless another creature trespasses or tries to steal from them. You must admire that, eh?"

"I admire their physiology." The Doctor continued past the tanks, distorted squid shadows reaching for him plaintively as he moved down the long corridor. "And the ones you catch are worth much more to me alive than as an appetizer."

"Let's talk about how much they're worth," said Cragg. "I've noticed you expanded the operation."

"What makes you say that?" The Doctor looked at Cragg over his shoulder. He wasn't smiling but his eyes were. "Just because I wanted to borrow a few more of your tentacled friends?"

Cragg shook his head. "That could just be your research. I meant your visit."

"Maybe I came for the fried food." The Doctor followed the curve of the hallway toward the steps to the undersea grotto. "Got tired of being served live eels in China. Slippery buggers."

"You're a bit slippery yourself, Doctor."

"Cragg, I thought you liked me."

"I like you just fine." Cragg stepped in front of the Doctor to unlock the metal door at the bottom of the stairs. "But if we're to remain business partners, I need to trust you're not holding out on me."

"An armored car gets jacked, and you're asking *me* questions?"

"I'm not talking about the car," said Cragg.

"Who did it?"

Cragg kneeled to secure the door. The hallway ahead was lit only by a watery glow emanating from the grotto, pale light reflected off silvery fish swimming endlessly. No finish line in sight, but they never stopped racing. "I don't know much about cars. Ships, on the other hand, I could tell you something about those."

"Can we cut the bullshit?"

"Can we?" asked Cragg, slowing his pace so they walked shoulder-to-shoulder. "The lines at the donut shack have gotten longer."

"So *that's* what you wanted to talk about. What sharp eyes you have."

"The lines are longer, and some of the regular customers aren't looking too good," continued Cragg. "There have been more seizures."

They moved into the heart of the tunnel, fish on all sides, kelp overhead, Oscar at his perch standing watch. The Doctor craned his neck and stared at the creature for a long minute, like a reverent at the feet of the Buddha. When he turned his attention back to Cragg he looked almost serene.

"Seizures." He repeated the word slowly, as if saying it aloud gave it power. "How do you know that?"

"I read the local paper," replied Cragg. "Maybe you should get a subscription yourself. Even in a city that considers recreational drug use an inalienable right, a sudden spike in emergency room visits gets reported in the police blotter."

"You're practically an amateur sleuth," said the Doctor. "I thought I was just talking to a fisherman."

"You're not talking to me," said Cragg. "You're talking to the pier. You're talking to your business partners. The consortium."

"Is that what we're calling it now? I always liked syndicate better. Or maybe cartel, no, that's taken. How about cabal—"

"—is there something wrong with the drug?"

"Drugs," said the Doctor. "Plural, there's more than one drug in circulation. I'm…*we*…we're testing a bunch of different formulations. And no, there's nothing wrong. Everything's going according to plan."

"*Whose* plan?"

"There you go, getting suspicious again." The Doctor shook his head sadly, leaning against the side of the tank. "Don't pirates have a code? A tacit agreement to not fuck each other?"

"You know, I was thinking about that just the other day." Cragg paused as an eel almost eight feet long navigated its way through the kelp. The Doctor was standing with his back to the glass, so the eel seemed to emerge from the kelp and swim right into the Doctor's ear, taking up residence in the contours of his brain. "Problem is, you and your foreign friends aren't pirates. I thought you were businessmen."

"And..."

"...now I'm wondering if we're really in the same business." Cragg let that sit as he turned and continued down the tunnel.

The Doctor didn't say anything. He pushed off the wall to follow the flickering navigation lights toward the end of the conveyor. Cragg led as they ascended a short stairway to another room filled with cylindrical tanks. It was the last exhibit before the gift shop and the exit onto the pier.

All the tanks were filled with jellyfish. Purple-striped jellies were on the left, their bells pink and diaphanous, undulating in the half-light like a swarm of nightmares looking for a host.

On the right were moon jellies, fifteen inches across. Lit from below, moon jellies were blue and white, pulsating and drifting in an aimless quest to find a way out. Their tentacles were short and stringy, more like cilia, their bodies wholly translucent. No matter how many times Cragg came into this chamber, he marveled how something so fragile could be such a perfect predator. This room was always quiet, even when tourists crowded the floor and the lights were on. There was something about the movement of jellyfish that triggered a primal instinct to remain still and not make too much noise.

The Doctor stood in front of the moon jellies and studied them for a moment, neither man speaking. Then he turned and crossed his arms over his chest.

"You know how much it costs to launch a new drug, Cragg?" He held up a hand and stopped himself. "Never mind, you know how long it takes? *Twelve years* on average, with all the red tape and regulations. Then only ten percent will make it past clinical trials to human testing. After that, only one in five get past the bureaucrats at the FDA."

"And you're not a patient man, are you, Doctor?"

"Guess how many people are going to die from Alzheimer's in that time frame, in the U.S. alone? Maybe millions, not counting those undiagnosed." As the Doctor shifted against the tank, his arms gesticulating, the moon jellies drifted in the background. Though they didn't have eyes, jellies responded to vibrations and were attracted by his manic energy.

"Don't think I'm not interested in your little project. As a man getting on in years, I truly am." Cragg scratched at his chin. "But the mercenary in me has to ask, how much are you saving your colleagues by bending the rules?"

The Doctor quieted his movements, a sardonic smile on his face. One of the largest of the jellies drifted upward, moving past his shoulder and behind his head. In the dim light, it glowed an unearthly white.

"You want to know what business I'm in?" he asked. "I'm in the business of saving the world." The Doctor leaned back against the glass, and as the bell of the creature expanded, it resembled a halo.

Cragg didn't say anything.

"*You're welcome,*" said the Doctor. "Tell that to your money-laundering friends."

Cragg considered the man in front of him and couldn't decide if he was an actor or a zealot. In the end, it didn't really matter.

"It occurred to me that a suspicious man might think the money isn't changing hands in an equitable manner," said Cragg soothingly. "Because these drug companies, I seem to recall you telling me, they spend billions on drug testing, isn't that right? Billions, with a B?"

"Finally," said the Doctor. "A negotiation I can handle, but an *interrogation?* Kiss my ass."

"The question stands."

"Am I talking to you," asked the Doctor mildly, "or the cabal?"

"Consortium."

"Whatever."

"I believe it's just you and me here." Cragg made of show of looking around the empty room. "Unless you count the jellies."

"I'm paying you for your pets," said the Doctor. "And for violating about a dozen animal protection laws, I suppose."

"You said it yourself, nobody likes bureaucrats."

"Plus, you get a share of the overall operation, like the other partners."

"But I seem to know more about it than they do," said Cragg. "Since I heard you were coming to town, I've been doing my homework. Like you said, I've got sharp eyes. Which is why we're standing here, alone." Nonchalantly, Cragg dropped his right hand to his belt, resting it on the hilt of a knife the Doctor hadn't noticed before. Cragg's thumb stroked the handle with a restless malice, the lines on his face jagged with intent.

The Doctor laughed abruptly, then caught himself. "You can be a threat or an ally. Not both."

Cragg moved his hand away from his belt. "So, what's the deal?"

"I'll make you a rich man," said the Doctor, "but I need more time. That means we did not have this conversation, and make sure you're not talking in your sleep or bragging in any bars. Until the next field test is completed, pretend you've had your tongue cut out."

"Who would I tell," asked Cragg, "besides you? If the rest of the partners get wind of this, I'm the one who'll walk the plank. You'll be off in China, or wherever the hell you're off to next."

"Okay," said the Doctor. "But there's one more thing."

Cragg waited for the question that he knew would circle back at him like a boomerang.

"The armored car," said the Doctor. The moon jellies rose as a swarm, as if coming to eavesdrop on their conversation. "Because somebody got greedy, we've got unwanted attention." The Doctor raised his eyebrows expectantly. "Tell me you've got a name."

"I've got better than that, I've got one of the rogues who did it." Cragg kept his face impassive but felt the tide shift, deep in his gut. The implacable undertow of what he'd known all along. He was going to have to kill Lou.

"I'm impressed," said the Doctor. "He give up the money?"

"Not yet."

"His partners?"

"Not likely." Cragg shook his head.

"You get rough?"

"Tried to feed him to a shark."

The Doctor raised his eyebrows. "That's pretty good."

"Seemed like a fine idea at the time." Cragg visualized a new task in front of him. Take a skiff from the pier out to the ship, slice Lou's throat and throw the damn fool overboard before things got even messier.

"I want to talk to him," said the Doctor.

"I'll arrange it." *I'll say he drowned trying to escape.*

"You understand that if you fuck me," said the Doctor, "you screw yourself."

"That did seem to be the basis of our conversation." Cragg cocked his head to one side. "You know much about ships?"

"Not a damn thing."

"But you know that a ship needs an anchor." Cragg held up his hands and interlocked the fingers. "Without an anchor, you're adrift, vulnerable, and then the only way to stay clear of trouble is to keep moving."

"Okay."

"Which means the chain that secures the anchor is your life-line." Cragg pulled his fingers apart, his knuckles cracking audibly. "So, if there's even a chance that there are any weak links in your chain—"

"—you get rid of them." The Doctor's smile was warm but his eyes looked as cold as the jellyfish behind him. "And you think we have a weak link."

"Maybe more than one. A consortium is just a bureaucracy by another name, wouldn't you agree?"

The Doctor turned to the jellyfish as if looking for advice. "You know much about drug testing?"

"Does drinking till you pass out count as testing?"

"Afraid not." The Doctor turned around. "If a new drug has the potential to cure something serious—a horrible, incurable disease—but the tests show a probability that *five percent* of the patients will die from side effects, what do you do? By the time that drug is distributed globally, that five percent could translate to hundreds of thousands of people. Maybe more."

"Tell me, Doctor." Cragg smiled ruefully. "What *do* you do?"

"You play the odds." The Doctor gestured expansively around the room. "And focus on the greater good."

"Was I questioning your motives, Doctor?"

"So we're on the same side."

"Sure," said Cragg. "Who doesn't want save the world?"

43

Cape just wanted to save his client from any more heartbreak.

He also wanted to procrastinate and avoid talking to her until he knew what the hell he was talking about.

The cross he found might have belonged to her boyfriend, or it might belong to someone else. A wayward monk with a passion for scuba. Perhaps one of the sea lions converted to Catholicism after learning it was permissible to eat fish during Lent. Or maybe Cape was too chicken to bring Vera more questions but no answers.

He decided to visit the Sloth.

A short drive over steep hills, west on Geary until he reached Thirty-Fourth Street. Linda answered the door before Cape could even knock.

She was probably a head shorter than Cape, her true height a mystery because of the tornado of hair swirling in all directions, giving her a presence that far exceeded her stature. As far as Cape was concerned, Linda was ten feet tall.

She was the best reporter he'd ever known, and also the only person—besides himself—who could talk to Sloth and make sense of the responses. Sloth lived somewhere on the spectrum between autism and ALS, blessed with an uncanny ability to spot patterns in data as fast as any computer, but severely limited in his ability to move beyond a twitch of a finger or blink of an eye.

"It's been a while." Linda turned from the door before it was fully open, heading into the interior of the house. "I worried you might be dead."

"I worry about that myself." Cape shut the door and followed, noting the back of her hair seemed to be keeping an eye on him with every bouncing step. "But if I was dead, I doubt I'd be in San Francisco."

Linda laughed. "This city may look like heaven—"

"—but we've both lived here long enough to know better."

Linda glanced over her shoulder as they entered the living room. Sloth sat at his command center, a curved array of computer screens and hardware that would make the NSA envious.

Sloth was the most unimposing figure imaginable, a rotund man of slight stature with thinning hair, a gentle smile, and watery eyes behind wire glasses. His right hand twitched as Cape crossed the threshold, and the screens lit up with welcoming type.

DID YOU TAKE YOUR SHOES OFF?

Cape looked down at the spotless rug, then at Linda's bare feet. "Sorry."

GOOD TO SEE YOU.

"Nice to be seen." Cape slipped out of his shoes and crossed the room, placing a hand on his friend's shoulder and giving it a squeeze. "Thanks for looking into my puzzle."

"It's more a maze than a puzzle." Linda stood a few paces away, never venturing too close to the terminals. One of the quirks of her relationship with Sloth was her healthy paranoia about electromagnetic radiation, in all its forms. Cape was surprised she didn't wrap herself in aluminum foil as soon as she stepped out of the shower. "You're practically Theseus in the center of the labyrinth."

"Sounds like a lot of bull," said Cape.

Linda groaned. "A dollar for the pun fund." She held out her right hand until Cape took a single from his pocket and laid it on her open palm. "Next one will cost you five." She nodded toward the computers. "Now pay attention."

A kaleidoscope of geometric designs blossomed across the screens. Lines flowed as if a subway map was being drawn by a psychopath with a grudge against mass transit. Cape watched as shapes shifted and blurred, new patterns emerging. Streaks of color collided, only to fade and then reappear somewhere else.

"What am I looking at?"

"What we excavated," said Linda. "The labyrinth."

"I asked you to look into the armored car."

"You're looking *outside* the armored car—at all the places the money *inside* the car goes."

Cape reconsidered the grid as it pulsed and flowed like a circulatory system. Sloth thumbed a touch pad and a world map materialized behind the colored lines. Paths circled major metropolitan areas, then blended and dispersed at port cities before zooming offshore, only to complete the cycle by darting across the ocean to another financial center. Some lines cut through places unidentified by name, outposts in northern Canada, Siberia, and inland China.

"Let's pretend I'm lost in your maze." Cape tracked a blue line from central Russia through China, then across the Pacific to San Francisco, where it wrestled with countless other lines in an orgy of color and purpose. "Actually, there's no need to pretend. I'm lost."

"Start here." Linda pointed at a pulsating knot over San Francisco. "Notice how that area is never clear, lines always coming and going?"

"Yup."

"That's because we built the map with Pier 39 as the hub. The armored car was collecting money from businesses on the pier, so that's our starting point."

Sloth did something to the program, and a spot in San Francisco near the pier glowed. Cape squinted—it was near the financial district, somewhere on California Street. A bright green ribbon emerged from that locus point and split into four, then sixteen, then sixty-four, and ultimately hundreds of lines branching across the globe.

"That's the bank that contracted the armored car," said Linda. "And all the paths of its investments—and investors. And that's why a simple maze turns into a labyrinth. The bank has a *highly* diversified portfolio."

"Which bank?"

"The People's Bank."

Cape arched an eyebrow. "Kind of a generic name for a global bank."

"Before the banking crisis it was Commerce Bank of China." Linda glanced at her notebook. "Then when it moved into business loans, mortgages, and local banking services, it opened a branch in Chinatown and became People's Bank of China for a while, but that sounded—"

"—too Cultural Revolution?"

Linda nodded. "So now it's The People's Bank."

"But who are the people who run the bank?" Cape tried to pick a single line and follow its course across the screens and around the globe. By the time it split and raced across four compass points, he was lost. He tried again with a different line, ignoring the secondary branches, but only got halfway around the world before losing the thread in the middle of the Mediterranean. Cape stepped closer to the screen and pointed at the rat's nest of color in the middle of the sea.

"What's that?"

CYPRUS.

"It looks like a Spirograph doodle."

Sloth titled his head almost imperceptibly.

HOME TO OFFSHORE BANKS. VERY POPULAR WITH RUSSIAN OLIGARCHS.

"Look at Panama," said Linda. "Another offshore haven."

Cape shifted to the western hemisphere and saw a tangle of lines throbbing with potential mischief.

"Ever hear of the Panama Papers?" asked Linda.

Cape shook his head.

"It was big news about a year ago," Linda replied, "but mostly in the U.K., Iceland, and Eastern Europe. The BBC ran a whole series on it, but it only got covered by business journals in the U.S. for a day or so."

"So what did I miss?"

"An anonymous source inside one of the largest offshore banking operations, Mossack Fonseca, spilled millions of confidential records onto the internet."

OVER 11 MILLION RECORDS, NEARLY 2.6 TERA-BYTES OF DATA.

"But who's counting?" Cape smiled at Sloth. "And?"

"And it turns out over a hundred world leaders, including the prime minister of Iceland, several Russian oligarchs, and a former prime minister of England apparently had offshore accounts to hide their investments from auditors. Most of the accounts were managed by proxy. In other words, low-profile acquaintances and relatives—a nephew, family friend, in some cases complete strangers—were made signatories on accounts worth millions of dollars."

"Money laundering."

PROBABLY.

"But not necessarily," said Linda. "Money laundering is incredibly difficult to prove, because the trail…" She waved at the screens, her hair nodding emphatically. "…the trail is notoriously difficult to follow. They might have been banking offshore simply to avoid taxes at home."

"So politicians who raise taxes on everyone else were dodging them?" Cape scowled.

"Not to mention the perennial puzzle," said Linda. "How does a public servant like the prime minister of Iceland make millions of dollars while in office?"

"Anyone go to jail?"

"A couple of other low-level Mossack Fonseca employees." Linda's hair swayed indignantly. "And an IT guy at the bank who was blamed for the data breach."

"The IT guy?" Cape turned to see if Linda was joking but her follicles looked deadly serious. "What about the politicians?"

"Some resigned, most just stonewalled," said Linda. "Investigations are ongoing, but the furor subsided as soon as the press lost interest."

Cape glanced at the miasma of color over Panama, then back toward Cyprus, letting his eyes drift out of focus until they found their way back to San Francisco. "So how does this compare?"

"We just got started," replied Linda. "But if you're asking if this is the normal pattern for cash flow at your local bank, the answer is no, not by a long shot."

WATCH THIS.

Lines started to fade into the background as the hubs glowed brighter, a constellation of transactions defining a network. Most of the dots were green as envy, a handful of others were blue. Cape pointed randomly at one of the green spots in the Pacific Northwest.

"What's that?"

"Pike Place Market in Seattle," said Linda.

"How about that one?" Cape gestured toward Florida.

DISNEY WORLD

Cape arched an eyebrow and waved toward Europe.

"Euro Disney," said Linda. "Sorry, I mean Disneyland Paris. I always forget they renamed it."

Cape looked befuddled. "Why?"

"Would you go to *Euro Disney*?"

"Now that you mention it, no," said Cape. "I wouldn't."

"That was the problem," said Linda. "Attendance was dismal till they changed the name."

A green dot beckoned from Canada.

"Give me a hint," said Cape.

"Six Flags," said Linda.

"There's a Six Flags in Canada?"

"Montreal."

"That's an even bigger mystery than this armored car heist," said Cape.

NOT QUITE.

"Clearly there's a pattern." Cape studied the highlights on the map.

Linda's hair nodded vigorously. "Major tourist destinations, minimum ten-to-twelve different nationalities converging on a single location, and a high percentage of cash businesses in the area."

"Looks to me like the spin cycle on one big-ass money-laundering operation."

"Us, too," said Linda.

"But you said—"

"—it's tough to prove." Linda made a curt gesture at the latticework on the screen.

NOT IMPOSSIBLE, BUT TOUGH

"Even in the case of the Panama Papers, with actual leaked documents, they barely made a dent," said Linda. "So, it probably wouldn't hold up in court."

"Good thing I'm not a judge," replied Cape.

ESPECIALLY CONSIDERING WE OBTAINED THIS DATA ILLEGALLY

"Good thing I'm not a cop," added Cape.

Linda didn't say anything. The hum of the monitors was the only sound as Cape stood silently and let the enormity of the pattern reveal itself. This was a global operation, organized and determined, and he was one man, disorganized and ambivalent.

"We were thinking about sending an anonymous tip to the FBI," said Linda, reading his thoughts. "You still on good terms with that agent, was it Johnson?"

Cape shrugged. "If he hasn't retired, but this is global. They're federal, they usually need a domestic angle."

"CIA?"

"Busy fighting terrorism."

"Interpol?"

Cape shook his head. "If we invite one to the party, they'll all want to come, and then—"

"—it's not your party anymore."

"What do you always tell me when I throw my trash in the wrong container and don't recycle? Think globally, act—"

"—locally."

"This is big," said Cape. "So we need to think small."

I LIKE THE WAY YOU THINK.

"Coming from you, that's no small compliment. Can you zoom in on San Francisco?"

The map shimmered and the center screen became one city, a lopsided square surrounded by water on three sides. Colored lines followed the streets, leading to midsized blobs scattered across the city. There was a noticeable contrast to the world map, a blatant lack of symmetry.

Three glowing orbs dominated this grid, as disproportionate to the rest of the dots as the sun is to planets in a solar system. The pier was the largest, followed by the bank, then two spots south of the city proper, between Potrero Hill and Hunter's Point.

Cape pointed at the southernmost blob. Before he could ask, Linda read aloud from her notes. "That just looks big because of the reduced scale of this map. Globally, it shrinks to normal size, but the pier stays fairly large like the other tourist hubs."

"But what is it, another bank?"

"No," said Linda. "It's one of the bank's biggest local depositors, Hopewell Pharmaceuticals."

Cape stared at the map as she continued reading.

"Headquarters are near UCSF. One of the city's biggest

employers, after you factor out the tech companies. Hopewell has multiple business loans with the bank, presumably for capital investment."

"Have you looked into it?"

YOU MEAN BEHIND THE WALL?

Cape nodded.

NO TIME.

"From the outside it looks clean," said Linda.

"As clean as fresh laundry?"

"Fair enough," Linda said. "I forgot how cynical you are."

"I'm not cynical, I'm inquisitive."

YOU MEAN NOSY.

"That, too." Cape gestured at the other unidentified orb. "And that one?"

"Pratas Construction," replied Linda. "Builders. The company is headquartered here but handles construction projects all over the world."

"What do they build?"

"The new UCSF library, and a hospital near San Mateo. A factory in China and a mining operation in Chile." Linda scanned her notes. "Some other business in Europe, China, and Central America—all big industrial projects, at first glance."

"Take a second glance," said Cape.

Linda looked at Sloth. "Give us a couple of days. These giant corporations tend to have pretty tight security."

A DAY SHOULD BE FINE, TWO AT MOST

"Can you zoom into the pier?"

A Technicolor grid coalesced, a city within a city. At the center was a massive blue dot, connected by ephemeral threads to green spheres, then tenuously linked to medium-orange blobs and red dots of lesser size.

"What are those?"

Linda looked at her notebook. "The big blue ball is the aquarium, the biggest tourist spot on the pier. The greens are the major restaurants, chains mostly. Orange are gift shops and smaller food stands, red are specialty stores."

Cape arched an eyebrow and turned to Linda. "You really want to make an anonymous tip?"

"I thought you—"

"—call the aquarium and all the green balls," said Cape. "If you have time, one or two of the orange ones."

"And?"

"Tell them you're calling to set up an appointment for me, to ask some questions," said Cape. "About money laundering."

I DON'T LIKE THE WAY YOU THINK.

"You can't take back a compliment," said Cape. "Once given, it's mine forever."

"This does sound like a bad idea," added Linda.

THAT'S BECAUSE IT IS A BAD IDEA.

"But it's the only idea I've got," said Cape.

"What about the bank?"

"Don't contact the bank. Not yet. Only their customers." Cape looked at the map again. "The biggest dots on the pier, plus the construction and pharmaceutical companies. Tell them I'd like to interview them as soon as possible."

"You could get sued for libel just for scheduling that meeting." Linda frowned. "Companies like that have lawyers for their lawyers."

"I'm desperate."

"Fine." Linda held his gaze for a long minute, her hair vibrating disapprovingly.

"Thanks," said Cape. He stepped over to Sloth and squeezed his shoulder again. "Don't get caught."

The maps faded as a single message scrolled across the screens until it ran off the edge.

HA HA HA HA HA HA HA HA HA HA HA HA HA HA HA HA HA HA

Linda walked Cape to the door. "You're his favorite," she said. "When I tell him to be careful, he just gets defensive."

"I've known him longer." Cape hugged Linda despite her hair's attempt to push him away. "Thanks again."

"What are you going to do now?"

"Play to my strengths," said Cape, "and piss people off."

44

"I don't want you to piss anyone off."

Sally didn't answer. Cape thought she might be smirking until he realized it could be a frown. It was so hard to tell when she was upside down.

Sally walked on her hands across the floor of his office, then rotated like a Ferris wheel onto her feet without missing a step. She looked back over her shoulder. Definitely a frown.

"I never annoy anyone," she said levelly. "That's your specialty. I either seduce them or—"

"—maim them."

"I suppose getting maimed could be considered—"

"—annoying, yes. That's my point." Cape pointed at the chair in front of his desk, but knew it was a futile gesture. Sally came in through the window and had been roaming like a cat since she arrived.

"You want me to visit your bank." Sally stood in the far corner of the office but her disembodied voice sounded like she was standing directly behind him. Cape thought it might be the acoustics but suspected it was one of her many tricks.

"It's not my bank," said Cape. "It's The People's Bank."

"But I already know this bank. It serves the community."

Cape knew "community" meant Chinatown. "I need to know something very specific."

"If you're looking for a criminal connection to anyone on the mainland, don't bother." Sally's floating voice sounded bitter. "The Triads have too many legitimate business interests."

"I'm looking for a reaction." Cape held up a sheet of paper. "Between the cops and Sloth, I've now got a list of names." Sally didn't move, so he folded the list into a paper airplane and sent it sailing in her direction. "Everyone who's anyone connected to the pier—investors, sponsors, board members."

Sally snatched the airplane midflight before it veered through the open window. As she unfolded the paper she asked, "Anyone in particular?"

"The list is prioritized, big donors and public figures at the top."

Sally raised her eyebrows. "Even I recognize some of these names."

"The landed gentry of San Francisco." Cape folded another paper plane and set it soaring, but it slammed into the wall before getting anywhere near the window. "The reason the same investors keep getting rich from San Francisco real estate isn't because they have better instincts, it's because they're friends with the developers, who are friends with the politicians, who become investors themselves in the development projects they approve. So, when city politicians green-light a new project—"

"—they tell their friends," said Sally.

"And the circle starts all over again," said Cape.

"Like a dragon eating its own tail."

"Or a dog licking its own balls."

"*Language,*" said Sally. "But I take your point."

"By the time you arrive, Linda will have called most of the bank's clients and given them a poke in the ribs."

"And your name."

Cape held his hands together in front of his chest, the Japanese gesture meaning please or thank you that he'd learned from using emojis on his cell phone. Sally didn't seem impressed, so he added, "I know it's a fishing expedition."

"I've heard some people fish by throwing sticks of dynamite into the water and waiting until dead fish float to the surface," said Sally. "But I never believed it."

"Was that sarcasm?"

"Not if you have to ask." Sally's mouth twitched. "I'm just suggesting that you're better at causing a ruckus than I am."

"Your Chinese is better than mine," replied Cape. "And according to Linda, the bank manager came from Hong Kong. He doubtless speaks English better than I do, but this should be a nuanced conversation, and when it comes to Chinese, I can't tell the difference between *moo shu* and *wushu*."

"One is shredded pork, and the other is a Chinese martial art."

"But which is which?" asked Cape. "Not only that, *which witch is the witch to which I could switch without a hitch*?"

Sally definitely smirked this time.

"Context matters," added Cape.

"So I'm considering a small business loan?"

"Your school is technically a small business," said Cape. "Seems plausible."

"Seems thin," replied Sally. "But defensible."

Cape nodded. "So, if they find their way back to me—"

"—then one of their clients must have contacted them."

"In a hurry."

"I take it back," said Sally. "This isn't like fishing with dynamite."

"Thanks."

"More like a grenade."

Cape shrugged. "I can't think of another play."

"*Hamlet.*"

"Funny." Cape stood and stretched. "If I go, the manager will just deflect, but while you're vetting the bank as a potential customer..."

Sally waved the list in her right hand. "I'm dropping names—"

"—like little sticks of dynamite."

"Boom," said Sally quietly. "I just hope you're ready for the blowback."

Cape let his eyes drift toward the window as he visualized the schematic of cash flowing across the pier. "When can you go?"

"About an hour." Sally glanced outside to gauge the position of the sun. "It's still early enough to go home and change into something—"

"—less intimidating?"

"Something that looks like I want my loan application to be approved."

"I hope I'm not wasting your time."

"That would be a first." Sally smiled.

"I just need an angle," said Cape. "The bank is at the center of everything, but I don't think it's *behind* everything. To be honest, I don't even know what I'm investigating anymore."

"That's why it's a mystery."

"I was always partial to thrillers," said Cape.

"You don't get to write your own story," said Sally. "You know that."

"Yeah," said Cape. "But the guy who's writing mine must be one sick bastard."

45

Linda felt sick as she hung up the phone.

While she was making calls, Linda was all business. She used her reporter's voice to push through any gatekeepers until she got an executive assistant, public relations department, or the personal voicemail of someone in charge.

But now that she'd finished calling a dozen businesses, on and off the pier, she felt nauseous. As if she'd set something inexorable in motion, a runaway train about to jump the tracks. She wished she could blame the buzzing in her head on radiation from the phone, but she was using a landline, and besides, Linda wasn't in the habit of lying to herself.

She glanced at the screens across the room, Sloth's hands twitching on his keyboard. The glowing orb of the bank swelled as data streamed through it, tentacles of color reaching across the map. Like a child's sketch of a sea monster, drawn with every crayon in the box. A psychedelic kraken.

Linda watched it pulse and spread, a single entity with impossible reach and insidious purpose. If the gothic novelist H.P. Lovecraft had ever dreamt about money, it would've looked something like this.

Linda had been a journalist long enough to know that phone

calls were a game of polite deflections and guilty inflections. A good reporter could catch them all, if they listened hard enough. But in the real world it was actions that counted, not words. Actions taken by desperate people with something to lose.

And in Linda's experience, nobody liked to lose.

46

Lou didn't want to lose consciousness.

A deathly chill as a wave shoved him underwater, but he bobbed to the surface with the passive buoyancy of an empty promise.

He couldn't feel his arms, so he stopped paddling, but the cold was keeping him awake and that gave him hope. When he stopped feeling cold, then he would probably stop feeling. Lou wasn't an optimist, but he was an opportunist, so he'd take anything he could get if it meant staying alive.

Lou was desperate when he jumped overboard, ready to walk away if he could just get away. Forget the cash if they could forget about him. But Lou knew they wouldn't forget, and he couldn't walk away without leverage. To them, he was the loosest of loose ends.

So now he was pissed, tired of spitting water like a dolphin with acid reflux. He was probably going to drown, and normally that thought would be terrifying, but Lou had been afraid of dying for the last thirty-six hours. His adrenal glands could only take so much. Death by pirate, then death by shark, and now death by drowning.

He could give in to the cold, the sea, and the sheer weight of his own guilt. Or he could float like a fishing lure, kick with the current, and plot his revenge.

Because revenge is like fish served cold.

Or a dish with mold.

A wish well told?

Maybe tuna fish not sold.

Fuck it, he could never get his idioms straight. Whatever revenge was before, it was Lou's watchword now.

They built a consortium, good for them. He would burn it to the ground.

Lou had never been a good guy, but he'd never been a total scumbag, either. He was just a selfish bastard trying to survive, like everyone else on the planet. But now he had a purpose, something to look forward to. Something best served cold.

That was it, best served cold.

Revenge was like ceviche or sushi.

Lou would be the steak tartare of revenge. *A lean, raw serving of vengeance that his enemies would choke on, their eyes pleading with Lou to administer the Heimlich of mercy...*

Another wave sent a torrent of seawater into his mouth. Lou coughed and spat, losing his train of thought. Just as well; he was getting swept away by his newfound purpose. And there wouldn't be a moment's revenge if he didn't beat the odds and make it to shore.

Lou flexed his fingers and gasped a lungful of air, mentally bracing himself against the cold before he rolled onto his stomach.

He had coasted long enough. It was time to start swimming.

47

Swimming through the crowd like a barracuda in heels, An spotted her prey and moved toward the window.

Her silk dress was the color of blood, slit to show as much leg as possible without revealing the throwing knife strapped to her thigh. Her necklace was loose enough to be removed easily with one hand, the jade pendant positioned so the wire strand could be used as a garrote. In the right hands, it could easily crush someone's windpipe, and the pendant hung at a length that gave men an excuse for their eyes to wander. A distracted subject is an easy target.

She always dressed to kill, but An didn't think she would need props tonight. By the time she got the call, the party was already underway. Now it was winding down, the host holding court with a thinning crowd on the balcony. He was young, handsome, and very sure of himself.

A judge's son with political aspirations of his own, he was a regular fixture at galas and gallery openings, rarely seen twice with the same woman on his arm. Tonight, a semifamous lingerie model was rumored to be his date, but she must have fallen ill because she never arrived. He was a bachelor for the evening.

One of his former paramours had caused a stir last year by

telling a local tabloid that he liked to get rough in the bedroom. There was talk of assault charges in the gossip columns, but once she left town, the rumors died. Another woman came forward but a settlement was reached and the case never went to court. Any mention of her story evaporated off the internet.

He never commented on the accusations and never looked back.

Tonight, the view behind him was spectacular. His apartment was on the top floor of the tallest residential building in San Francisco. Home to both a Super Bowl-winning quarterback and a right-fielder for the Giants, Millennium Tower had been mired in controversy since its inception.

Neighborhood arguments against a building of a such epic proportions went unheard by the city council after their palms had been greased, but it was impossible to ignore complaints from the tower's own residents.

The tower was sinking.

Built on pilings driven into mud and sand instead of bedrock, Millennium Tower was starting to resemble the Leaning Tower of Pisa. It had sunk sixteen inches since it opened only a few years ago and was tilting another six inches off the vertical.

Given the scale of the building and size of the apartments, it wasn't noticeable at first unless you were looking for it. Prospective buyers might roll a marble across the floor to see if it followed a straight path. The view from the balcony wasn't skewed, and there was no sense of vertigo. And yet, An couldn't help wonder what might happen when the next big earthquake rolled into town.

She imagined guests sliding off the balcony one by one, like leaves falling off a tree in late autumn. Slowly spinning as gravity brought them back to earth.

An had studied the building while researching the bachelor on the balcony. Then she made arrangements to ensure his date never made it to the party. The handsome host glanced in An's direction, and she smiled demurely before looking away. It was the second time they'd made eye contact.

On the third, An would approach and introduce herself.

After some chitchat, he'd ask what brought her to his party, and she would drop the name of one of his departed guests. She estimated only a few minutes of banter before his focus narrowed, and he began unconsciously excluding the other guests from their conversation. More small talk, during which An would subtly shift her position on the balcony so he would accidentally brush against her.

Maybe he would put a hand on her shoulder to emphasize something he was saying. She would touch her hair in response, alternately break eye contact and widen her gaze, stroking his subconscious and telling his id that she found him incredibly attractive.

It's no wonder that over half the assassins in the world are women.

An turned her attention to the view and counted to one hundred before glancing once again at the judge's son. She caught him watching and smiled, her eyes closing the distance between them. It was time to say hello.

An thought about leaves falling as she let the undertow of the crowd spin her around. She moved inexorably toward the balcony, where a beautiful collision was about to occur.

48

Lou worried an ugly collision was about to occur as the undertow spun him around like a leaf.

He dreaded slamming into one of the pilings of the pier, his rib cage shattering against a column of wood that couldn't care less if he drowned. He was too exhausted to swim, too dehydrated to cry for help, and too numb to close his eyes.

Flat on his back, arms outstretched, he looked like a man about to be crucified, but Lou knew that when he died it would be for his sins, and his alone. He wasn't a religious man but having Death as his swim buddy had broadened his spiritual outlook. After an hour in the water, he had prayed to anyone he thought might be listening, starting with the Big Guy and moving through eight of the apostles—he couldn't remember the other five, besides Judas, who was a total jackass.

Lou also gave a shout-out to Mary, a nod to Moses, and a desperate plea to Poseidon, Neptune, and King Triton from *The Little Mermaid*.

During a particularly rough patch, Lou attempted to contact Michael Phelps telepathically, but the dude wasn't paying attention. All those medals must have gone to his head, or maybe he was stoned. Lou kicked and swam as if a shark were chasing him, and, given his recent experience at the aquarium, that wasn't too hard to visualize.

Against all odds, rip currents, and the cold, his hapless strokes and desperate kicks put Lou on a course for land. If the boat had been on the far side of Alcatraz when he jumped, Lou would have been swept under the Golden Gate and out to sea. Now he was back where he started, human jetsam flowing into the marina.

A swell of the incoming tide lifted Lou like a rubber raft and pushed him between two pilings and under the elevated pier. Numbly, he turned his head, trying to get his bearings.

It was the dead of night, and running lights along the walkways of the pier were too faint for any depth perception. His arms felt like logs and Lou couldn't feel his feet at all. After a tentative jerk and wobble, he rotated his body counterclockwise. He was only yards away from home, but if he didn't keep kicking, the next ebb in the tide might suck him back into open water.

Lou gasped as water filled his mouth. His face submerged and he yelled, bubbles spewing forth as his words drowned. Struggling to recall what it felt like to have toes, he kicked spastically, neck twisting as he tried to suck some air into his sodden lungs. Oily water oozed beneath the pier, and Lou felt himself sliding forward.

His head smacked into something rubbery, probably a tire roped onto the piling to protect the boats. Lou bounced off, stunned and disoriented. He flipped onto his back, gasping. The blubbery obstacle bumped him again, this time with intent. It slapped him on the leg and leaned forward to give him a wet, whiskery kiss.

It was a sea lion, playfully tossing Lou around, like a toddler with a bath toy.

Lou surged another ten feet before crashing into the floating pier, the square island at the center of the marina. He was the only human in sight, stranded within shouting distance of the main pier. Desperately, he looped his arms around one of the pilings, the wooden platform only a couple of feet above his head. His hands were claws of ice, his breathing shallow, his vision limited to a few feet.

He could swim twenty yards to the main pier and hope to find a ladder he could climb, then crawl to the guard station for help. Or he could scramble onto the platform directly above him and hang out with the sea lions until dawn.

Lou felt his arms slip as another sea lion jostled past. An ill-timed bump could knock him clear of the platform, too exhausted to swim back. Then he'd sink and drown within sight of salvation.

With excruciating deliberation, Lou reached above his head and grabbed the edge of the platform. He held on more by instinct than feeling in his fingers. With cautious sweeps of his legs, he rocked back and forth until his torso began to clear the surface of the water. *One...two...*on the third pass, he kicked like one of the Rockettes and managed to hook his right foot onto the platform. He hung there for an eternity, until the next wave lifted him over the edge.

Sea lions snorted and shimmied, maneuvering for position. The platform was packed. Lou stretched across the nearest one and rolled, sliding between two cows that outweighed him by almost a hundred pounds each. They groused and grumbled but didn't bark or bite.

Lou wasn't in the open water, wasn't on the verge of drowning, and was comfortably sandwiched between two warm bodies. Not exactly the threesome of his fantasies, but he wasn't complaining.

As a final wave of exhaustion pulled him under, Lou closed his eyes and smiled.

49

Sally batted her eyes and smiled inwardly at the thought that the bank manager might actually give her a loan.

His name was William Chen. His face was broad, and his tie was as thin as Sally's cover story. His suit was expertly tailored. Sally had no doubt it was made custom in Hong Kong and suspected that she knew the tailor.

She was wearing a black pencil skirt and green blouse, her long hair pulled back into a ponytail. She'd considered wearing glasses but thought that might be a bit much.

They had moved past formalities into discussing the finer points of her small business loan, when Sally abruptly switched from English to Cantonese as if searching for the right words. She wanted Chen speaking his native tongue as she led him down a path of incendiary insinuation.

Lies might be bilingual, but lying wasn't. Sally didn't want his tells—the physical cues that he might be lying—masked by an accent or confused with a stumble over an unfamiliar collection of vowels.

Sally's outward expression was placid, her eyes full of gratitude as Chen answered her questions. After a particularly tedious explanation of the advantages of a term loan with floating interest,

Sally knitted her brows and introduced a subtle note of intensity into her voice.

"The bank's reputation," she began, "is well known in our community."

The bank manager smiled as if auditioning for a jack-o-lantern competition. "Our fortunes have been very good."

"My lawyer—"

"Lawyer." Chen's pupils contracted almost imperceptibly.

Sally looked earnest. "He suggested I speak to some of your largest clients—"

Chen nodded and opened a desk drawer to retrieve a list of names, typed on a sheet of bank stationery. "We have an approved list of clients who have agreed—"

"—but he thought the bank might be reluctant to give out their names." Sally produced her own sheet, the list of names Cape had given her. "So he did some research and provided a list of people I should call."

"A list." Chen's face blanched, as if the word triggered instantaneous blood loss.

"But I thought I should speak with you first."

Chen regained some color. "Very wise."

Sally smiled in acknowledgment but didn't say anything.

"May I see the names?" Chen reached across the desk with an assumptive air, the sleeve of his jacket pulling back to reveal the inside of his left wrist.

Sally pulled the list back quickly enough for him to come up short. "Perhaps it would be better if I read them to you?" She smiled demurely.

"Of course." Chen straightened his sleeve as he sat back in his chair, but Sally had spied the triangle tattoo just below his wrist. She kept her eyes moving and her expression neutral, but that geometric shape was something she hadn't expected to see on a bank manager.

Heaven, Earth, and Man. The three sides of the triangle.

As a young girl, she'd seen similar markings on the chests, backs, or arms of her instructors. Often the triangle would hold the Chinese character *Hung* within its borders. The symbol for the Heaven and Earth Society.

Just another name for the Triads.

Chen glanced at Sally, but she had lowered her eyes to the sheet of paper.

"Shall I begin?"

Sally had memorized the names, so glancing upward as she recited them was as natural as blinking. She could study Chen's reactions as they occurred.

It was likely that one of the names would get a response, if only because the manager would consider it indiscreet to discuss the bank's elite clients. But now that Sally had seen heaven, earth, and man, she took particular delight in enunciating each name with excruciating slowness.

What surprised her wasn't any particular twitch, blink, or tic—it was the sheer number of them. By the time Sally read half the names she had eight hits, and when she moved from corporations to individuals, Chen went from sallow to florid to apoplectic.

When Sally used the honorific Judge before one of the names, Chen almost came out of his chair to interrupt her.

"Your lawyer," he began. "Can you…"

"Yes?" Sally looked up from the page and locked eyes, her smile radiant. It took Chen a moment to compose himself.

"You never told me his name."

Sally bowed her head slightly. "My mistake." She reached into her bag and removed a business card, which she presented to Chen with two hands. It was embossed with Cape's name and phone number, but no mention of his real profession. The card stock was thick, and Chen turned it over in his hands before placing it carefully inside his jacket.

"I'm not familiar with the name," he said. "Have you worked with him before?"

"Many times." Sally's mouth almost twitched but she maintained her composure.

Cape would be impressed. Sally hadn't killed anyone since arriving at the bank, and she'd been there for almost an hour. She would wrap this conversation in the next few minutes, put the loan forms into her bag, and thank Chen for his time.

Sally now had a short list of names that warranted a closer look, and Chen had a business card with a tracking chip embedded in it.

Maybe things were finally falling into place.

50

Sergey smiled as the last tumbler fell into place and the lock sprang open. He opened the door to Dave's Donuts, grinning at his sister like a madman.

"I practiced lock-picking for six months," he said proudly. "And you thought I was just jerking off."

"I never think about you jerking off," replied Eva. "It would turn me celibate." She jutted her chin at the security guard standing behind her. "You sure he's okay?"

Sergey gestured for them both to follow him inside the donut shack before answering. The pier was empty at this hour, but you never knew. After he'd shut the door, he glowered at Eva. "Nastya says Tony doesn't talk much."

"So he's dumb."

"Don't be mean," said Sergey, smiling apologetically at Tony, whose expression didn't change. "Nastya has him on our payroll."

Eva glanced at Tony. He stood just over six feet tall, stocky in his blue uniform. He had a Taser, flashlight, and walkie-talkie on his belt. Short blond hair, brown eyes too close together, a flat nose, and a cigarette hanging precariously from his lower lip.

Eva looked back at Sergey, unconvinced. "You should tell him to put out his cigarette. Someone might see us."

"Why don't you tell him? He's standing right next to you."

"I don't think he speaks *sister*," said Eva, keeping her scowl aimed at Sergey. "Besides, for all we know, he's on a lot of payrolls. He works for the pier, too."

Sergey stepped close to the guard, who remained expressionless. "Tony, are you on the take for anyone else?"

Tony shook his head, causing the ash from his cigarette to fall onto the floor.

"Is he really mute?"

Sergey shrugged. "Why don't you ask him?"

"*Gospodi.*" Eva pushed past her brother into the cramped interior of the diminutive donut factory. She pulled out a flashlight and swept the room.

Sergey followed, leaving Tony standing by the door. "He guards this section of the pier until four a.m., so as long as he's on duty, we are invisible."

"Shouldn't he be outside, keeping watch?"

"I don't trust him *that* much," said Sergey. "He might wander off or fall asleep. You know how security guards can be. This way I can keep an eye on him."

"You're kidding."

"Someone comes to the door, he can say he found it ajar and came inside to investigate."

"He doesn't even talk—"

"—so we hide in the dark while he chases them away, or we slip out while he distracts them."

"Does *he* know that's the plan?"

"He nodded when I told him." Sergey shrugged. "What do you want from me? He's the only guard we own."

"He should put out his cigarette," repeated Eva. "This place looks flammable." She indicated the conveyor belt where the donuts got made, a mobile ramp which ended in a straight drop into a vat of cooking oil. The lid was off the vat, rainbow patterns forming in the beam of Eva's flashlight.

"You think they clean that out in the morning or use the same cooking oil over and over again?"

Eva stuck out her tongue. "One of the many reasons I don't eat the donuts."

The flashlight bounced along powdered sugar on metal shelves, sealed containers of oil stored against the nearest wall, and trays of dough in a refrigerated section of the shack toward the back. After they made a circuit of the room, Eva turned the flashlight on Sergey.

His chin glowed but his eyes were in shadow, like a treat-or-treater trying to scare his friends. She tilted the beam so it caught him directly in the eyes.

"What is your brilliant plan, Brother?"

Blinking furiously, Sergey said, "We are here to cause trouble."

"We discussed this," said Eva. "Trouble is not a plan. Be specific."

"We find the stash of drugs and take them."

At the word *drugs*, Eva looked over his shoulder and caught Tony staring at them, his eyes barely visible but his body angled in their direction. As she watched, the stoic sentinel took the butt from his mouth and used it to light a new cigarette.

"He should not be in here with us," Eva hissed.

"You're so tense," said Sergey.

"Please just find the drugs," sighed Eva.

"Give me the flashlight." Sergey snatched the light and got on his hands and knees, aiming it under the shelves. He crawled a few feet before heading toward the front counter and the walk-up window.

Eva followed a few paces behind but remained standing. "We sold him these drugs, so why are we stealing them?"

"We put a little dent in Dave's cash flow. Who knows, maybe we sell them back to him after he admits to ripping us off."

"We don't know him," said Eva, "or that he ripped anyone off."

"And we won't find out unless we have leverage," said Sergey. "Or get someone to make a move."

"By make a move, you mean start a war."

"A skirmish," said Sergey. "Dave thinks someone is picking a fight, maybe he'll fight back."

"But with whom?"

"Who would you pick?" Sergey directed the light under the counter.

Eva stood in the dark while her brother crept along like a drunken rat in a cellar. After a moment, she said, "I would blame the *khuliganami* at the aquarium."

"So would I!" Sergey smiled at what he considered a moment of bonding. "Pick the biggest kid on the playground and punch him in the nose, then nobody messes with you."

"That's what I was thinking, but—"

"—it doesn't matter," said Sergey. "He could go after anybody, one of the big restaurants, the banana stand, anyone on the pier who's part of the group. All we want is enough chaos to bring some order to this situation. Dave might call the meeting himself, but he will never suspect us."

"Because we sell him the drugs."

"Bingo," Sergey cried. It took a second before Eva realized he wasn't responding to her but had discovered something. A wooden cabinet mounted under the counter, secured with an old padlock. "Hold the flashlight."

Eva stole a glance at Tony. It was hard to tell in the murky gloom of the shack, but the glow from the ash lit his face less brightly than a moment ago, making her believe he was on his third cigarette. She muttered something under her breath and crouched below the counter, grabbing the flashlight from Sergey as he unwrapped his lock picks with loving care.

It took four tries and seven minutes before the latch popped open, but Eva had to admit her brother had finally developed a useful skill. Inside the cabinet was a plastic container of the type common to kitchens everywhere for storing flour or sugar. It held a jumble of small packets that resembled tea sachets, along with a plastic bag filled with a white powder that Eva knew wasn't confectionary sugar.

Sergey handed Eva the container, which she slipped into the oversized purse on her shoulder. He closed the cabinet and relocked the padlock. Even in shadow, he had a deeply satisfied look on his face.

Eva let a smile displace her familiar scowl. "Let's get out of here."

They reached the door and Sergey opened it a crack, peering outside. As he gestured for them to follow, Tony paused to light his fourth cigarette, the butt from his third held carefully between the thumb and forefinger of his right hand. His sullen face glowed in the amber light as he greedily sucked in the nicotine.

Eva's scowl reappeared as her right hand shot forward involuntarily. Before she could stop herself, she had smacked both cigarettes sideways, sending them spinning like batons.

The shorter butt landed on the conveyor and bounced once, twice, and a third time before landing on the trail of powdered sugar, which simmered and spat like an incendiary camel.

"Oops." Eva looked apologetically at Tony, who wasn't mute after all.

"Oh, shit," he said.

Eva lunged for the door.

She spared a glance over her shoulder as the longer cigarette completed its slow-motion arc, landing in the vat of cooking oil like Esther Williams, headfirst with barely a ripple.

An orange ball of flame expanded like a star going supernova, followed by a heatwave that slammed the door shut with a resounding whump. Eva grabbed Sergey by his shirt and dragged him across the pier.

They managed to stumble-run almost thirty feet. The siblings dove behind a cement planter topped with miniature palm trees—an instant before a secondary blast sent a shock wave that Eva felt in her chest. The first explosion must have knocked the lid from one of the spare oil drums, a hungry fire foraging for fuel.

In middle school Eva watched movies about the history of the Cold War. Atomic bombs tested in deserts and mock cities, wooden towns built to demonstrate the destructive power of the United States and her own Mother Russia. Mushroom clouds as big as the sky, smoke and fire eclipsing anything on the horizon, radioactive fallout as heavy as summer rain.

Eva remembered hearing that the energy of an atomic bomb was needed to trigger fusion in a hydrogen bomb, a codependent conflagration that takes you all the way from Bikini Atoll to Hiroshima. But the films from her childhood were black and white, poor production values. Propaganda films from a half-forgotten place and time. For Eva, this was all too here and now, as the series of explosions inside the shack became a chain reaction.

Dave's Donuts reached critical mass.

The fireball was as bright as day, as hot as the sun, and as loud as a used car salesman's tie. Eva felt something burn her cheek and realized the palm trees were on fire, their fronds disintegrating overhead. She swatted ash out of her hair and kept her head down, body sprawled across Sergey, who was yelling wordlessly against the thunderous wave rolling across the pier.

Then came the fallout.

Donuts rained from the sky. Raw dough had been flash-cooked and launched skyward. Golden-brown harbingers of doom plummeted back to earth like gluten hail.

Splat-splat-splat. Donuts sounding like hoofbeats, but Eva could hear sirens in the distance and knew the cavalry wasn't coming. She and Sergey were pinned down, but they had to get out of there.

A final chthonic wave shook the planks of the pier as the last vat of cooking oil turned to plasma, blasting the walls of the shack to splinters. Eva and Sergey were jolted backwards as something slammed against the far side of the planter.

Eva wondered if the motor from the conveyor belt or a section of the roof had nearly crushed them, but she waited a full minute before unclenching her eyes and gingerly rising onto all fours. Prepared to duck if anything that didn't have wings was airborne, she peered cautiously around the smoldering palm trees.

Tony the security guard was smoking, but for once there wasn't a cigarette in his mouth.

Tendrils of flame danced along his torso, wisps of smoke poured out of his ears, nostrils, and mouth. He was deep-fried and crispy.

Tony's eyebrows and lashes had burned off, the lids open and melted in place. His eyes were wide in disbelief that cigarettes had actually killed him. Irony lay across his steaming corpse like a burial shroud.

Eva crouched behind the planter and tugged on her brother's shoulder. Sergey kept yelling at the top of his lungs until she smacked him on the side of his head. The sirens were getting closer.

"Get up." Eva smacked him again, more gently. "Now."

Sergey rose to his knees and looked at the crater where the donut shack used to be. "What the hell happened?"

"I got Tony to quit smoking."

"Where is that *perebezhchik*?" Sergey stood shakily. "Did he take off?"

"Oh, yes," said Eva. "Like a rocket."

51

Cape's first thought was that a rocket had been launched from the pier.

He saw the flash of light before hearing a thunderous wave that shook the planks beneath his feet. A glimpse of something hurtling skyward, a frenzy of bottle-rockets launched in the middle of the night. Maybe an explosion at a fireworks store, he couldn't guess.

When donuts started to fall from the sky, Cape wondered if a childhood wish had finally come true.

Undeterred, Cape climbed the steps to the second level of the pier. The silver cross was dangling from his right hand, the chain wrapped around his palm like a rosary. It was late, but Cape was suddenly anxious to finish the conversation he'd been avoiding all day.

He had hoped the police would have found one of the missing drivers, but neither Beau nor Vincent had called him back. Linda and Sloth probably made progress following the money trail, but there was no point checking until tomorrow.

He took the stairs on the south side of the aquarium to avoid the gate at the main entrance. Tourists didn't realize the sides of the pier were always open to foot traffic so business owners could come and go as they pleased. All the stores were closed and the promenade lights extinguished as Cape walked along the open balcony leading to Vera's place.

Though already a safe distance from the donut shack when the fireball lit up the pier, it shone brightly enough to illuminate everything in his immediate vicinity. Vera was standing in front of her store, watching him approach.

Cape wondered if she'd rushed outside at the sound of the blast or was already getting some night air when the shack went boom. Vera looked like she'd been waiting there all night, as if this sort of fireworks display happened like clockwork. Either way, Cape wouldn't get away with just leaving a note on her door.

Instinctively he wanted to run toward the fire. Lose himself in something physical and leave the wreckage of the human heart up here, where it was someone else's problem. But the flashing lights at the end of the pier meant professionals were already on the scene, people trained to deal with conflagrations and calamities.

Their job was down there. His job was standing right in front of him.

Vera tracked his progress, her expression shifting with the light and shadows cast by the distant flames. When her gaze landed on the cross, Cape could see fire dancing in her eyes and felt like he was hand-delivering her own personal hell.

She let her fingers slip off the railing as Cape unwrapped the chain and gently lowered it into the palm of her left hand. She clenched her fingers until the knuckles were white. The reflected glow from the fire expanded as her eyes welled with tears, but before the first had fallen, Vera turned wordlessly and stepped across the balcony into her store.

She left the door ajar, but Cape waited, standing outside until the sirens stopped. The emergency vehicles kept their flashers on, a beacon for any stragglers from the firehouse. It was mesmerizing to watch the lights without their caterwauling soundtrack. Cape counted to one hundred before following his client into the store.

Red and white staccato flashes were the only illumination as Cape navigated his way past the counter to the back room. Vera was already sitting on the bed facing the window, her legs straight across the mattress, back against the pillows. Her eyes were fixed on the middle distance between the aquarium and the marina. Scaffolding covered the near side of the aquarium up to the roof, but the work site was as dark and empty as the rest of the pier.

The last time Cape was here, the room had felt almost cozy. Now it seemed small and sad. Her jacket was strewn across the desk chair. The cross lay on the desk, its chain across the back of her cell phone. The phone screen pulsed softly in the darkened room, barely visible under the edge of the phone case—the light from a fairy trapped in a box.

Cape sat down on the bed and tried not to breathe.

Vera sounded too tired to utter more than one syllable at a time.

"Where?"

Cape told her about his undersea tour of the docks, the position of the cross relative to where the truck fell into the marina. When he had finished, she spoke softly.

"You think Hank swam away from that crash?"

Cape couldn't tell if she sounded hopeful or hopeless. "I simply told you where I found it."

"I can't believe you found it at all."

Cape waited until she turned away from the window, then said, "They didn't find a body in the truck, but that doesn't mean he's alive."

"You think Hank is hiding…*from me*?"

"I didn't say that either," said Cape. "But if he isn't, he's probably dead…"

"Those are my choices?" Vera's eyes flashed in the dark. "Accept that he's dead and innocent—or believe that he's alive and guilty? That isn't good enough."

"No, it isn't."

"But that's all you've got."

"For now." Cape shifted on the bed. "Vera, do you know anything about money laundering?"

"What?" The question caught her off guard, diffusing her anger. "What's that got to do with finding Hank?"

"If I can't find him," said Cape, "maybe I can find a motive."

Vera shook her head slowly from side to side.

Cape pressed. "You sent me to speak with Harkness for a reason."

"Maybe I thought you were left-handed."

"I'm not." Cape laid his right hand on hers. "And you're not answering the question."

Instead of pulling away, Vera rotated her wrist so her fingers wrapped around his. She held fast, as if afraid she might fall.

"Everyone on the pier knows there's skimming," she said. "Some of the restaurants don't even try to hide it, encouraging customers to pay with cash, offering discounts if they do. But for those of us selling hard goods, it's not so easy, is it?"

"Not to mention illegal."

"And the little fish always get caught first," replied Vera. "So, a lot of us mind our own business. We're not invited to the party, but we don't call the cops to complain about our neighbors, either." She paused, glancing out the window again. "Nothing illegal about that."

"I'm not talking about running a cash business and lying on your taxes," said Cape. "Harkness can chase that dog all he wants, he can even run to the IRS and they'll yawn in his face. Half the restaurants in town exaggerate their cost of goods and underestimate their income, and there's no way of checking unless you go there and eat three meals a day for a year."

Vera's brow furrowed. "Hank was just a driver."

"A lot of money flows through the pier," said Cape. "And Hank's one of the few people who saw just how much. That might have made him a liability."

"Clean money and dirty money look the same, isn't that what you're telling me?" She let go of Cape's hand and ran her fingers through her hair. "How would he know the difference?"

"Maybe he didn't." Cape took a deep breath, feeling the smallness of the room, frustrated that every question only raised another. "Maybe his partner did." He stood abruptly and said, "Why don't—"

The wall behind Cape exploded.

A searing pain across his cheek. Cape instinctively let his knees buckle to fall forward. He grabbed Vera by the sleeve on his way down, dragging her from the bed onto the floor. Cape twisted to land on his back and Vera fell on top of him, the wind knocked out of both of them. Plaster-dust filled the room like smoke.

His ears caught up with his other senses, and Cape realized he never heard a shot. Just the *kachunk* of glass punched inward and the subsonic eruption of plaster vaporizing. Cautiously, he raised his head a few inches off the floor and looked across the bed at the window.

A jagged hole the size of a dime stared back at him.

Cape kept his left arm around Vera to hold her close to the floor. He considered removing a shoe to make a throw at the light switch but didn't want the shooter to know that anyone was still here, alive or dead.

Cape felt tears running down his cheek. He looked at Vera, who was staring at him—wide-eyed but dry-eyed. He'd been shot at before and wasn't typically this emotional, so gingerly he touched his cheek. His fingers came away red.

"Here." Vera rolled onto her side and touched his face. Her hand was trembling but she was clearly intent on what she was doing, grateful to focus on something beyond fear. Cape felt a sharp stabbing sensation directly below his left eye, a tugging, then a renewed flow of crimson tears.

Vera held a shard of glass in her hand, only half an inch long but sharp as a needle. A fraction higher and he'd be wearing an eye patch.

"Thanks." Cape blinked and dabbed his cheek with the cuff of his shirt, then with his sleeve until the bleeding slowed. His dry cleaners already hated him, after years of blood stains and powder burns. He wondered if they'd finally had enough and decided to take a shot at him. Not the likeliest of suspects, but at least they had a motive.

He looked at the wall opposite the window. Where the plaster had been smooth, now there was a divot that could have been made by a sand wedge. Six feet off the floor as if it had always been there. Cape hoped the bullet hit a stud and was buried in the wall, just waiting to be excavated.

"Did someone just *shoot* at us?" Vera's voice was more even than the look in her eyes.

"I don't think they were aiming at you." Cape smiled with one corner of his mouth. "You smell nice, by the way."

Vera flushed, then coughed out a laugh. "Lavender shampoo." She shifted her body to look at Cape without tilting her head. "Are you trying to distract me so I don't freak out?"

"I don't have a lot of filters." Cape craned his neck to look at the window again, which inadvertently pressed them closer together. When he looked back at Vera, she was staring at him.

"Am I bleeding again?" He raised a hand to his cheek.

"No." Vera caught his hand in hers and held it. "You think they're gone?"

"I would be."

"How long should we stay on the floor like this?" Vera glanced at the door as if gauging the distance, then at the window. "To be *safe*."

"Let me see." Cape started to untangle his legs from hers, but Vera squeezed his hand and shifted her hips against him.

"Not yet," she said. Her eyes locked onto his, impossibly large and incredibly close.

Cape felt a sense of vertigo, as if he was falling forward rather than leaning in to kiss her. She tasted like lavender, though he couldn't have told you before this moment what lavender tastes like.

Vera pulled him closer, her breath coming fast as she released his hand and reached for his belt. Cape reciprocated as an inner voice started reciting all the reasons this was a bad idea.

This is a response to the adrenaline rush of a near-death experience. Because feeling alive matters more right now than worrying about death. Because you're an idiot with horrible judgment and no sense of professional stan—

The blood rushing through his ears drowned out his inner voice, until the only sound he could hear was the warning drum of his own heart as shoes and clothes slid across the floor.

Vera swung her left leg over Cape and grabbed the back of his head with both hands, pulling his hair as she slid on top of him.

Cape pulled her close and whispered in her ear.

"This doesn't seem very safe."

"So shoot me," said Vera.

52

Sally shot a glance at the screen strapped to her wrist and confirmed what she already knew. William Chen, the decidedly duplicitous manager of The People's Bank, was still at home.

Sally perched as motionless as a gargoyle on the roof across the street, five stories up with an unobstructed view of the main entrance. Chen lived in a doorman building on Stockton Street, near the Ritz-Carlton and only a few blocks from Dragon's Gate, the symbolic entrance to Chinatown. He was in Sally's backyard, the neighborhood that his colleagues with triangle tattoos claimed as their own.

The business card with the tracking chip might be on an end table, or in the pocket of his jacket draped over a chair, but Sally doubted it. She visualized Chen pacing the floor, holding the card in one hand while gripping his cell phone in the other, trying to decide whom to call first.

Sooner or later Chen would leave, or someone would come to him. As Sally waited, she emptied her mind and let the susurrus of the street shape the rhythm of her breathing. Memories to calm her, and the past to always keep her present.

Sally is twelve, barely as tall as the bow she strains to hold, the arrow pointing at her instructor's chest instead of the target.

Chinatown had more foot traffic than most San Francisco neighborhoods, but the street below couldn't be called crowded by the standards of a big city like New York. Small clusters of people came together to clog the sidewalk like human plaque obstructing an artery, only to break apart into couples or sole pedestrians meandering in opposite directions.

Age fifteen, stalking a man through the streets of Kowloon, wondering when the poison will take hold and drop him to his knees.

Sally believed that if Chen was going out, he would have left right away, and almost thirty minutes had elapsed. She opened her senses and tried to give a name to the nagging feeling in her gut. Sally had been taught that answers to what might happen next always lay in the past. What once was pain is now perspective.

Alone in the rafters of the great hall at school, eavesdropping as the Dragon Head warns her instructors about getting too attached to their students, because all the girls are disposable.

A vitriolic shout echoed off the buildings and broke into fragments of profanity directed at a woman staring at her phone, shambling like a zombie across the middle of the intersection.

Standing on a balcony in Tokyo, watching a crowd on the street below point skyward as they wonder if the broken man at their feet jumped or fell.

A figure moving along the sidewalk broke Sally's reverie. It was a woman whose feet didn't seem to touch the ground. While everyone else shuffled or strolled, she moved with a fluid grace around her fellow pedestrians, gliding like a river flowing around rocks.

The blond wig was a nice touch, thought Sally, and the sunglasses unremarkable in a town of intermittent sunshine and perpetual pretense. But Sally could spot someone from her alma mater a mile away if they didn't truly mask their appearance, change their gait, and lose themselves completely in a borrowed identity.

Sally knew it was An who stepped into the lobby of Chen's

building, disguising herself just enough to confuse the amateurs—the police, the men of the Triads, or whomever was paying them. That meant An knew Sally might be watching and didn't care, or more likely, she cared very much and wanted to be recognized for who and what she was.

An wanted to be seen, and she wanted Sally to follow her.

53

"Follow me," said Cape.

He reached across Vera to snag his left shoe and her pants, then rolled onto his stomach and belly-crawled to the door, gesturing for her to follow.

Like two caterpillars in no particular hurry, they cleared the threshold to the store. After a few feet Cape extended a hand to help her up. They stood naked in the front room, surrounded by children's clothes.

"This seems vaguely inappropriate," said Cape.

Vera smiled and shook her head as she reclaimed her pants and slipped them on. After pulling on her shirt, she ran both hands through her hair and looked over her shoulder at the back room. "Should we call the police?"

"Probably." Cape stepped into his shoes and looked at the wall adjacent to the back room, scanning for a bullet hole. Then he turned to Vera and took a deep breath.

"I just wanted to say, this isn't part of my usual—"

"—services?" Vera leaned in to kiss him on the cheek. "Then don't make me pay for it." She stepped over to the counter, resting her hand near the register and exhaling loudly. "Has this happened to you before?"

"Sleeping with a client?"

Vera smacked him on the arm. "Getting shot at."

Cape shrugged. "Not lately."

"My God." Vera studied him as she rested her weight against the counter. A range of emotions coruscated across her face, the repercussions of the shot hitting home. "For a man with a target on his back, you seem awfully complacent."

Cape tilted his head to one side. "That's because I'm finally making progress."

"Someone tries to kill you and that's *progress*?"

"Murder is rarely motivated by apathy."

"Wow." Vera let her back slide down the front of the counter so she could sit on the floor. "Your job really sucks."

"Tell me something I don't know," said Cape.

54

Lou didn't know what woke him and he didn't care.

Kaboom. He awoke with a start, disoriented. Then an over-powering smell brought his memory rushing back through his nose.

He was pinned between two sea lions. Neither dead nor eaten alive, just squeezed like a sardine by his aquatic roommates.

Lou had been dreaming that every tourist and merchant on the pier had assembled to celebrate his return. The brave explorer and hero, lost at sea but safely returned. There had been a big parade and fireworks in his honor.

Fireworks.

Lou raised his head to peer over the nearest sea lion. The night sky was suffused with orange light emanating from the pier. Red and white strobes pierced the amber haze and bounced off the clouds.

Lou flared his nostrils to detect anything besides sargasso and sea lion. The smell of charred wood drifted over the marina, along with an undercurrent of something more familiar.

Lou felt a sudden pang of hunger.

He rose onto his knees and rested his arms gently across the back of the nearest cow to steady himself. The sea lion wobbled and grunted but didn't budge. Lou peered through the indigo night and squinted at the pale objects floating in the marina. Hundreds of them, bobbing on the waves like Lilliputian life preservers.

Donuts.

Lou had thought his odyssey was over but was clearly mistaken. Things were getting weird on the pier.

He took a deep breath to gather his strength, regretting it instantly. His eyes started to water and he felt dizzy. He waited a full minute before standing shakily. Gingerly, he stepped between the dormant sea lions, tiptoeing as he tried to avoid stomping on anyone's whiskers. An angry cow could bring his journey to an end with one butt of the head.

At the edge of the floating platform, Lou looked across the water at the pier. It was thirty yards to the nearest ladder, give or take. That meant he had to swim when he could barely stand. He stalled by trying to count the donuts, but his stomach cramped at the sight of all that dough. He wondered how many donuts it would take to support a man's weight.

Lou sat on the edge of the platform and decided he'd swallowed enough seawater to drown his fear but not his anger.

He had given enough to these bastards. It was time to take it all back.

55

"I take it back."

"Apology accepted," said Sergey.

Eva elbowed him in the ribs. "She wasn't apologizing to you, *durak.*"

"I wasn't apologizing to either one of you," replied Anastasia.

Sergey and Eva looked at their older sister expectantly.

Anastasia gestured at Sergey. "I said you were a fuckup, but that was unfair." She turned her obsidian stare on her younger sister. "Because you are *both* fuckups."

Sergey held up a hand. "Now listen, Nastya—"

"Don't try to talk your way out of this." Anastasia let her eyes drift to the nesting dolls lining the store shelves. Maybe the *matryoshka* would listen to her. "I send you on two simple tasks, and you kill two security guards."

Sergey shot a thumb at Eva. "She killed one of them."

"It was an accident!"

"So was mine."

Eva snorted in derision. She pulled a packet of gum from her pocket and popped three rectangles into her mouth.

"You know," said Sergey, "I was thinking—"

"Don't," said Eva. "You thinking is what got us—"

"—hear me out." Sergey waved his right hand like a white flag. "I was thinking these security guards are like the red shirts on Star Trek."

Anastasia frowned. "What are you talking about?"

"Every time Captain Kirk and Spock beam down to a planet, they bring security guards wearing red shirts."

"So?" Anastasia said impatiently. "Our security guards wear blue."

"That's not the point."

"What is the point?" asked Anastasia.

"These guys always die," said Sergey. "Within five minutes of landing on the planet, they get incinerated, eaten alive, or turned into a block of salt."

"Salt?" asked Eva.

Sergey held his hands six inches apart. "About this big."

"Cool," said Eva. "I never saw that episode."

"Stop talking," snapped Anastasia. "Both of you."

Sergey and Eva tried to look remorseful. The nesting dolls looked skeptical. Anastasia looked pissed.

"No one saw you?" asked Anastasia.

Sergey and Eva glanced at each other before shaking their heads.

"The police and fire trucks are still here," said Anastasia. "You left nothing behind?"

"Not even this." Eva reached into her purse and revealed the canister of white powder. "We even remembered the drugs."

Sergey produced the ziplock bag of tea satchels he'd removed from the shack. "Don't forget the single-serve instant highs."

Anastasia's expression changed to grudging admiration. "We can resell the powder."

"What about the satchels?" asked Sergey. "Who needs Dave or his donuts? Let's cut out the middleman."

"I think we cut out Dave when we blew up his shack," said Eva.

"No," said Anastasia. "The satchels will connect us to the shack."

Sergey looked at the satchels as if they were gold bullion. "But—"

"Don't be greedy," said Anastasia. "Throw them away."

"Cousin Viktor has connections," said Sergey. "He could move them in a day."

"*Nyet.*" Anastasia waited until he met her gaze. "Did the explosion damage your hearing, Little Brother?"

"*Bez raznitsky.*"

"Don't *whatever* me," snapped Anastasia. "What do we think Dave will do?"

"Have you ever met Dave?" asked Eva.

"Now that you mention it, no," replied Anastasia. "We drop off the drugs at the shack, they get mixed into their packets, sold, and then—"

"—we get paid," said Eva.

Anastasia shrugged. "I think our uncle made the deal with the original owner of the shack."

"Maybe there is no Dave," said Sergey.

"Maybe it's an acronym," said Eva.

"Is that like an idiom?" asked Sergey.

"No, it could be an abbreviation for Drugs Are Valuable Everywhere."

"Eva, you're as bad as he is," said Anastasia. "Please focus."

Sergey sat up straighter. "Maybe it's Dealers Are Very Energetic."

"It doesn't matter!" Anastasia slapped her right hand on the counter. "Someone owns the donut shack. Maybe more than one someone. Either way, I'm sure our uncle has met them at the consortium meetings."

"Let's refer to them as Dave," said Sergey. "Just to keep things simple."

"Brilliant." Anastasia flexed her fingers and let her hands drop to her side. "So what will our erstwhile business partner, this so-called Dave...what will he do?"

"Call his insurance company?" said Eva.

"No," said Sergey. "Dave will worry."

Anastasia nodded in approval. "Worry about…"

"Losing his customers," replied Sergey. "There are plenty of other places to buy synthetic pot in this town."

"Will he call a meeting of the consortium?" said Eva.

"He might," replied Anastasia. "Or he might think he's getting squeezed out."

"He can't rebuild the donut shack fast enough," mused Sergey. "Dave will be the one to call a meeting, because he needs another base of operations."

"Who would you turn to?" asked Anastasia.

"We don't get enough foot traffic here at the store," said Eva. "A long line of addicts shopping for nesting dolls might look suspicious."

"Stoners hanging around theme restaurants without sitting down and ordering a meal would seem just as sketchy," added Sergey.

"The banana stand is too small—"

"—and too exposed."

"The dragon store?" asked Eva.

"A dragon sculpture costs a lot more than a donut."

"The Alpaca store is in a discreet location…"

"There's an alpaca store?"

"Level two, just past the kite store," said Eva. "You need to get out more."

"I didn't know it was legal to own an alpaca," said Sergey. "I could ride one to work."

Eva snorted. "They don't sell alpacas, *tupitsa*, they sell their wool. Hats, scarves, shawls—"

"The niche retailers aren't the answer." Anastasia laced her fingers and rested her hands atop her head. "The *only* place on the pier that gets enough customers is—"

"—the aquarium," said Eva and Sergey simultaneously.

Anastasia nodded. "They have a gift shop on the ground floor.

You don't even have to visit the exhibits—it's accessible without a ticket right from the pier. Always crowded but also cluttered, no clear lines of sight."

"With a counter running the full length of the store," added Sergey.

"Sounds perfect," said Eva.

"I take it back," said Sergey. "Dave, if there is a Dave, won't call a meeting. He'll just negotiate directly with the aquarium."

Anastasia smiled. "That's what I would do."

"Maybe we should talk to them, too," said Sergey.

"Nastya, how well do you know our contact at the aquarium?" asked Eva.

"Well enough not to trust him."

"Why not?" asked Sergey.

"Because he's a pirate."

"I always wanted to be a pirate," said Eva.

"It's never too late," said Sergey. "You're still young."

Eva tried to elbow him again, but Anastasia waved her off with an open palm, as if she were about to bless them both. "Sergey," she said, "you have been inadvertently insightful this evening."

"I have?"

"*Da.*" Anastasia nodded and stepped away from the counter. "Eva, I want you to go to the aquarium and talk to this pirate."

Eva stopped slouching and swallowed her gum. "To represent the family?"

"No."

Eva frowned. "What do you want me to do?"

"I want you to betray us."

56

Cape didn't want to betray his feelings in front of the police, but he was very disappointed the CSI technicians weren't better looking.

He dealt with cops all the time and knew the harsh realities of police work, but like most Americans, Cape couldn't avoid the subversive influence of television. He didn't watch much TV, but after the launch of *CSI: New York*, *CSI: Miami*, *CSI: Las Vegas*, and *CSI: Cyber*, it was inescapable.

Even if you didn't watch any television, the ubiquitous posters on buses and taxi tops would brainwash anyone into thinking all CSI departments were staffed by women with perfect figures and men with broad shoulders, cleft chins, and personal stylists.

The whole country was watching models with microscopes, but Cape was watching two middle-aged men with rubber gloves crawl around Vera's store, looking for clues.

Cape knew one of them fairly well, a paunchy guy named Stuart. His colleague was named Stan, and Cape made it a point to stand in front of Stan at all times, because the back of his head looked like someone sprayed silly string onto his skull while he was sleeping. It was disconcerting.

A detective named Sullivan watched over them. He had gray

at both temples, slack in the jowls, and lassitude seeping out of his pores.

"Detective Sullivan, are you leaving soon?" Vera emerged from the front of the store and joined them in the back room. "I'm sorry, I don't mean to be rude, it's just...it's been two hours, and I have to open in the morning,"

"We're about done," said Sullivan. "Photographer's left already, I got your statements, just waiting on those two." He jerked a thumb at Stuart, who was standing on a stepladder with a flashlight in his mouth.

"Almost finished here," Stuart mumbled as Stan crawled along the baseboard at the foot of the ladder, a plastic bag in one hand and tweezers in the other.

Vera nodded her understanding as she stepped over to Cape. She rested a hand on his chest as she looked up at him, but he couldn't read her expression. Maybe she was thinking that she was glad he didn't get shot, or maybe she was worried she'd collapse from exhaustion if she didn't lean on him.

As if in answer, Vera moved past him toward the cot, where she sat down heavily, looking like she might fall asleep sitting up. She raised a water bottle to her lips, realizing too late she'd forgotten to remove the cap. She sighed and laid it on the bed unopened. Behind her, the broken window cast a dim reflection of the room, a jaundiced image of her new reality.

Cape drifted over to Stuart and asked, "Find anything?"

Stuart took the flashlight out of his mouth and glanced down at Cape. "Not much more than a hole in the wall."

"Bullet flattened on impact?" asked Cape.

"If there was a bullet," mumbled Stuart.

Still on his hands and knees, Stan shook his head impatiently. "Because if there was, we'd find bullet fragments."

Sullivan snorted derisively. "Maybe you're not looking hard enough."

"Frangible," muttered Stuart.

Sullivan clearly thought he'd just been insulted. "What did you say?"

"*Frangible*," said Stan, groaning slightly as he leaned against the wall and stood up. Stuart bent down and handed him two plastic bags, which seemed to contain a mixture of dust, dirt, and baby powder. "A frangible bullet is specially designed to disintegrate on impact."

"Did you just make that word up?" asked Sullivan.

"How long you been a detective?" replied Stan.

"It does sound made up," said Cape.

Stuart gave him a look. "Don't push it. Civilians aren't normally allowed to linger at a crime scene."

"I *am* the crime scene," said Cape.

"On that we can agree," said Stuart.

"A frangible bullet is a nasty piece of work," added Stan. "Hits like a brick but doesn't pass through like a full metal jacket, so it doesn't hit the person standing behind the victim—"

"—which is pretty considerate, if you think about it," added Stuart.

"But it's untraceable," said Stan. "Which makes our job a lot harder."

"What's it made of?" asked Sullivan.

Stuart shook one of the baggies. "Powdered metal usually. Zinc, tin, or tungsten, after it's cold-bonded or *swaged*."

"Now that word you definitely made up," said Sullivan.

"Squeezed into a die-cast form," said Stan impatiently. "Shaped, liked dough in a cookie mold. The army even started experimenting with plant material."

"Biodegradable bullets?" asked Cape.

"That's the idea." Stuart nodded. "Some government greenie decided all those bullets fired by the military were getting into the soil and polluting the earth."

"What about all the dead bodies?" asked Sullivan.

"Biodegradable," said Cape. "Remember?"

"So they're making small batches of bullets out of fibrous plants?"

"Like kale," added Stan.

"Kale?" Sullivan looked impressed. "About time someone found a use for that stuff, it's fucking inedible. And you know what's even wor—"

A *thunk* followed by a rolling sound interrupted them.

All four men turned to find Vera on the cot, asleep. The water bottle had fallen off the bed and was slowly heading toward them. Cape picked it up and set it gently on the desk. Without a word, he moved to the front of the store and waited while the police silently packed up their gear.

Once they were ready, Cape followed them through the front door before closing it behind him. He turned to Stuart and Stan.

"Thanks, fellas."

"Lucky you're not dead," replied Stuart.

"Assuming there was a bullet," said Stan. "And it wasn't some kid throwing a rock."

Cape snorted. "That kid would have one hell of an arm. He'd be pitching for the Giants."

"That window saved your ass," said Stan. "Even glass can mess with the trajectory of a—"

"—frangible," said Cape.

Stuart patted Cape on the shoulder. "You're better than most," he said. "I'd tell you to stay out of trouble, but then you'd be unemployed."

The CSI techs headed for the stairs, Stan giving a half-hearted wave over his shoulder without looking back. "Sullivan, we'll let you know when the tests are back, which won't be tomorrow, so don't nag."

Cape turned to Sullivan and asked, "You going to have a uniform outside?"

"I'll ask one of them to keep an eye on the store for a bit." Sullivan jutted his chin over the railing toward the smoldering ruin of the donut shack. The smell of caramelized sugar lingered in the predawn air. Most of the emergency vehicles had left, only a medium-sized fire truck remaining with its lights off. Two uniformed cops milled about, one of them smoking.

"Thanks," said Cape. "I doubt she's in any danger."

"Agreed." Sullivan smiled. "If I only had one shot, I'd definitely be aiming for you."

"You're almost as funny as Beau," said Cape. "When you see him, tell him my feelings were hurt that he didn't come down himself."

"Beau usually works homicides. This was only *attempted* homicide. Besides, he and Vinnie are busy tonight."

"What went down?"

"Not what, but who?" Sullivan pursed his lips and made a whistling sound like a bomb falling in a Wile E. Coyote cartoon. "Someone took a header off Millennium Tower."

"Who?"

"Jesse Cranston."

"I recognize the name." Cape frowned. "But can't place it."

"You read the society pages?"

"I tend to stick with *Peanuts* and *Family Circus*."

"Jesse was an up-and-comer on the political scene, offspring of a San Francisco power couple. Mom was Judith Cranston, passed away a couple of years ago, but in her day ran the San Francisco Opera. Big on the charity circuit."

Cape felt a knot tying itself around his gut.

"Maybe you've heard of the father," said Sullivan. "William Cranston."

"That name I know." Cape visualized the list he'd given to Sally. If memory served, Cranston's name was near the top. "He's in politics too?"

"You could say that," said Sullivan. "He's a judge."

57

"I'm not one to judge," said the Doctor, "but you sound like a bunch of spineless cephalopods."

The man at the far end of the table worked his jaw with the fervor of someone worried about swallowing a cherry pit. He was hungover, having celebrated his sixtieth birthday the night before, but was feeling queasy for another reason. He was chairman of the board, but when the Doctor showed up, he wasn't in charge of anything.

He scanned the table for support, but the five other board members refused to make eye contact, having developed a sudden and intense interest in their own hands, their empty notepads, or their shoes.

The boardroom was simultaneously conservative and opulent. Wood on the floors, walls, and ceiling. The table was a mahogany ellipse only slightly larger than the orbit of Saturn. On the left sat one woman and two men about his age, with two younger women on his right.

The board had taken years to assemble and included George and Elaine, two African-Americans. *Check.* One Asian woman, Doris, *check.* Three Caucasians, counting Pat, Kerry, and himself, and he'd made an additional contribution to inclusion with an artificial limb. The left leg below the thigh, due to a drunken motorcycle accident when he was a teenager. So the disability box got checked, and if you looked closely, you'd notice the raised Adam's apple on Kerry, the raven-haired woman who used to be a man. Transgender gets a check mark. Next year he planned on swapping out Elaine for a gay Latino he'd met at a networking event, but even now it was a perfectly inclusive board of directors, demonstrably diverse and therefore beyond reproach.

Not to mention political diversity. Two Democrats, two Republicans, a registered Green Party member, and even a Libertarian, but every single one a capitalist at heart.

To criticize the company was an attack on all of them, and in these politically correct times, no one would dare.

Unassailable in every way, until this lunatic started calling them all jellyfish.

"We're just being cautious," the chairman said reasonably. "You have to admit—"

"I admit that I thought you, Steve, of all people…" The Doctor shook his head disconsolately. "I thought you had the backbone to see this through."

Doris looked up from the table. "We are still committed—"

"Time doesn't wait for committees, Doris," said the Doctor impatiently. "And neither do I."

"I said *committed*," objected Doris.

"Tomato, tom-ah-toe," said the Doctor. "I look around this table and see a bunch of bureaucrats. I'd call that a committee." He smiled wickedly and added, "Or a consortium." He looked pointedly around the room. "That's a much better word, don't you think?"

George shifted uncomfortably in his chair and cleared his throat. "Doctor, in this forum, in this room, the board cannot condone or acknowledge any collusion omitted from our annual report. Hopewell Pharmaceutical Company is a publicly traded enterprise, as you know."

"I love it when you guys call it an enterprise," said the Doctor. "As if a giant drug company is a fucking starship on a five-year mission. You're on a mission to get your ass reamed by Wall Street if you don't launch a new drug in the next fiscal year."

Kerry's cheeks squeezed together like a pair of angry lemons. "Which is why we turned to you."

"Exactly," said the Doctor.

"We just want to slow down the trials," said Elaine. "The seizures—"

"Statistically insignificant." The Doctor waved a dismissive hand. "And not connected to us at all. The users—the test subjects— are three steps removed from any path that leads back here. San Francisco has more than enough junkies to muddy the waters."

"But what if there *is* an investigation?" asked Kerry.

"What if there's a lawsuit?" asked Doris.

"A *class-action* lawsuit," added George.

"We own a judge," said the Doctor curtly. "We own *the* judge— any case brought against us will go to the State Superior Court and land on his bench."

George furrowed his brow. "But the donut shack exploded."

Steve nodded emphatically. "It blew up."

"The pier was on fire," added Elaine histrionically. "It was all over the news."

Pat exhaled loudly. "Praise God it wasn't the banana stand."

"Are you serious?" asked the Doctor incredulously.

Pat shrugged. "I love me some fried bananas."

Doris and George nodded their agreement.

"I'm not talking about the goddamn bananas!" said the Doctor. "Or the donuts." He rolled his neck until a loud *crack* brought his eyes back to the table. "You nimrods are worried about the donut shack? Say the police stumble across some caramelized contraband, you seriously think any reporters—even Woodward and Bernstein—could connect a pissant dealer to one of the biggest pharma companies in the Bay Area?"

"It's not just the press," said Steve, in his best chairman-of-the-board baritone.

The Doctor's eyes glinted like winter sun on a broken windshield. "Go on."

"We got a phone call."

"So that's it." The Doctor nodded to himself and stood up. Moving to a whiteboard mounted on the wall, he pulled a Sharpie from his jacket pocket, ignoring the erasable markers in a tray mounted beneath the board. "I know about the phone calls."

"Calls?" Steve was aghast. "Plural, as in more than one call? What other calls?"

"Your partners on the pier," said the Doctor mildly. "They got calls, too."

"*This* call mentioned money laundering," said Kerry testily.

"Yup, that's the one," said the Doctor. "We'll handle it."

"How?" asked Pat.

"You don't really want me to answer that," said the Doctor. "Do you?"

"People could go to jail," insisted Pat.

"I don't care if half the consortium gets locked up for money laundering, as long as the drug tests stay on schedule. That's why this thing is a double-blind." The Doctor spun the marker across the back of his knuckles like a magician performing sleight of hand. "The Russians import our magic ingredients—"

"—unregulated pharmaceuticals," muttered Doris.

"You want to be a global company, then ignore the local laws," snapped the Doctor. "Manufacturing and R&D are handled in China, and our angel investors from Hong Kong make sure all the profits are squeaky clean by running everything through their Chinese laundry."

"That's our point," said George, eyebrows on full alert. "A reporter called about money laundering, and you're not concerned?"

"It probably wasn't a reporter."

"Who then?" asked Pat and George simultaneously.

"We have a theory."

"'We have a theory'?" Steve seemed to swell in his chair. "You keep saying we, but who's *we* in this scenario?" He waved furiously around the table. "I thought we were the only *we* that matters."

The Doctor turned to the whiteboard and took the cap off his pen. "I think it's time we discussed roles and responsibilities." With the care of a surgeon making an incision, he drew a perfectly straight line from the top of the board downward at a sixty-degree angle.

"Is that a permanent marker?" asked Kerry.

"Yes." The Doctor took a step back to judge the angle before drawing a second line horizontally across the board. "Yes, it is."

"That shit will never come off," muttered George.

"The erasable markers are *right there!*" said Steve, jabbing his finger. "You know what that board cost?"

"It's replaceable." The Doctor turned to face them and lazily rotated his wrist so the pen took them all in. "Just like this board." He smiled. "Just like all of you." A graceful turn on his heels and he faced the whiteboard again, to draw the third and final line. "And like the lines on this board, it's important for you to understand that some decisions, once they've been made, cannot be erased."

Elaine cocked her chin forward. "Are you threatening us?"

The Doctor gave her a sympathetic look but ignored the question as he stepped to the side of his sketch. "Now what do you see?"

Six faces stared at him, nonplussed.

"It's a triangle," said Steve, an undercurrent of understanding in his voice.

"Very good, Steve," said the Doctor. "No wonder you're the chairman of the board." He capped his pen and traced it through the air along each side of the perfectly formed triangle. "Heaven. Earth. Man."

Six nervous faces looked around the room, reliving the

childhood nightmare when the teacher is going to call on you, only you forgot to do your homework.

"Symbolism is very important to our investors in Hong Kong," said the Doctor mildly. "And so is honoring your agreements."

"We're not suggesting we don't launch the drug," said Steve, holding up his hands in surrender. "But perhaps another look at the data—"

"You want a look behind the curtain?" The Doctor surveyed the room as if making a decision, sizing each of them up in turn. "This is a one-way ticket, my friends."

The room looked at him expectantly, but no one spoke.

The Doctor continued. "You want a new, one-of-a-kind drug—"

"—to fight disease—" began Doris.

"—to corner the market," said the Doctor. "To box out your competitors, hold up the insurance companies, and generate enough cash to lobby Congress to prevent any over-the-counter competitors from showing up for at least a decade."

"We're just looking to fast-track FDA approval without setting off any alarms," said George. "That's our business model."

"I'm not criticizing," replied the Doctor with a smirk. "But your partners in China, you do know what *their* business model is, don't you?"

Doris almost raised her hand but caught herself. "Low-cost manufacturing at scale?"

"You actually think the Chinese Central Committee is a bunch of wannabe capitalists?" asked the Doctor. "Just because the Soviet Union collapsed into an orgy of oligarchs—getting their rocks off by fucking with our elections—doesn't mean the Chinese have taken their eyes off the prize."

"The prize?" asked Kerry.

"Um, let me think...*the global economy*? Try watching Bloomberg or CNBC every once in a while." The Doctor shook his head at their naivete. "You can't take over today's world with H-bombs, tanks, or an army—even an army that outnumbers Justin Bieber's twitter following."

"You're generalizing," protested Steve. "That's got nothing to do with us."

"It's got everything to do with you. It's the only reason you're profitable." The Doctor's stare was evangelical. "You want me to stop generalizing, fine, I'll get specific—what happens if a patient takes one of your drugs and has an adverse side effect? Say, for example, their life-saving cholesterol medication causes erectile dysfunction?"

"Well, the prescribing physician might give them a PDE inhibitor," Steve said slowly, clearly wondering where this was going. "Like Viagra or Cialis."

"But what if that triggers depression?" asked the Doctor. "Then they might also prescribe…what?" He looked around the table. "Anyone?"

This time Doris did raise her hand. "An antidepressant."

"Exactly!" said the Doctor gleefully. "So, if you sell a drug with negative side effects, and you're the drug company, *you get to sell more drugs*. If the condition is chronic, we're talking six-to-eight different prescriptions a month, easy. I'd say that is one hell of a business model, wouldn't you?"

"It's not that simple," said George, frowning.

"Actually, it's entirely that simple," said the Doctor. "You hypocrites are pissing your pants over a bunch of seizures? Eliminate side effects and you nimrods are out of business. That is what you need to understand before you start talking about gathering more data or taking it slow."

"You can't tell us what to do," Steve said unconvincingly. "This board is an independent body."

"Sure, it is," said the Doctor. "We're all independent. Some of us want to cure Alzheimer's, while others want to sell more drugs, and that's fine. But consider this—some might get their jollies from controlling a fifth of the U.S. economy by making sure the

American public gets addicted to drugs manufactured overseas." The Doctor paused for effect. "*Everyone* gets something out of this deal, which means *nobody* gets to back out."

No one said anything in rebuttal, and for a long moment the boardroom was as somber as a eunuch's bachelor party.

The Doctor returned his attention to the indelible triangle, tapping the bottom of the pen sharply against the board until all eyes fixed on his hand. With excruciating deliberation, he traced the lines of the triangle in reverse.

"Heaven. Earth. Man."

He tapped the board three more times. "In this instance think of yourselves as *man*—no sexism intended, ladies—man, as in mortal. *Mortal*, derived from the Latin word *mortalis*, meaning death, or in this case, *capable of dying*."

"I told you he was threatening us," said Elaine, looking around the table for validation.

The Doctor's finger lovingly traced the second line. "*Earth*. For our purposes, think of this as our foundation—the consortium, our partners, and the bank."

Steve worked his jaw. "And the last line?"

"*Heaven*." The Doctor spread his hands like a Baptist minister. "Where the power lies, where everything was put in motion so long ago." He brought his hands together so they were pointing at the table. "Where God watches…all…of…*you*."

"Don't you mean all of *us*?" asked Doris, gesturing back at him.

"Did I stutter?" asked the Doctor.

"Are you suggesting you're God?" asked Steve, at the same instant that Elaine asked, "Are you threatening us again?"

"Yes," said the Doctor, a beatific expression on his face.

"Damn," said Steve.

"I knew it," said Elaine.

58

"I knew it," said Eva. "You're jealous of me."

Sergey scoffed. "I just don't like your outfit, that's all."

"I think you wish that you were going to the aquarium," Eva raised an eyebrow. "Or maybe you want to dress like a pirate."

Sergey shook his head. "I'm not into cosplay."

"Then why did I catch you watching television and masturbating to Wonder Woman when we were kids?"

"This is a bad example," said Sergey.

"Fine." Eva spread her arms and looked down at her suede boots, leggings, wide leather belt, low-cut blouse, and waistcoat. "If I'm going to seduce a pirate, I need to be dressed appropriately."

"You look like you're going to a Renaissance Faire."

"Very funny." Eva pulled a Slim Jim from her belt and unwrapped it testily, biting it in half as her brother sized her up.

Sergey idly ran his finger across the top of one of the nesting dolls, wondering if it would leave a trail of dust, but it was as immaculate as the rest of the store. He wondered if dust was as terrified of his older sister as he was.

But Nastya wasn't here. She put him in charge of helping Eva prepare for her rendezvous, and this was one job he wasn't going to screw up.

"And no one said anything about *seducing* anyone," he added. "You are supposed to be talking business."

Eva rolled her eyes. "I could wear a hat," she said, "the one shaped like a triangle."

"Then you'd look like George Washington." Sergey scanned the shelves until he found a nesting doll painted like a pirate. He had to admit, Nastya had everything in this store, from dolls painted in the traditional manner—old women and young Russian girls—to dolls painted like politicians, celebrities, even comic book characters. From Donald Duck to Donald Trump, Popeye to Putin, anyone could be turned into *matryoshka*.

He took the tiny pirate and started breaking it apart, laying each successive doll on the counter. The largest looked like Blackbeard, eyes fierce and beard scraggly. The next was a corsair, a handsome rogue with a curved sword. The third looked like one of the Village People.

Sergey frowned. If he was going to help his sister, he needed some kind of visual reference. He looked at Eva.

"Was there a pirate in the Village People?"

Eva furrowed her brow. "Policeman, Indian chief—"

"—Native American," corrected Sergey. "Don't be so culturally insensitive."

"*Vyrezat*," snapped Eva. "Policeman, chief, construction worker and…"

"…and…"

"…and…?"

Sergey snapped his fingers. "Soldier!"

"Nice." Eva nodded. "I forgot about him. But there was one more, wasn't there?"

The siblings paced around the store for a couple of minutes, heads down, until Sergey smacked the counter. "Was there a guy in leather?"

"Yes!" Eva frowned. "What was he supposed to be?"

"I think he was supposed to be gay," said Sergey.

"Brilliant," said Eva. "I never knew that when I was a kid, though."

"Me, neither," said Sergey. "Wasn't I the construction worker for Halloween, when I was ten?"

Eva shook her head. "That was Bob the Builder."

"American culture is very confusing," said Sergey. "Even now."

"We grew up in two worlds."

Sergey nodded. "So, we have the cop, chief, construction worker, soldier, and gay leather man." He sighed in resignation and glanced at the nesting doll. "No pirate."

"No pirate." Eva shrugged.

"Never mind," said Sergey, reaching for the doll. He broke it apart, muttering under his breath. He almost gave up until the fifth-smallest doll emerged. Sergey beamed as he hit pay dirt with a meticulously painted female pirate. She scowled at Sergey as if she wanted him to walk the plank. He looked her up and down, then held the doll aloft like Indiana Jones holding a golden idol.

"Who needs the Village People when you have Russian craftsmanship!"

Eva looked quizzically at the doll, then at her brother expectantly.

Sergey glanced from Eva to the doll, then back again. His eyes narrowed as he scrutinized his sister.

"Lose the vest," he said. "And the belt."

"But—"

Sergey held up a hand for silence. "And untuck the blouse."

Eva complied.

"The top of your boots," he said, "roll them back up. You want to be an authentic pirate, not an extra in a Johnny Depp movie."

Eva took a step back, hands on hips.

"Not bad," said Sergey, checking the doll to make sure he didn't miss anything. Painted along the waist of the tiny pirate girl was a rapier on her left hip and musket on her right. "Wait a minute."

"What?" asked Eva, but her brother had set the doll on the counter and disappeared into the back of the store. Eva heard him rummaging around before he cried out triumphantly. A minute later he was standing in front of her with both hands behind his back.

"Hold out your left hand," he said.

Eva studied his expression before cautiously extending her hand, wondering if her brother would revert to his puerile instincts and drop an ice cube or ball of slime into her palm. But Sergey was full of surprises lately.

"Put this in your boot." Sergey put something slim and heavy into Eva's hand. Looking down, she recognized it instantly.

"Your knife," she said. "I forgot about that one."

"Remember, it's a switchblade." Sergey took it back from her, holding it gingerly in his right hand. The blade was concealed, the handle made of horn grips with a recessed button on one side. Sergey swung his thumb over the button and pressed. Eva jumped backwards as the blade snapped open. One second it was an innocuous pocket knife, the next it was a cobra about to strike.

Sergey showed her how to release the catch that locked the blade in place, then folded it back into the handle until he heard a *click*. "When you press the button your hand should already be in motion, stabbing. Unless you just want to show off and intimidate someone."

Eva took the knife and moved her hand up and down, getting used to the weight. Then she bent down and slid it into her right boot, flexing her calf until it settled.

"Now turn around," said Sergey.

Eva looked at him suspiciously. "Are you going to look at my ass?"

"There isn't much to look at, *mladshaya sestra*."

"Hmph." Eva spun around and felt her brother's left hand on her hip, then something slipped into her waistband at the base of her spine. She guessed what it was even before she reached around and pulled it free.

Eva turned to face Sergey before looking down at the gun in her hand.

It was a slim .32-caliber semiautomatic that fit neatly in her palm. A logo that looked like a Z enclosed by a C was stamped into the plastic grips. The metal of the slide felt as cold as a Russian winter.

"Where did you get it?" Eva asked.

"It's Nastya's," replied Sergey. "I know where she hides it." Then, seeing the look of concern on his sister's face, he added, "Don't worry, Eva, just bring it—and you—back in one piece, and Nastya won't mind."

Eva looked at her brother as if seeing him for the first time, then stood on her toes and kissed him on the cheek. "*Spasibo, brat.*"

Sergey blushed. "You're welcome." He wiped his cheek in mock annoyance. "And remember, Eva, never trust a pirate."

Eva slid the gun behind her back. "Don't worry, I'll keep the safety off," she said, "and my eyes open."

59

Vera opened her eyes and knew something wasn't right.

She lay on the cot in the back of the store, her head across her right arm. She awoke with the sensation she'd been crying in her sleep. Rolling onto her back, she twisted her neck to see the window. There it was, a hole punched through the glass. Raising her hand to her face, she touched her cheek below the left eye and visualized the blood streaming down Cape's face.

That wasn't a dream, she thought. That wasn't even a nightmare.

Then she glanced at the floor and smiled at the memory of rolling around like a pair of teenagers. That wasn't a dream, either.

Vera wondered what time it was.

Her body felt stiff, neck complaining that she'd slept on her arm instead of a pillow. A faint creak as she sat up, and for an instant she wondered if the sound had emanated from her tired bones instead of the springs on the cot.

Creak. Pause. *Creak.*

It wasn't the cot.

Footsteps, it sounded like footsteps at the front of the store.

Vera took a deep breath to clear her head and listened more closely, but it was impossible to gauge distance. Someone was pacing outside the store, each footfall squeezing a creak or groan from the wooden planks of the pier.

It occurred to Vera that Cape would have let himself in, so she stood up, realizing a policeman might be posted outside her door. *Might as well say hello.* She ran her hands through her hair and tried to blink the sleep from her eyes.

The light coming through the window was murky and gray, the lamps on the pier reflected upward by the fog. As dawn approached, the fog always thickened, wrapping around the buildings like a straitjacket.

Vera stepped from the back room into the store. It was brighter here because of the size of the front window and the reflective surfaces of the clothing displays, but the view outside was an impenetrable wall of filthy cotton.

As she approached the counter, the front door opened suddenly.

A man was silhouetted against the fog, one hand on the doorknob, the other outstretched in a half-hearted wave.

"Cape?" Vera came forward but stopped as if she'd walked into a wall.

The invisible barrier was a smell unlike anything Vera had ever encountered, an olfactory onslaught that made her eyes water and throat constrict. She took a step back as the store filled with a blend of rotting seaweed, damp fur, and brine.

If Poseidon had taken a thousand sea lions to indulge a sudden craving for Taco Bell, only to realize in the middle of the night they were violently allergic to cheese, this is what it would smell like. And somewhere in that miasma of nautical nausea, Vera also detected a faint smell of soggy donuts.

"Who the hell is Cape?"

Vera gasped as she recognized the voice.

Lou stepped into the light and smiled crookedly.

His pants were torn, his shirt disintegrated, and his skin as pale as an albino shark. He wore the odor of the bay like a cologne, and the seaweed on his head resembled hair extensions. His shoes were bobbing in the waves near Alcatraz, but he stood at a jaunty angle as he leaned against the counter.

Vera shook her head in disbelief, but her nose told her this wasn't a nightmare, she was wide awake.

Lou stepped further into the store as Vera felt her back press hard against the counter. She had nowhere to go, unless she turned her back on the apparition in front of her.

Vera calculated her chances of making it to the door or screaming loud enough for anyone to hear, assuming the pier wasn't deserted at this hour. Her cell phone was in the back room. She gauged the distance to the store phone and the letter opener she kept near the register, but for now they were both out of reach.

Her only option was right in front of her.

Vera gritted her teeth and forced herself to look into Lou's bloodshot eyes.

"We need to talk," he said.

60

"I hate talking to you."

"Since when?" Cape tried to look offended but there was no bullshitting a cop, and he had known Beau too long. "I thought we were friends."

"Friend's got nothing to do with it," said Beau. "We can talk about sports, movies, even relationships—"

"I'd rather not talk about relationships," replied Cape, a little too quickly.

"Our conversations about work tend to be lopsided." Beau shrugged. "That's all I'm saying."

"But I'm buying you breakfast," said Cape. "Again."

"You're on an expense account."

"It's the gesture that counts."

"Then count this one." Beau held up his right hand, middle finger extended. "Maybe I'll pay this time," he added, "if you tell me *what-in-the-fuck* is going on."

Cape caught the eye of a passing waitress as Beau attacked his French toast like a Panzer Division under Rommel.

"I see you gave up your diet," said Cape.

"I never give up," said Beau. "I'm using reverse psychology on my body."

As their waitress ensured they were both fully caffeinated, Cape glanced at the other patrons. Not surprisingly, everyone was more interested in bacon than in anything he might have to say.

The Hidive was never very crowded this time of day, known more as a waterfront bar than a place to grab breakfast. Located in the shadow of the Oakland Bay Bridge and adjacent to the garish yellow of Pier 28, the neon martini glass above the front door conjured an image of a dive bar from the 1940s.

Beau took some bacon and popped it into his mouth. His biceps stretched the fabric of his black T-shirt as he rested his elbows on the table, eyes on Cape.

"Someone almost shot me," said Cape.

Beau nodded as he swallowed. "I heard."

"They missed."

"Obviously." Beau chuckled, a bass rumble that almost shook the table.

Cape shoveled some eggs into his mouth, blue eyes only faintly amused.

"You sure they were aiming for you?" asked Beau. "You even sure it was a bullet?"

"I'm not sure of anything at this point."

Beau took another bite. "The guys at the crime scene said the best angle for a shot would be from the roof of the aquarium. You rattle any cages over there?"

"It's on the list," said Cape. "I've been busy."

"Me, too."

"Doing what?" asked Cape. "Tell *me* something."

"Nice try." Beau shook his head. "You haven't told me anything I don't already know."

"Know anything about money laundering?"

"That's another question," replied Beau. "You're doing all the asking and none of the telling."

"I play to my strengths."

Beau gave him a cut-the-shit stare. Cape laughed.

"You told me the donut shack was a front for drugs," said Beau. "Soon after that...BOOM!" He spread his fingers theatrically. "It's raining donuts."

"I'm surprised more cops didn't show up."

"Hilarious," said Beau. "I have to wonder—since I'm a cop and don't believe in coincidences—if you know anything about that little incident?"

Cape shook his head. "If someone thought they were being investigated, seems like a dumbass way to cover your tracks."

"Drug deals always go bad," replied Beau. "Maybe somebody has a grudge."

"Maybe."

Beau drained his fourth cup of coffee and waved for another round. Cape noticed his own was empty and tried to recall if he'd slept at all last night, then realized that if he couldn't remember, the answer was no.

"Why'd you ask about money laundering?" said Beau.

Cape told him about the money trail discovered by Sloth and Linda, the skein of currency changing hands across the pier. He handed Beau printouts of the schematics that Sloth had been building.

Cape left out Sally's visit to the bank and did his best to skip anything that might make Beau uncomfortable, like hacking past the firewall of a global bank.

When he finished, Beau looked like a Sphinx with a hangover.

"Run that last part by me again."

"Which part?" asked Cape.

"The part where you called these places," said Beau, "*and you gave them your name?*"

"Oh, that."

Beau reached under the table, pulled his gun from its holster, and laid it on the table between their plates. It was a Sig 9-millimeter, a semiautomatic pistol that looked angry just sitting there. The waitress, on her way back to their table, froze when she saw the gun until Beau took the badge off his hip and held it up. She spun on her toes like a ballerina and headed in the opposite direction.

"Take my gun and shoot yourself," said Beau. "That will really confuse the hell out of whoever is trying to kill you."

"Put that away," said Cape. "Or the waitress will never come back."

"I've had too much coffee already," answered Beau. "Maybe you could go to that place on the pier that does face painting for kids? You could drop your pants and ask them to paint a target on your ass."

"You did suggest I rattle some cages."

"But you didn't pick a target." Beau took the gun and returned it to his hip. "You called so many places, you've got no idea who took the shot."

Cape made a rueful face. "I was getting impatient."

"You don't know if the drug trafficking is connected to money laundering."

"Drug money always has to get cleaned," said Cape. "Doesn't it?"

"Maybe," said Beau. "But speaking as a sworn officer of the law, you've got fuck-all when it comes to evidence that would stand up in court."

"You just said you don't believe in coincidences."

Beau slurped his coffee loudly and stared at Cape over the rim.

"If it's all connected," said Cape, "then everybody wins."

"So why 'jack a truck?" said Beau. "Is that what you're asking?"

"What can you tell me about the Millennium Tower jumper?"

Beau paused long enough to give the impression he wasn't going to answer, then said, "That hasn't hit the papers yet."

"That's one advantage of getting shot at," said Cape. "You get to hang around gossipy cops in the middle of the night."

"What's the question?"

"The victim was the son of a judge—Judge William Cranston, right?"

Beau nodded. "Superior Court judge, got re-elected last year."

"I thought judges got appointed."

"Not to the Superior Court—have to run for that office like any state politician."

Cape stared at the mottled surface of their table for a minute, trying to find a pattern. "So he'd have to raise money for his election campaigns like everyone else."

"Yup, every election cycle," said Beau. "Why?"

"When you and Vinnie told me about the heavy-hitters behind the pier, you said investors included a state senator and a judge," said Cape. "He's the judge on that list."

Beau drummed his thumb against the table as if sending a distress signal. "Slipped my mind while I was watching the forensics team scrape his son's brains off the sidewalk."

"Did the kid leave a note?"

"Most people don't."

"So you think it's a *coincidence* his dad is connected to the pier."

"Did I say that?"

"We should call the Feds."

"This is my backyard," said Beau testily. "What are you gonna show the Feds—your illegally obtained financial information that leads to nowhere, or the disappearing bullet that might not have been a bullet, or maybe some water-logged donuts—"

"—fine," said Cape.

"The Feds won't act on a hunch, and the only crime I'm authorized to investigate is the armored car heist, because, so far…it's the only crime."

"You find the drivers?"

"You think I'd be sitting here if I had?" Beau cracked his knuckles. "My guess is they're either dead or long gone."

"It's all connected," said Cape.

"I'm not saying the pier doesn't look fishy."

"You either believe these are totally unrelated events, or—"

"—you've stumbled onto the greatest criminal conspiracy in the history of the city," said Beau.

"I never stumble," said Cape. "I just flail around."

"I noticed."

"This case has too many moving parts."

"I noticed that too."

Cape sighed. "I feel like I'm boxing an octopus."

"Then turn it into a knife fight," said Beau. "And cut off its arms."

61

"Cut off its arms," said the Doctor. "It'll be a lot easier."

He leaned into the webcam and imagined his face looking huge and distorted on the other end, but he was trying to make a point, and no one seemed to be listening. On his laptop the display was split into quadrants, each showing a different view of his lab in the middle of the Pacific Ocean.

His humorless assistant, Joy, stared disapprovingly from the upper right corner of his screen.

"This is our last specimen of *Hapalochlaena maculosa*," she said. "It would be foolish to kill the creature for one sample when we are so close to finding the right protein sequence, and your supplier in Australia—"

"That's a blue-ringed octopus," said the Doctor.

Joy looked perturbed. "That's what I said. *Hapalochlaena mac—*"

"I wasn't finished," snapped the Doctor. "I'm not there to perform the procedure myself, and that little critter is the fourth most venomous creature on the planet. The neurotoxin in its saliva may be key to the sequencing, but it would be foolish to handle that animal without taking precautions."

"Killing it seems to be an excessive precaution," replied Joy, her monotone polite and humorless. Through the speakers on his laptop she sounded more like Siri or Alexa than ever.

"Suit yourself."

"We could wait until you return to the lab."

"Absolutely not," said the Doctor. "We've got too much invested, and we're close to a breakthrough. If today's test works, we're going to expand trials beyond San Francisco."

"But if it doesn't," said Joy, "you'll regret having killed the animal."

The Doctor pressed his thumbs into his temples until they turned white. He wasn't as worried about the danger as he was about the procedure getting botched. He couldn't afford a day trip to the Spratly Islands.

If today's test looked promising, his associates would expand trials to Seattle, Orlando, San Diego, and eventually Montreal, Paris, and Tokyo by the end of the year. Things had gotten messy in San Francisco, and time wasn't on his side.

On the screen in front of him, the octopus floated in its tank as if it had all the time in the world. Maybe six inches long, covered with brown and yellow bands, its body mottled with blue rings. Its tentacles seemed luminous against the seawater of the tank.

"I'm sure it will be fine," said Joy. "We have wire mesh gloves."

"Swell."

"Stewart will be very careful."

The Doctor almost asked who-the-hell-is-Stewart until he glanced at the lower left of his screen and saw a tall, pale technician moving from the main lab toward the examination counter. The resolution on the laptop wasn't the best, but the Doctor thought he detected a ribbon of sweat on Stewart's upper lip.

The Doctor clucked his tongue. "He looks like a man with acrophobia stepping onto a tightrope."

"He is very qualified," insisted Joy.

"Tell that to the octopus."

The last quadrant featured a view of the entire lab from a

camera mounted on the wall across from Joy. Sliding his thumb
and forefinger over the track pad, the Doctor adjusted his view to
zoom into where the action was about to take place. By scanning
the four squares he could track every moment of the operation.

"Showtime," said the Doctor.

Another technician entered the lab. He approached the tank
with a grabber stick, the type of grip-activated mechanical arm
sold in drugstores around the world to reach things on impossibly high shelves. This one had been modified—instead of
a plastic claw on the end, a net held by a wire ring opens or
closes with every squeeze of the handle. Tied to the fabric of
the net was a tiny crab, a common bait for octopus traps. The
rig was inspired by the clay jars and cages used by fishermen
from Europe to Asia.

The technician was compact, with a physique somewhere
between a rugby player and an end table. He held the stick with
the calm assuredness of a conductor, assuming that conductor
was an epileptic under attack by bees.

"Who's that guy?" asked the Doctor.

Joy stepped into frame and looked directly at the camera.
"That's Chris. He is very competent."

The Doctor started to say something but caught himself. It
was hard enough finding a cure for incurable diseases, but finding
talent willing to work under duress at a top-secret laboratory while
committing every known human rights violation in the process,
well, that was beyond him.

"Tell him I say hi," mumbled the Doctor. "Stewart, too. Thanks,
guys."

Joy's enormous face looked approvingly from the screen. The
Doctor made a mental note to do a better job remembering people's names. He had forgotten that tidbit from his professional
coaching. Just a tiny bit of acknowledgement, and you could get
people to do almost anything.

"Remember, Joy," said the Doctor, "the venom is stored inside the salivary glands, behind the beak, so you have to spread the arms wide before you use the syringe."

Joy nodded. "Chris will use the stick to remove *Hapalochlaena maculosa*—"

"—stop showing off," said the Doctor. "Just say octopus."

"Chris will remove *the specimen* from the tank," continued Joy. "And Stewart will hold it down and separate the tentacles while I use the syringe to extract the venom."

Chris climbed onto a step stool next to the counter and moved the stick over the opening of the tank. It knocked against the sides with a hollow clunk the Doctor could hear clearly through the laptop speakers. As the net slid into the tank, the octopus moved effortlessly to the side, its arms undulating. The little crab kicked and clacked its claws in agitation, two of its legs held tight with monofilament.

"Now leave it there," the Doctor commanded. "Our little kraken is curious by nature, just give it a moment."

The stick continued to wobble back and forth until Chris hooked the end onto the side of the tank, letting go of the handle. This left the net suspended about halfway down the tank, almost level with the octopus.

It was impossible to tell where the octopus was looking, but its arms waved methodically, each containing olfactory nerve endings. It was like having nine noses. It drifted idly, sizing up the situation, then extended two arms into the net and pulled itself inside. Once clear of the edge, it opened like a flower, bringing the beak forward to begin its feeding.

Chris lurched at the stick, almost knocking it from its perch, but his hand grasped the handle before the octopus finished the crab. The net closed as the octopus pulsated, the bands around its head shifting in color from dark brown to pale beige.

"No time like the present," said the Doctor.

"Understood," said Joy. "Stewart, get into position."

Stewart stepped to the opposite side of the counter from Chris and gave a final pull on his mesh gloves.

"That species can survive out of the water for almost an hour," said the Doctor. "So take your time and do *not* fuck this up."

Joy pursed her lips but didn't respond to his motivational speech. She stepped away from the camera as Chris slowly lifted the net from the tank. As it broke the surface of the water, the octopus swelled and contracted like a beating heart. The rings on its skin turned iridescent, as if each tentacle had a dozen blue eyes glaring angrily at their captor.

"Oh, he's pissed," said the Doctor.

When the net was level with the counter, Chris glanced nervously at Stewart to make sure he was paying attention. Joy stepped into frame, syringe at the ready, stainless steel glove on her left hand.

Chris squeezed the handle and released the net. The octopus hit the metal counter and bounced like a ball, its arms springing outward on impact. Stewart lunged forward, grabbing the head with his right hand and pinning it to the table. The Doctor heard a chorus of three gasps as if a bomb had been defused.

"So far, so good," he said. "Now flip him upside down."

Stewart rotated his wrist and inverted the octopus, unfurling half the tentacles with his left hand while shifting his right from the head to the other four arms. With its arms spread, the octopus looked less threatening but more obscene, an alien caught with its pants down and legs open. The twin rows of suckers on each arm pulsated suggestively.

At the center of this unholy flower was the beak, more reminiscent of a parrot than a pocket-sized sea monster.

"Joy, you're up."

Joy cautiously placed her left hand on the counter, gloved fingers extending over the nearest arms of the octopus as she brought the syringe forward with her right hand. Peering closely at the tissue around the mouth and beak, she picked a spot and inserted the syringe. The blue rings on the octopus went full neon and the mottled skin shifted from light to dark like an angry Rorschach test.

"Venom extracted," Joy announced.

A collective sigh from the lab. Joy moved out of frame to inject the neurotoxin into a test tube. The Doctor leaned back and released the breath he'd been holding. Chris wiped sweat from his eyes and smiled broadly.

Then Stewart made a terrible mistake.

He wasn't a trained marine biologist, or he would have handled the creature more roughly. The flesh was so gelatinous, the texture so squishy, he worried about crushing the animal if he squeezed too hard. And the octopus was so tiny, barely wider than his hand. He was being cautious but naturally assumed it lacked the strength to free itself from his grip.

A marine biologist would have known that even a one-pound octopus was capable of lifting forty pounds if it gained enough leverage. So, when Stewart relaxed his grip, the octopus sensed its chance, and instinct took over.

Two of the arms wriggled free of Stewart's left hand and writhed in the air, looking for purchase. Without thinking, Stewart moved his right hand to contain them, which let another two arms slide from underneath his fingers. It was like squeezing Jell-O just hard enough to keep it in your hands, but not so hard that it oozed through your fingers. Panicking, Stewart changed his grip again as all four arms on the right side escaped.

The octopus swung its free tentacles sideways with enough momentum to flip itself onto Stewart's left wrist, where it landed heads-up like a bad penny.

Stewart still had a feeble grip on half the arms, but the rogue tentacles wrapped themselves around his left wrist just below the cuff of his mesh glove.

"Oh, that's not good." The Doctor watched, mesmerized, as Stewart started to shout.

"Get it off…get it off… *get it off me!*"

"Easier said than done," muttered the Doctor.

Joy saw what was happening and ran into frame, then stopped

short. Chris stood on the opposite side of the counter, rigid with fear, his mouth agape. Stewart waved his arm back and forth, but the octopus held fast.

Stewart realized he was still clutching half the tentacles, so he opened his left hand and swung his arm wide. Like a seat belt that locks into place from the physics of a crash, the octopus didn't budge until Stewart bent his elbow for the backswing and momentum reversed, then halted. At that instant the creature slid up past the glove, and Stewart screamed as the beak found the soft flesh of his forearm.

He whipped his arms like a stuntman on fire, and this time the octopus decided to let go. It flew across the counter like a giant ball of snot, tentacles akimbo.

It smacked Chris squarely in the face.

The tentacles snapped around Chris' skull on impact, two latching onto his ears with gymnastic precision. The bulbous head of the octopus landed directly over his gaping mouth. Somehow Chris remained standing, like a boxer taking a punch to the face, too stunned for his brain to get a message to his legs that it was a knockout.

Over the tinny speakers of his laptop, the Doctor heard a gargled scream followed by an aquatic gagging sound before Chris fell backward out of frame.

Joy's face ballooned onto the screen, her eyes huge as she looked into the camera pleadingly, as if she could summon the Doctor to teleport through the webcam.

The Doctor reflexively shifted to lecture mode.

"Victims may experience dizziness," he said, "or a feeling of intoxication. A common side effect is sudden fatigue, followed by muscle paralysis and shortness of breath."

The Doctor realized he sounded like the mandatory warning heard at the end of every drug commercial ever made, a litany of side effects so dreadful that it was a wonder anyone took a single pill. The drug industry had finally learned what Las Vegas casinos knew a long time ago, that people would play the odds, even though everybody knows the house always wins in the end.

In the lower quadrant of the screen two legs kicked spastically, the shoe flying off the right foot. The next instant, the legs disappeared.

"I don't think Chris is doing too well," said the Doctor.

Joy looked to her left reluctantly.

"The octopus remains on his face," she said. "But at least Chris has stopped kicking." Joy narrowed her gaze and shook her head disconsolately. "Actually, he might have stopped breathing." She stepped out of frame and then returned, her expression one of resignation. "He's dead."

On the far side of the counter Stewart was turning as blue as the rings on the octopus. He had been holding his left wrist with his right hand, as if covering the wound might cause it to heal, but now he moved his right hand to his throat while steadying his trembling frame against the counter. Joy and the Doctor stared with morbid fascination as both arms went rigid, then Stewart fell sideways like a redwood at a lumberjack camp.

"He's done," said the Doctor. "That's the *tetrodotoxin* shutting down his nervous system, the active ingredient in the venom you extracted. You did get the venom, didn't you?"

Joy finally blinked, in disbelief at the question. It took her a moment to find any words before she simply said, "Yes."

"Thank God," said the Doctor.

Joy looked as pissed as he'd ever seen her.

The Doctor conjured an earnest expression and added, "I meant thank God, but at what cost…"

"That is *not* what you meant."

Behind her, the octopus was moving up the side of the counter.

Against the white cabinets, its skin was paler than before. With tenacious determination, it suckered along with surprising alacrity. A slimy tarantula ascending Everest.

"Turn around," said the Doctor.

Joy started and took a quick step backward but kept her cool, considering the circumstances. The octopus perambulated across the counter until it reached the tank. Extending two tentacles, then a third and fourth, it pulled itself forward and up, up, and up the glass column. Moments later it was drifting placidly in the water, a sated vulture on the wind.

"Hey, Joy," asked the Doctor, "remember when I said it has nine brains?"

Joy sighed. "We took every precaution—"

"—but you know what it *doesn't* have?" The Doctor paused for dramatic effect. "Opposable thumbs." He wiggled his thumbs at the webcam. "That gives us the upper hand, so to speak."

"Understood."

"So next time," said the Doctor, "cut its fucking arms off."

Joy nodded but didn't say anything.

"Run the tests," said the Doctor. "And call me when you have the results."

"I'm a bit short on lab assistants."

"Remember, we're trying to save lives."

Joy was nonplussed.

"It wasn't your fault," added the Doctor reassuringly. "This kind of thing always happens when you strive for the greater good."

"What always happens?" asked Joy.

"Somebody dies."

62

"Everybody dies," said Sally.

"Exactly," said Cape. "That's what I'm worried about."

"That doesn't make any sense." Sally pressed the headphones further into her ears. She was still on the roof across from Chen's apartment and couldn't tell if the background noise was on her end of the call. "Are you driving?"

"Yes."

"With the top down?"

"How'd you guess?"

"Because I'm asking you to repeat every other sentence." Sally took her hand away from her ear and sat down on the edge of the roof, legs dangling over the side of the building. "I said the banker hasn't moved."

"And I said I don't care about the banker!" Cape raised his voice against the wind. "Well, I do, but at the moment I want the—" A rush of wind, static and then, "—udge."

"Fudge?"

"What?"

"You just said you wanted fudge."

"That's not what I said."

"I've just never known you to crave sweets."

"I said *judge*." Cape was yelling into the phone. "The priority is the judge, not the banker."

"Why?"

"You said the banker is in on this."

"Whatever this is, yes." Sally visualized Chen's triangle tattoo. "He's all in."

A rush of wind answered her, followed by, "—dead!"

"What?" asked Sally. "First everybody dies, and now somebody's dead?"

"Who's dead?" asked Cape. "Did you kill someone?"

Sally looked at Cape's name on her phone. "I'm thinking about it."

"*What?*"

Sally counted to ten. "Can you put the top up?"

"I'm driving."

"Pull over."

"Talk louder." A whoosh and a horn preceded Cape adding, "—think they killed his son."

"Whose?"

"The judge," said Cape as a truck horn reverberated. "As a warning."

"Why now?"

"He must've threatened to go to the police, or the press," said Cape, "when things started to go sideways on the pier."

"Things went sideways the minute that truck went into the bay." Sally looked across the rooftops for a moment before adding, "This isn't your fault, you know."

The wind in her headset was the only reply.

"This judge," said Sally. "Married?"

"A widower," said Cape. "I had Linda check—but he's got a daughter and grandkids in San Mateo."

"So that's the threat," said Sally. "Spill your guts to the press—"

"—and everybody dies," said Cape. "I said that already."

Sally stood up and glanced across the street at the apartment building. "He might find another way out, if he's desperate enough."

"Beau says the cops haven't told the judge about his son yet."

"The bad guys might have told him," said Sally. "Or sent him a photo."

"That's why I'm calling," said Cape. "The papers don't have a name yet, but the police are contacting the judge today, asking him to ID the body."

"What do you want me to do?"

"Get to his house—it's the weekend so he's not in court—before he has any other visitors, welcome or otherwise," said Cape. "Just get there before they do."

"And?"

"Take him off the board."

Sally listened to the rushing of the wind and wondered if it was the blood coursing through her veins. "You sure?"

"He's already dead," said Cape. "It's him or his daughter."

Sally studied the front door of Chen's building and considered the possibility of a rear entrance. An had been inside long enough, and her blatant dare might have been a ruse. Get Sally thinking An wanted to be followed, when in reality she'd already left.

"I'm on my way." She started moving toward the fire escape on the far side of the roof before asking, "What are you going to do?"

"I'm going to visit an aquarium."

63

"Welcome to the Aquarium by the Bay!"

Cragg bowed with a flourish and waved his arm as if doffing a hat, though his tangled hair was uncovered. He smiled like a shark who just heard that the all-you-can-eat buffet was open late tonight.

Eva resisted the urge to curtsy and merely nodded. Instinct told her this was a dangerous man, but experience taught her that he was still just a man. Men weren't complicated, even when they were strange.

"I like your outfit, lassie."

Of course you do, thought Eva. That's why I dressed this way. "I came to talk business, not fashion."

"Fair enough," said Cragg. "I won't say a word about your *dungbie*, but I'm guessing you do want to talk about our lost booty."

"I understood about half of that," said Eva curtly. "*Prekratit' igrat' v igry.*"

"Come again?"

"See, it's frustrating, like someone speaking a foreign language." Eva put a hand on her hip, suspecting she resembled a model for Captain Morgan rum. "After all, it's not September 19th, is it?"

"What's that got to do with anything?"

"That's International Talk-like-a-Pirate Day," said Eva. "I looked it up."

"There's a day for that?" Cragg seemed genuinely surprised. "Like Mother's Day?"

"You're saying *you* didn't know there's an official day on the calendar for talking like a pirate?"

Cragg shrugged. "Every day is talk like a pirate day."

"There's also a national popcorn day," said Eva. "A day for bittersweet chocolate. Darwin Day, Pi Day, clean-out-your-closet day, nap day, paper airplane day, and on and on. There's even a national day for telling jokes."

"You know any good jokes?"

"Knock-knock," said Eva.

"Who's there?"

"A bunch of Russians."

"A bunch of Russians who?"

"A bunch of Russians who think you're trying to rip us off."

Cragg smiled with one side of his mouth. "That's not very funny."

Eva let her hand slide off her hip. "I agree."

Cragg turned on his heel and walked slowly toward the hall of jellyfish. Eva fell into step beside him but kept an arm's length away.

"Where are all the people?" asked Eva, scanning the empty floor and listening for distant footsteps. Groups of tourists had been moving away from the aquarium when she arrived, but she hadn't paid much attention. "The tourists?"

"Didn't I mention we closed early?" asked Cragg. "Chased all the visitors away when I heard you were coming, cut the day short. Didn't want us to be interrupted."

"I see."

Cragg gestured reflexively at the glowing tanks but didn't provide any commentary. The jellyfish bobbed and undulated with indifference. Without breaking stride, Eva angled her foot so the switchblade pressed against her calf reassuringly.

"There's a sign on the door saying repairs are commencing in the undersea tunnel—the grotto—and we're closed till tomorrow." Cragg raised a hand in greeting to one of the jellyfish, a blue and yellow apparition eight inches across. "Not entirely untrue. We're overdue for an inspection of the Plexiglas and support structure under Oscar, so we'll to take a look."

"Oscar?"

"He's the real star of the aquarium, I'm just the sideshow," said Cragg. "Come on, let me introduce you."

They reached the top of a narrow flight of stairs. Standing at the bottom of the stairs was a man with a gun.

"I'd like you to meet the Doctor," said Cragg. "Doctor, this is Eva, one of our erstwhile business partners."

The Doctor nodded in greeting. He had an average build, a forgettable face, and a semiautomatic pistol in his right hand.

Eva braced a hand against the railing but remained at the top of the stairs.

"*Chert poberi*," she said sullenly. "I thought we were going to parley."

"Oh, we are, we are," said Cragg.

"Just being cautious," said the Doctor. "You never know whom you can trust."

Eva looked from the Doctor to Cragg. "Is this what you did to Dave?"

"Who the hell is Dave?" asked the Doctor.

"Dave?" said Eva. "Dave's Donuts?"

"Oh, that Dave," said Cragg. "There is no Dave."

Eva nodded. "Sergey was right."

"I guess I'm Dave," said Cragg. He gestured at the Doctor. "So is he...and you, for that matter...if you take my meaning."

"Well, *Dave*," said Eva, in a tone as flat as she could manage. "Our donut shack exploded."

"You know anything about that, young lady?"

Eva scowled the way she had seen Nastya do a thousand times.

"I came here to ask you the same question," she said testily. "That shack was where you distributed our product, and I want to know what the Hell you're doing about it."

The Doctor lowered the gun but held it loosely at his side. "I like her, Cragg."

"So do I," said Cragg. "But can we trust her?" He gestured down the stairs and looked pointedly at Eva. "Let's have that parley, shall we?"

As Eva took the first step, Cragg put a hand on her shoulder, as if helping her down the stairs with an avuncular gesture, but his fingers slid abruptly down her back, and before she could react, he snatched the gun from under her shirt.

"Give that back," said Eva.

"Oh, I will." Cragg weighed the compact pistol in his hand, then dropped it into his coat pocket. "Don't hang the jib, missy. I'll give it back as soon as we finish our business, I promise."

Never trust a pirate.

Eva realized she was more pissed-off than afraid. Pissed at herself for losing the gun, pissed at her family for taking a backseat to a bunch of faceless criminals. And pissed that she finally met a pirate, but he turned out to be just like every other man she'd grown up with. All smiles and charm until you got behind closed doors.

Fear could be crippling, but anger? That she could work with.

Eva smiled at her captors and continued her descent, wondering what was waiting at the bottom of the stairs.

64

At the bottom of the stairs sat the judge's house.

It was a mansion with a view to die for, but An hesitated only an instant before taking the stairs to the front door, her feet barely touching the flagstones. She rang the bell and rapped on the window alongside the door, then moved swiftly to the side of the house before anyone could answer. She didn't want to be seen just yet, even by the man she was calling on.

The neighborhood was quiet this time of day. Sea Cliff held the distinction of being the priciest neighborhood in a city known for exorbitant real estate. Prices were driven by the eponymous cliff abutting the neighborhood. Behind each home was a ribbon of backyard and a short path to a cliff overlooking China Beach two hundred feet below.

The view of the Pacific had lured celebrities, musicians, artists, and billionaires. Most didn't know China Beach was named for the immigrants who came with the Gold Rush to work the railroads and the mines. The rocky beach, sheltered but too rough for swimming, was a safe place to fish. Today's residents simply knew they had an unbroken view of the Golden Gate Bridge and a resale value that would outpace inflation until the end of time.

An crouched under a side window and listened, but no one

came to the front door. Peering over the edge of the windowsill, she saw a large drawing room with leather couches and a desk fronting a bay window in the back. She counted to ten, then slid to the rear of the house.

The back door was wide open.

There was a screen door attached, so it hadn't been left open for an ocean breeze. A path of bluestone cut across the backyard toward the cliff, but An noticed that grass alongside the stones was compressed, as if someone had veered off the path while walking in a hurry or, more likely, running.

She could only think of one reason why someone would run toward a cliff.

Ignoring the open door, An glided across the lawn to the edge of the cliff and looked down.

The body of a man lay sprawled on the rocks below.

Legs splayed at odd angles, he looked like a marionette whose strings had been cut. Blood mixed with seawater had painted a scarlet halo around his skull. As sunlight bounced off the rocks, a million rubies seemed to mourn his passing.

An couldn't see his face from this height, but the man's identity wasn't a mystery. She turned away from the cliff and headed toward the front of the house. It was only a matter of time before one of the neighbors took their dog for a walk along the beach.

She had warned her associates this could go one of two ways after the son was put in jeopardy. The men working with the Triads assured her the judge wasn't the self-destructive type. They were sure that once he got the message, he would play ball.

An didn't play ball, so the metaphor was lost, and she knew better than most that enough pressure could make anyone the self-destructive type.

The over-confidence of men never ceased to amaze her.

She took one last look over her shoulder at the Pacific Ocean. Almost seven thousand miles over the horizon sat Hong Kong, a city from which a secret society controlled her movements as sure as the moon did the tides. That sensation of being tethered remained even after An turned her back on the ocean.

Maybe it was a view to die for, after all.

65

The view from Cape's office didn't tell him a damn thing.

He could see the entrance to the pier, with people milling about as usual, and the aquarium, but he didn't have X-ray vision. He wouldn't know what was going on inside that place until he got over there.

First, he had to find his gun.

Cape figured the invisible shot that almost took his head off must have originated from the roof of the aquarium or the scaffolding on the side of the building. Initially he was more intrigued by the timing of the attempt than its source, but there was no way Cape was going to walk into the aquarium unarmed.

As he rummaged through his desk, Cape put his phone on speaker and dialed Vera at her store. No answer. The store should be open, even if one of her assistants was minding the register. Cape tried her cell and it went straight to voicemail.

He tried her cell again.

It's Vera…leave a message, but if you do, text me to let me know or I might never get back to you.

Cape texted but didn't wait for a reply. He'd be over there soon enough.

The gun was in the middle drawer on the right.

The revolver was a .357 Ruger with a three-inch barrel, matte silver frame with black grips. The barrel was angled below the front sight, as if the pistol's chin was tucked into its chest and wanted nothing more than to head-butt you into oblivion. It weighed more than a guilty conscience.

Cape wasn't self-destructive but would be the first to admit that he put himself in far too many situations in which he was shot, stabbed, strangled, and punched. He bought the gun to scare the shit out of anyone he pointed it at—in hopes of never having to pull the trigger.

He holstered the revolver and clipped it to his belt, then slid on a jacket and stepped into the hallway. He didn't wait for the elevator but took the stairs two at a time. Cape had the feeling that no matter how soon he arrived, he was already late to the party.

Either he had completely lost perspective on this case, or things were finally coming into focus.

66

Sally focused on the dwindling figure of An until it rounded the corner at the end of the street and vanished. Presumably a car was waiting a short distance from the judge's house.

Sally wasn't overly concerned with following her. She might never see An again, or they might cross paths very soon. Her own desires meant nothing if fate had plans of its own.

Sally slid off the roof, landing like a panther on the back lawn. She stayed on the stone path as she moved to the edge of the cliff to admire her handiwork.

No wonder An neither lingered nor climbed down to the beach. The judge looked like a broken jar of tomato sauce that slipped from a grocery bag. Sally may have gotten overzealous with the letter opener, but there hadn't been much time for finesse.

Someone would have to treat the cut on his forehead after he revived, but a few stitches seemed like a good bargain compared to eternal rest.

The judge had already heard about his son's death when Sally arrived, which meant his handlers weren't playing around. He was distraught, desperate, and in denial. He was convinced he could protect his daughter simply by playing along.

Sally convinced him otherwise.

She assured him there were only two options. Sally could help him fake his own death, or she would gladly kill him, now, with her bare hands. She gave him sixty seconds to decide.

The judge chose Option A.

They walked three houses away and took a switchback path to the rocks below. Once they reached a spot directly below his backyard, the judge looked nervously up the face of the cliff to see if they were followed. Sally punched him in the throat just hard enough to drop him to his knees. Then she struck both sides of his temple as if banging two cymbals together. He hit the rocks like a seagull's leftovers.

Sally took the letter opener and sliced his forehead laterally. The nice thing about head wounds is they bleed profusely, but with no arteries involved, it's messy and not mortal. The rocks were damp but the tide was out, so it took Sally only a few moments to configure his limbs to suggest gravity had done its job.

Ten minutes after Sally climbed the roof, An rang the doorbell.

Things would have gotten complicated if An had visited the beach. A part of Sally had been rooting for complicated, but as much as she loved a challenge, she realized in that moment that she didn't want to hurt An if she could avoid it.

Clearly, An had somewhere else to be. So did Sally.

Now she watched as the waves extended their fingers toward the base of the rocks. She estimated the tide would come in after two hours, and odds were the judge would regain consciousness within the hour. Sally decided to leave the judge where he was.

She was always willing to play the odds.

67

Sergey knew he was playing the odds by climbing the scaffolding without a harness, but he couldn't think of a better plan. No way he was going to leave his kid sister alone with a pirate.

He agreed with Nastya to send Eva by herself, but that was before people vacated the aquarium. Sergey had watched from the pier as throngs of tourists exited the building, the front entrance was locked, and a sign taped to the door. Now Eva was alone in that cavernous building where no one could hear her scream.

Sergey paused on the second level of the scaffolding and looked across the pier, holding tight to the metal pipes of the temporary structure. Painters didn't work over the weekend, so no one paid any attention once he scrambled beyond the first level.

Sergey paused to catch his breath. *Where can no one hear you scream?*

It wasn't underwater, so the answer wasn't *Jaws*. Shark movies always featured someone screaming underwater, bubbles exploding from mouths gaping in terror. And it wasn't a horror movie, because those tended to be nothing but wall-to-wall screaming.

In Space. Sergey felt the endorphin rush of a puzzle solved, relieved that piece of trivia wouldn't be gnawing at his subconscious as he climbed. *In space no one can hear you scream.* From the movie *Alien.* A classic.

Then he thought of the scene when the alien bursts from the guts of the astronaut, and Sergey felt a sudden wave of nausea. Or maybe it was vertigo. Sergey resisted the urge to look straight down. Either way, there were creatures just as creepy as that alien, swimming around inside the aquarium.

Good thing he was armed.

Wrapping his fingers around the next rung of pipes, Sergey climbed past the third story, gritting his teeth as he reached the top. He managed to get his shoulders and then his torso over the edge of the roof where the scaffolding was anchored. Then he rolled from the edge of the roof to the skylight.

Sergey patted his jacket pockets to make sure he hadn't dropped anything. Eva had the only gun he could obtain on short notice, plus he had gifted her the switchblade. He almost brought the scissors they kept behind the register, but that seemed lame. Sergey decided his best weapons were the element of surprise and a handful of projectiles.

He had grabbed the biggest and heaviest nesting dolls on display. After some stretching and tearing of fabric, he managed to fit four into his pockets. Much like in life, the figures with the biggest heads were politicians, so Sergey grabbed a *Putin*, a *Bush*, an *Obama*, and a *Mao Zedong*. (The Bush was a *G.W.*, since the senior Bush *matryoshka* had been sold the week before to an elderly couple from Texas.)

As a Russian, Sergey was naturally cynical about politicians, so throwing them away seemed both symbolic and pragmatic.

The skylight was a rectangle twenty by ten feet, segmented into panes of glass just wide enough for a man to slip through. Sergey knelt down and peered through the nearest corner, waiting for his eyes to adjust. The floor was only ten feet down, and the room below appeared to be deserted.

It was time to crash the party.

Sergey pulled the sleeve of his jacket over his right hand and made a fist, cocking his elbow as he prepared to punch through the glass.

68

The glass would have broken easily but Cape decided to try the
doorknob first. Lights were out in the front room of Vera's store,
and a printed sign on the door promised Back In A Few Minutes.

Cape figured he could sidle up to the door and slip the latch,
and if that didn't work, punch through one of the glass panes.
But there was enough foot traffic on the pier to make timing a
bit tricky. Tourists were walking along the upper level, and stores
adjacent to Vera's were open for business.

The door was unlocked, which in itself was a bad sign, but as
soon as he stepped inside, Cape realized it wasn't the only one.
On every previous visit to Giraffe's Best Friend, the store had
been immaculate. Clothes were refolded the instant a customer
set them down, the diorama of stuffed animals rearranged every
night.

The first thing Cape noticed was disarray around the register.
A pencil holder had been upturned, a pair of scissors a few inches
away from the cup. Papers were scattered as if someone had swept
an arm across the counter. There was also a faint whiff of decay,
as if the window had been open during an algae bloom in the bay.

He moved to the back room, but no one was there. Vera's cell
phone lay on her desk, near where he'd seen it last. He turned it

over. On the lock screen, two missed calls from a local area code. Cape took out his own phone and Googled the number.

Sparing a glance at the cot, he crossed the room to stare out the broken window. The roof of the aquarium was just a stone's throw away, the near wall covered by scaffolding that anyone could climb.

Cape pocketed the phone and locked the door on his way out of the store.

He took the stairway to the main thoroughfare and headed in the direction of the aquarium. As he passed the window of the left-handed store, he caught a glimpse of Harkness standing behind the counter, berating one of his customers. Cape glanced to his right toward the magic shop and wondered what feat of legerdemain Davik was performing.

Farther up the pier was the smoldering crater that had once been the donut shack. Tourists circumnavigated orange cones marking the perimeter. The banana stand and pretzel cart had filled the void and were doing a brisk business.

Cape arrived at the aquarium to find the stairs empty of the usual throngs, only a handful of people sitting on the steps, eating. The sign on the front door raised his suspicions even more. Why close an entire aquarium just because one room is under repair?

He circled around the east side of the building, where the freight entrance opened onto the service road that ran along the marina. The exact spot where the armored car had crashed through the railing of the pier into the bay.

That car had pulled on an invisible thread as it sank, unraveling a conspiracy that was hidden until now. Cape was back at the beginning, and he still didn't know how the story was going to end.

He moved along the building until he reached a rectangular window set adjacent to a metal door. The window was two by three feet, broken into six squares, the top of its frame at the height of his shoulder. The room beyond was dark. Peering inside, Cape could just make out a desk and phone. On a normal business day, someone manning the desk could look outside and see when their delivery arrived.

The rays of the afternoon sun were blocked by the building, the road in shadowy half-light. No cars were around and only a few people could be seen farther up the narrow strip of asphalt— employees from one of the shops on a smoking break.

Cape didn't care if the window was wired for a security alarm. There was an upside either way. He didn't want anyone inside to know he was coming, but a little backup never hurt. He removed his jacket and wrapped it around his right arm, with the thickest part of the fabric at the elbow. Turning his back to the window, he snapped his arm and broke the glass.

Cape listened for distant sirens or nearby footfalls. The only sound was the bay sucking hungrily on the pilings of the pier.

Cape thought about the unrelenting hunger of the sea. He almost drowned once, after someone cut his brake lines and he drove off the end of a pier. Maybe that was why everything in this case felt out of his control. There was a familiar undertow of inevitability.

As he cleared glass shards from inside the frame, Cape looked at the water the way a deer stares at a passing car. He knew it was only a matter of time.

Swinging a leg over the windowsill, he climbed over the desk and stepped into darkness.

69

Eva stepped into darkness and felt a fleeting sense of panic.

The hallway between the bottom of the stairs and the undersea grotto was pitch black, but Cragg knew precisely how many steps until they reached a steel door. As he yanked it inward, an ethereal light danced across the floor and dappled the toes of Eva's boots. The light was moving in waves, gentle sine curves of indirect sunlight interspersed with bluish-black stripes.

As soon as they crossed the threshold, Eva held her breath, an involuntary response to being underwater.

"Welcome to the grotto," said Cragg, amusement in his voice. "Normally we would've entered from the other side, just like the tourists, but the fire door was closer to the stairway. Go ahead, take a gander."

Eva nodded absently as she stared at the ceiling—or what should've been the ceiling. At first she didn't know where to focus, up at the ceiling or along the Plexiglas walls. Fish as small as her fingers swam in tightly packed schools, followed by a random assortment of larger fish in hues of silver, blue, and red.

"One fish, two fish, red fish..." the Doctor sang softly. "Cragg, can we get down to business?"

Cragg held up a hand. This was his temple, and he demanded a moment of awe and wonder as tribute.

The Doctor shrugged. Eva ignored them both.

Eva knew she should keep her eyes on the pirate and the doctor, but a childhood fascination with the sea hypnotized her a moment longer. Seaweed waved in the half-light, warning her to look over her shoulder. She pivoted on her heel and made sudden eye contact with Oscar.

Involuntarily, she took a step backward and heard Cragg chuckle quietly.

The giant Pacific octopus moved a tentacle in greeting, or maybe Eva was being dismissed. It was hard to tell. Oscar seemed to settle lower on the ceiling, the way someone might sink into a couch after a long day. The width of the tentacles expanded against the Plexiglas.

"There," said Cragg, close enough that Eva started. "See those seams where the walls meet the ceiling? Barely visible until Oscar moves, and totally invisible unless the main lighting is off, as it is now." He gestured at various points above. "We check those from time to time—though this is the Aquarium By the Bay, we don't want the bay *inside* the aquarium."

Eva tore her eyes from the ceiling. "You mean we're not inside a giant fish tank?"

"We're under the bay," replied Cragg. "That's why there's so much kelp, and the fish move so fast." He waved at the walls of the chamber. "Just like a tunnel for cars that runs under a river, this is a tunnel for people. The only difference is you can see through the walls."

Directly before them was a conveyor that moved visitors the length of the chamber, right to left from Eva's perspective. It was currently motionless, but she noticed green and red Start-Stop buttons at either end.

To their left was the exit where the people-mover would flow into the main hall of the aquarium. On their right, the on-ramp from the street entrance, where gaggles of school children streamed daily into the grotto for the first time. Directly across the room was another fire door like the one they'd come through.

Eva made a mental note that there were four ways in and hopefully at least one way out for her. She looked up at Oscar.

"Why doesn't he escape?"

"Some man-made barriers connected to the ceiling structure, just the right configuration to let fish in but keep Oscar here at home."

"So, he's trapped," said Eva, thinking she knew just how that felt.

"He got too big, and that was his undoing." Cragg slipped his hand into his pocket and removed the small semiautomatic he'd stolen from Eva. "Wouldn't you agree, Doctor?"

As the Doctor opened his mouth to respond, Cragg side-stepped Eva and backhanded him across the face with the gun.

"Cragg, what the *shit*—" The Doctor staggered but remained on his feet. A trickle of blood emerged from the corner of his mouth. He started to raise a hand to his face, but Cragg wagged a finger like a warning metronome.

With a nonchalance that belied the speed of his hands, Cragg worked the slide on the pistol to feed a cartridge into the chamber, then aimed at the Doctor's forehead. "Your sidearm. I'd be obliged if you dropped it."

Not wanting to get caught in the crossfire, Eva stepped to the side, but she stumbled and fell to one knee as the Doctor's pistol fell to the floor. Cragg kicked it out of reach before Eva could even think about making a grab. It skidded across the conveyor to the opposite side of the room.

Eva stayed down, hands on the floor—as submissive a pose as she could manage.

"Relax, lass," said Cragg. "We're just going to talk." Eyes on the Doctor, he added, "Nothing personal, Doc, just feels better being the only one holding a gun."

"We had an agreement," said the Doctor, dabbing at the edge of his lip.

"We still do," said Cragg evenly. "And I intend to honor it. But since we don't know what this young lady is about to tell us, I'm just hedging my bets."

The Doctor looked past the barrel of the pistol and smiled cynically. "*You* took the money?"

"Not exactly."

"Reckless bastard." The Doctor spat blood. "Double dipping son of a—"

"Mind your tongue, Doctor," said Cragg soothingly. "After all, it's an optional piece of equipment."

Eva felt the tension building, as if the two men were succumbing to the water pressure outside the chamber.

The Doctor was beyond indignant. "You put this whole operation in jeopardy for a robbery?"

"This was before our new arrangement," said Cragg defensively.

Eva smirked but kept her head down. "Never trust a pirate."

"You got that right!" An unfamiliar voice echoed across the grotto, and all eyes jumped to the street entrance.

At the edge of the conveyor was a man in tattered clothes, standing next to a woman with auburn hair who looked like she'd rather be anywhere else.

The tattered man was holding her left arm at the elbow, but as soon as he had the room's attention, he released her and brought both hands to bear on a formidable weapon.

The man was pointing a spear gun at Cragg's heart.

The pirate didn't lower his gun or shift his stance away from the Doctor. He stayed motionless, reluctant to be impaled. It was obvious that Cragg knew his uninvited guest.

"Lou," he almost whispered. "Thought we'd lost you, lad."

"You salty sociopath." Lou moved the spear gun up and down suggestively. "Hope you don't mind I borrowed this—took it off the wall of your holding tank—remember that place? Where you dunked me in the pool?"

The Doctor raised his eyebrows. "This the guy you fed to a shark?"

"Afraid so," muttered Cragg.

"No wonder he's pissed."

"You've got no idea," said Lou. He took a step closer and sighted down the spear gun like a rifle. To his right, the woman scanned the room nervously. Eva noticed her eyes landed on the gun at the far side of the room.

All three men were staring at the tip of the spear.

Eva saw her opening. Keeping her left hand on the floor, Eva snaked her right hand into her boot and found the switchblade. In a seamless arc, she whipped her arm over her head and pressed the release button.

The blade snapped into place as she lunged sideways at Cragg.

The knife penetrated the leg of his pants just above the knee. Cragg howled as the point scraped along his patella until half the blade disappeared into his thigh. Eva felt herself losing her grip and twisted the knife clockwise like an angry watchmaker.

Cragg spasmed as if electrocuted, arms shooting upward, hands clenching in agony. The pistol discharged once, before it slipped from his contorted grip. A spiderweb of luminous cracks appeared under Oscar.

The pirate fell onto his side, desperate to wrench the knife from his leg. Blood was pumping thickly through his fingers.

Thank God he didn't have a wooden leg. Eva rolled to her right but careened into the Doctor, who fell heavily on top of her. She tried to shove him off but their legs tangled, and he was pulling in the opposite direction. Eva twisted and tried to wriggle free, elbowing him in the side of the head for good measure.

The smelly lunatic with the spear gun was getting closer, but his eyes were solely on Cragg. Eva's pistol was diagonally across from the pirate, so she turned her attention to the Doctor's gun that Cragg had kicked across the room.

The auburn woman was already halfway there.

With a final heave, Eva rolled clear of the Doctor and they both scrambled to their feet. Their eyes met—he clearly had the same idea.

Whoever got to a gun first would control the room.

They had reached the conveyor belt, the midpoint of the race, when the fire door on the far wall slammed open. A man holding a massive revolver in his right hand stepped into the room.

Not quite six feet tall, with sandy hair and bluish eyes, he assessed the scene quickly and pointed his gun at Lou, since the spear gun was the only weapon in play. Eva thought the stranger took in the chaos with admirable calm until he caught sight of the woman heading for the gun near his feet.

"Vera."

"Cape." The woman looked relieved. "Thank God."

Lou lowered the spear gun to half-mast but didn't drop it. He was looking at the woman named Vera, but she was staring at the man with the gun. Eva and the Doctor stood side by side on the conveyor.

Nobody moved except Cragg, who writhed and cursed in guttural tones as he tried to staunch the bleeding. It was a frozen tableau of unfulfilled anarchy, just waiting for another catalyst to arrive.

The sound of pounding footsteps from the main hall came out of nowhere. Everyone turned as the beats grew louder and faster. A lone runner, heading in their direction, someone without care for the hazards of inertia.

Eva recognized those footsteps.

Sergey burst into the room and slid across the floor like a bear on ice skates. He was holding two nesting dolls as if they were grenades.

"What did I miss?" he asked breathlessly.

"Who the hell is he?" asked the Doctor.

"That's my brother," said Eva proudly.

"*Privet sestrenka*," said Sergey. "Are you hurt?"

Eva shook her head and smiled. She had never loved her brother so much.

The man called Cape tracked Sergey's heroic slide like everyone else, so he hadn't noticed when Vera bent down and grabbed the Doctor's gun. Neither had Eva, who only realized what was happening when she heard the *click* of a hammer.

Now she and everyone else saw that Vera was pointing a gun at Cape.

70

Cape was disappointed but not surprised to see a gun pointing at his chest.

Vera looked at him apologetically as he lowered his revolver and let it drop to the floor.

"You knew," she said simply.

"I suspected." Cape let his gaze drift to her gun hand. "And now I know."

Vera nodded. "What was it?"

"You left enough breadcrumbs to start a bakery," said Cape.

He scanned the room, trying to sort friendlies from accomplices. The only person Cape recognized was Lou, the other missing driver, and he didn't seem friendly at all.

Vera sidestepped so no one was in her blind spot. Sergey put his nesting dolls back in his pockets but stayed where he was. Cragg seemed to have passed out.

Everyone sensed that what happened next would depend entirely on the outcome of this conversation. Vera turned her attention back to Cape.

"Tell me."

"There are three crimes," said Cape. "The armored car. The drug trade. And the money laundering. Two of them are perfect."

"Damn straight," muttered the Doctor.

"The money laundering operation is a work of art," said Cape. "It's so fully baked into the local economy that it's invisible."

Vera half smiled. "You're a lot smarter than you seem at first."

"I get that a lot," said Cape. "If someone is laundering hundreds of millions of dollars, why steal a few million? The armored car is small potatoes."

"Because they're morons," said the Doctor. Vera looked at him without shifting the gun from Cape, but her eyes made it clear the Doctor was in her sights.

"No," said Cape. "This wasn't stupid, it was deliberate." He looked at Vera without acrimony. "You wanted to blow it all up."

"It wasn't about the money," said Vera.

"The hell it wasn't," said Lou.

"That's what threw me," said Cape. "*You* turned me on to money laundering by sending me to Harkness and his conspiracy theories. You even made it clear you resented being cut out of the pier's underground economy. So why hire me in the first place if you stole the money?"

"I was told that you'd never quit," said Vera.

"But you still gave me a push," said Cape. "When things weren't moving fast enough, you had someone take a shot at me."

"Sorry about that."

"It was my own fault." Cape touched the cut on his cheek. "I was sitting next to you, but the shot was taken at eye level. If I hadn't stood up when I did, they would've missed by three feet. The only sniper who misses at that distance is one trying to miss, and the only person who knew I'd be at your place was, well…you."

"I knew you were the right man—"

"—for the wrong job," said Cape. "Your cell phone was glowing when I came into your office, before the shot. Could've been someone texting you, or maybe you texted someone to say I'd arrived." Cape patted his jacket pocket. "Oh, before I came here, I found your phone on your desk—you often get calls from the aquarium, or just today?"

"I knew I forgot my phone," said Vera, glancing at Lou. "But I left in a hurry."

Cape regarded Lou but addressed Vera. "Your sniper?"

"No," said Vera. "Just a partner in crime." She flicked her eyes toward Cragg, still curled into a ball. "I had a pirate do the dirty work."

Cape nodded. "He was your inside man?"

"We were neighbors on the pier," said Vera, "and pirates like to tell fish stories when they're drunk. A few bottles of rum and I knew everything he knew. And Cragg knew where all the bodies were buried."

"The silver cross was a bit heavy-handed," said Cape. "How many did you scatter under the marina, anyway?"

Vera smiled bitterly. "I'm not as cynical as you think."

"I didn't say you were," said Cape. "But he's dead, isn't he?"

"I got Hank out." Vera's tone hardened. "Just not fast enough."

"Buried at sea," said Cape. "No wonder I couldn't find him."

"You were never supposed to," said Vera.

"Did he know?"

Vera shook her head. "Hank wouldn't go along with my first plan." She jutted her chin at Lou. "So I had to go with plan B."

"And killed Hank."

"He died." Vera almost spat. "There's a fucking difference. That's what always happens to people I care about."

"I'll take that as a compliment." Cape turned to the room full of felons. "And these are your loose ends."

"Come again?" said Lou.

"*Vot dermo*," muttered Eva.

"Hold the fucking phone, Hercule Poirot," said the Doctor. "This has nothing to do with me."

"I wouldn't be so sure," said Vera. "*Doctor*."

"Who the hell are you?" asked the Doctor.

Vera adjusted her grip on the gun and changed her stance so the Doctor stood within the sweep of her arm.

"Vera, I meant to ask you," said Cape, "how your daughter died."

Vera's head swiveled back to Cape like a gun turret. After a pause that seemed to last a lifetime, she forced a breath and worked her jaw into a grim smile. "Something tells me you already know."

Cape shook his head. "I just know this must be personal."

"A doctor killed her," said Vera, eyes back on her target. "She got sick, really sick, but she was finally getting better." Vera pointed the gun like a finger at the Doctor's heart. "Then some doctor decides to *adjust her meds*—says it just like that, like he's a mechanic tuning an engine—and next thing you know, after one fucking pill—she's gone."

"I'm sorry," said Cape.

"It wasn't me," said the Doctor.

"It might as well have been," said Vera. "Guess who manufactured the drug?"

Cape didn't have to guess. "Hopewell Pharmaceuticals."

"Oh, shit," said the Doctor.

Vera blinked as if wiping away a memory, then looked at Cape with an opaque expression. "What you called a work of art, this criminal cabal—"

"—it's a consortium," said the Doctor irritably.

Nobody moved but Cape knew everyone wanted to, all at once. He gauged the distance to Vera and considered his chances of rushing her.

"When I realized what was behind it," said Vera, "I decided to steal from them, just like they stole from me." She waved the gun toward the Doctor. "Because I knew money was the only thing that would get their attention. The only thing that would bring *him* here."

The Doctor looked like a man invited to his own wake. "There are bigger forces at work here," he said. "I'm trying to save the world."

"Can my sister and I leave?" asked Sergey.

"No," said Vera.

"I'm not kidding," said the Doctor. "I'm about to—"

"—you're about to die." Vera brought her hands together around the pistol's grip in a shooter's stance. Cape had no illusions she could miss at this range.

The gunshot came, but the Doctor didn't fall.

Vera rocked backward, red mist flying off her shoulder. She spun like a drunken ballerina but didn't drop her gun. Cape felt the snap of a bullet passing within inches of his head as a second shot missed its mark. A giant snowflake of cracks appeared in the wall as aftershocks ricocheted around the room like hornets.

Cape dropped to the floor and rolled until he found the shooter.

Cragg was sitting in a pool of his own blood, propped against the translucent wall. The pirate was struggling to hold the small pistol as if it were an anchor. He steadied his hand and tried to squeeze off another shot, his face a rictus of revenge.

The concussive twang of the spear gun preceded a tiny harpoon appearing in Cragg's chest. It was like a magic trick—a bloody pirate one moment, a skewered scallywag the next.

Cragg clawed at his chest, the pistol skittering across the floor until it hit the conveyor. A wheezing sound emanated from the wound.

Lou dropped the spear gun and took a step closer, not blinking until Cragg's hand stopped moving and his head fell forward onto his chest.

"*Aarrrgh,*" said Cragg, and then he died.

"A pirate to the end," said Eva.

Lou kicked at Cragg's boot. "See you in Davy Jones's locker."

Cape realized Vera was still on her feet.

The bullet had only grazed her shoulder, and she had her bearings. Cape was three feet away from his revolver when their eyes met. Still on all fours, Cape held up a hand.

"Isn't this the moment when you ask me to run away with you?"

"You're a good man," Vera said, making it sound like the biggest character flaw in the history of humanity.

She looked almost sad as she raised the gun and took aim.

71

Oscar almost felt sad as he watched the humans fighting.

He was less emotional by nature than the bipeds he watched in his zoo, the crystal cave through which these strange creatures traveled every day. He sometimes wondered how they felt to be trapped on the other side of the wall, unable to swim freely like Oscar.

Oscar could travel to the open ocean anytime he wanted. Most creatures didn't realize that even a giant octopus could collapse into a ball the size of a sea anemone, or slip through a crack no wider than a frond of coral.

Oscar lived here because he wanted to—plenty of food, no natural predators, and a front row seat. Never dull.

Some of the bipeds were familiar to him. The ones who passed through daily, pointing or waving at Oscar as they guided others through the maze. Like the one resting below him right now, sitting on the floor of the cave. His aura was dimmed for some reason, so Oscar had a hard time discerning movement.

The other creatures were radiating tension in all directions, dark hues of purple, red, and orange coloring their every move.

One of them in particular held Oscar's attention, a figure near the center of the room. Insofar as Oscar ever wondered about these creatures' mating habits, it seemed to be a male. Slight stature, an unremarkable specimen in every way, except for the energy around him. A vortex of conflicting colors swirled around his body, alternating between light and dark.

Oscar didn't have strong feelings, but he did have good instincts—and he decided that he didn't like this biped, not one bit. Even through the wall, Oscar felt this creature might be some kind of threat.

Oscar realized that if they ever met on his side of the wall, one of them would have to die.

72

Cape realized he was about to die.

The thought really pissed him off. He had suspected he might be walking into a trap yet somehow still ended up on the floor with a gun pointed at his head.

The odds of reaching his revolver before Vera fired were worse than the state lottery—but Cape had always been a gambler. He made the lunge.

As Vera squeezed the trigger, George W. Bush hit her in the face.

The nesting doll split apart on the bridge of her nose. Dick Cheney and Condoleezza Rice fell to pieces at Vera's feet. She staggered back on her heels as the gun discharged.

The nine-millimeter was exponentially louder and more powerful than the tiny semiautomatic Cragg had fired. When the bullet hit the ceiling, fissures ran like tributaries off the spider web made by the previous shots.

Cape grabbed his revolver and slid across the floor, twisting to find a clear angle. Vera pivoted and was about to fire again when Vladmir Putin knocked her in the jaw. Her shot went wide, carving a divot the size of a snow cone into the wall behind Cape.

"Godammit!" Vera kicked Putin across the floor and shifted

her attention to Sergey, who was wielding two more nesting dolls. He cocked his arm and threw as hard as he could.

Barack Obama fell apart halfway through his arc as if reliving the midterm elections. Before Obama could even come close to kicking Vera in the head, Joe Biden and Hillary Clinton were competing for airtime. The nesting doll fell in unequal halves on either side of its intended target.

Vera pointed her gun at Sergey's crotch.

Sergey froze, Mao Zedong trembling in his right hand.

Cape didn't have time to stand or aim, so he stayed close to the ground and took the only clear shot he had.

Cape shot his client in the foot. He had shot himself in the foot so many times on this case, it seemed only fair. The bullet tore through Vera's left shoe in a geyser of leather, bone, and blood.

Vera tumbled sideways and hit the floor, landing hard on her right side.

Cape swallowed a wave of nausea and guilt as he lined up his next shot.

Vera howled as a searing rage, kept under pressure for years, boiled over. She thrust the gun forward, pointing at the entire universe. At everyone who ever fucked her over. At fate. She pulled the trigger again and again, until the clip was empty and bullets flew like molten hail.

Cape felt a metallic fist punch him in the side, hard enough to send him sliding backward across the floor.

Sergey doubled over like a wallet snapping closed. His right hand clutched his thigh where a crimson bloom was spreading.

Mao Zedong spun on his head, his view of the world forever upside down.

Eva felt her heart stop as her brother fell. She ran toward her gun, which was only inches from the dead pirate. She spared only the briefest glance at Lou as she passed.

Lou stood frozen, mesmerized by Vera's turn to savagery, unsure of whose side he was on anymore. Bullets zipped past him as giant snowflakes appeared on the walls and ceiling. Brilliant fractals expanded rapidly, as if a sudden frost had come to their undersea kingdom.

Cape clutched his side to staunch the bleeding and felt a cascade of water on his neck. He worried about going into shock, but the cold slap revived him. He rolled onto his back to catch some water on his face.

Eva had bent over to grab the gun when she sensed the Doctor behind her. His arm was around her neck before she could turn. He slid the inside of his left elbow against her larynx, knowing just where to apply pressure. Eva swung her right arm backward, turning the barrel of the gun toward what she hoped was the Doctor's leg, but his right arm caught her wrist and held it fast. She might fire into the floor but wouldn't hit him.

Eva would be unconscious soon or her neck would be broken.

Fortunately, she had an older brother, and most of her life had played with his friends—the kind of boys that her sister told her to avoid. Adolescent assholes who believed they could take whatever they wanted by force.

Eva raised her right leg until her knee was almost at her chest, then drove the heel of her boot into the Doctor's shin, scraping all the way down before stomping on his instep like a jackhammer. The Doctor yelped and Eva ducked, slipping her head through his arm.

Clutching her pistol like a pair of brass knuckles, Eva pirouetted and punched the Doctor in the throat. He fell on his ass like most of her brother's childhood friends.

Eva rushed to her brother's side but the heel of her boot slipped on a puddle of seawater and she landed on top of Sergey, knocking the wind out of both of them. The pistol flew from her hand and skidded across the floor. Eva took no notice. She hugged her brother hard enough to make sure his heart was still beating.

Cape sighted down the barrel of the .357, aiming for Vera's

shoulder, but didn't even cock the hammer on his revolver. He waited until his ears stopped ringing to confirm what his eyes were saying. Vera was dry-firing, squeezing the trigger on an empty gun, trying to shoot the world.

Cape groaned as he crawled to her. Blood from his wound fell like rain through his fingers while the downpour from above soaked his back.

Vera raised the gun, but Cape knocked it aside, the swing of his arm sending liquid pain running down his side. He collapsed onto his right shoulder, still holding his gun, his face directly over hers. She didn't meet his gaze until Cape wrapped his arms around her, less to restrain her than to let her know someone was there. He watched Vera's rage melt into pools of pure sorrow.

"Sorry I shot you," said Vera.

"I shot you first," said Cape.

Cape's hair was drenched, seawater running down the sides of his face and into his mouth, tasting like tears. As he shifted his weight to pull her closer, a voice came between them.

"You ruined everything."

The Doctor was standing ten feet away, Eva's pistol in his right hand. He was looking straight at Vera. He rubbed idly at his crotch with his left hand, then turned his head and coughed.

Cape still had the revolver, but his right arm was pinned under Vera's left shoulder. Their eyes met as he cocked the gun slowly.

"Nobody has to die." The Doctor took a step forward. "Don't you get it?" Water spat from the ceiling in jagged bursts and drenched him where he stood, but the Doctor didn't seem to notice. "Not from cancer, not from heart disease, not from Alzheimer's. We can cure all of it…me…*I can cure all of it.*"

Cape felt blood oozing from his side. He bit his lip and blinked water from his eyes as he scanned the room, trying to map where everyone was standing. He wondered if there were any more guns in play.

"I'm trying to save the world." Disdain for humanity was

etched onto his face but the Doctor's ire was focused on Vera. "And you want to tear it apart because of one dead kid?"

Cape rolled onto his back and fired.

The roar of the .357 was a sonic boom, and the Doctor jumped despite not being hit. He hesitated as Cape fired again, then a third time, each shot an anvil thrown straight at heaven.

A seismic bolt of lightning tore across the ceiling, connecting all the cracks in a constellation of ruin. The room imploded with a roar that only the ocean could make. Before the Doctor could recover, all 187 quintillion gallons of the Pacific Ocean pushed San Francisco Bay into the room.

As the air turned to water, Cape wrapped his arms around Vera and took a deep breath.

73

Oscar spread his arms and took a deep gulp of water as the ground shook and worlds collided.

He was directly above the bothersome biped, the one with an aura out of sync with the natural world. Always black or white, no color or nuance to indicate harmony with its surroundings.

This creature stood apart, and to Oscar, that marked it as a predator.

A vibration like a rogue current ran through the crystalline surface beneath Oscar's arms. As the pressure became an inexorable tide, he felt himself falling faster than he had ever swum in the open ocean. Oscar extended his tentacles as far as they could reach, instinctively trying to slow his descent.

He opened his beak as he fell. Oscar could tell he was going to land on top of the creature, and he wanted to be ready.

74

The Doctor wasn't ready to die, and he wasn't the hugging type.

The octopus flew at him like one of those forest spiders from *Lord of the Rings*. The Doctor's primal instincts screamed *run* but there was no time to dodge, so his frontal cortex switched the command to *kill!*

He fired into the torrent of water, hoping to burst the gelatinous balloon of Oscar's head. The Doctor fired four shots in rapid succession.

The octopus spun like a hallucinogenic pinwheel as bullets ripped through one of the tentacles. By the time the creature landed on the Doctor, the shredded arm was torn in half.

Blue blood flowed like wine.

The Doctor crumpled onto his back. The octopus weighed over three hundred pounds and felt like a Buick made of Jell-O parked on his chest. A sudden stabbing pain near the sternum, the animal's beak or a popped rib. The Doctor started kicking like Quint in the final scene of *Jaws,* but there was no escape.

The water rose and the air-to-sea balance tipped in Oscar's favor. The Doctor slipped his right arm free and reached for one of Oscar's eyes, knowing that if he could get a hand in there, the creature might release him. His fate depended on which of them was more determined to survive, and who was smarter. His brain against Oscar's nine. The Doctor knew it could go either way.

75

Cape knew it could go either way. They could drown or get out alive. He hugged Vera with both arms as the water raged to reclaim the land.

The room was disintegrating faster than Cape thought possible. The deluge from above tossed them toward the front entrance like a pair of empty bottles. They bobbed and sank, slamming against the floor as waves collided.

His eyes screamed against the saltwater but Cape strained to keep them open, fighting an urge to black out. The water was deathly cold but his side was on fire. He gasped at every opportunity, gulping as much air and as little seawater as he could manage.

He glimpsed the Russians clutched in a similar embrace, getting swept in the opposite direction, toward the main hall. Somewhere in the primal part of his brain, Cape wondered what would happen to all the glass tanks when the tsunami hit. There was already so much blood in the water.

An amorphous shape soared overhead on a cross current, narrowly missing them. The water displacement created a vortex, and before Cape realized what was happening, he and Vera were spinning like lily pads in a whirlpool.

The shadowy horror drifted upward toward the open ocean,

a blood-orange cloud with nine arms, two legs, and two heads. A much smaller figure was being drawn in the wake of the monster. Cape couldn't be sure but guessed it might be the driver, Lou, getting sucked into the bay.

They were completely submerged now. Cape saw flashes at the corners of his vision, his nervous system's way of signaling imminent death. He kicked with the current, knowing water would do what water does and push everything out of its way. Vera was limp in his arms, a maroon ribbon streaming from the wound in her foot.

A tidal surge slammed against the outer doors, the wave using their bodies as a battering ram. Doors burst apart and Cape lost his grip on Vera as they were hurled across the gift shop. He sucked air and foam into his lungs as his face broke the surface. The outer glass doors were coming up fast.

As the rogue wave propelled them forward across the narrow space, they picked up speed. Cape could see the steps outside leading to the pier, but there was no way to change his velocity. Out of the corner of his eye, he saw Vera crash into a table full of stuffed animals—cuddly jellyfish with no sting and smiling sharks with no bite. He grabbed desperately at a clothing rack, but T-shirts tore off the hangers as the wave rocketed him toward the glass windows.

Cape tucked his head into the wave and grabbed his knees, hoping to become a cannonball before hitting the windows. A scream of bubbles escaped his lips from the pain in his side.

Talons of ice tore into his back as glass shattered. He made landfall in a cataclysm of broken windows, torn clothing, and stuffed animals, tumbling down the concrete steps like a Slinky with a drinking problem.

Cape hit the pier headfirst as the angry ocean chased him down the stairs.

76

Sally headed first to the pier but was too late.

Surveying the bedlam around the aquarium, she realized there was nothing she could do, and that was the worst feeling in the world.

Pools of water eddied across the pier like packs of dogs chasing a ball. Tourists tried to capture carnage selfies while uniformed police established a perimeter around the aquarium. A colorful assortment of sea creatures littered the ground—some were stuffed toys and others actual animals free of their tanks. Two ambulances had pulled onto the access road, their lights still flashing.

Sally watched as paramedics loaded Cape onto a gurney.

Though Sally stood some distance away, she could tell he was unresponsive. The blue sheet they wrapped around his body revealed lilac splotches across his torso, but Sally took solace from the fact they didn't pull the sheet over his face.

Cape's chances depended on the kindness of strangers and the whims of fate, and Sally didn't trust either. She would visit the hospital later, but there was nothing she could do here. No one she could save, and no one left to kill.

Sally headed back to Chinatown.

Sing Chong and Sing Fat were waiting for her at the corner of Grant Avenue and California Street, looking down on her and everyone else.

These two iconic buildings had been guarding the intersection and protecting the neighborhood for over a century. After the 1906 earthquake and fire nearly destroyed the city, opportunistic politicians tried to relocate Chinatown away from the heart of the city. The Chinese immigrants responded by building Sing Chong and Sing Fat in record time, marking their territory and rebuilding the neighborhood that had become their home.

Straddling the main cable car line, both buildings featured traditional Chinese architectural flourishes designed to celebrate their heritage and attract tourists. Extravagant designs reminiscent of temples on the other side of the world—yellow brick and red tile, sloping roofs with towers at the corners overlooking the street.

As Sally ascended the steep incline of California Street, she realized Sing Chong was calling to her.

The building was surrounded by bamboo scaffolding as used in Hong Kong for short-term construction and repairs. Sally spent enough time on rooftops to know that the tar on the older buildings was resealed every year before the rains came. Once the tar cooled, water was run continuously through hoses spread across the roof to check for any leaks.

Water streamed over the edges of the Sing Chong roof. The sky was clear, yet this building had its own rain cloud. A waterfall of tears cascaded over the bamboo, sluiced along the fire escape, and pooled at the edges of the sidewalk before splitting into streams that flowed into the gutter.

The building that cries.

A weeping house.

Sally sidestepped a gaggle of tourists, swung herself onto the first platform of scaffolding, and was climbing up the fire escape before anyone took notice.

She considered the layout of the building and trusted her gut. The logical place would be the tower, its sweeping curves and open columns so familiar to anyone who grew up in Hong Kong. A pagoda with sides open to the elements, capped by a roof with eaves that turned upward at the corners like a genie's slippers. The crenellated design was distinctly Chinese, and it reminded Sally that no matter how far she may have come, her childhood was always right behind her.

The roof was deserted. A tangled web of hoses pulsed rhythmically in warning. Sally stepped over them as if they were snakes and moved laterally toward the tower.

Sally could tell no one was inside the tower even before she glanced over the low wall. The energy felt dormant. A cursory perusal of the walls and ceiling for trip wires or optical sensors revealed nothing, but the lacquered box resting on the floor signaled the real puzzle still awaited.

Sally stepped inside the tower and knelt before the box, its mahogany surface almost invisible against the black floor. It was three feet wide and shallow, only ten inches across and less than six inches high. An ornate hasp of bronze was latched by a metal pin as wide as Sally's palm. She began to slide the pin to the left but stopped before the latch was released.

Sally spun the long box clockwise so she would be positioned behind it when it was opened, as if presenting a gift to an imaginary friend. She slid the pin from the hasp and grabbed the top of the box, hands shoulder-width apart, and slowly raised the lid.

A barely audible twang preceded a series of *thunks* as a flock of darts flew into the ceiling. They were smaller versions of the deadly barbs that Sally deployed in her apartment.

Not exactly a box of chocolates.

Sally spun the box around and looked inside to find…another box. The second was walnut with a cinnamon finish. Sally lifted it free of the first box with deliberate slowness, as if handling nitroglycerin.

Chinese nesting boxes were an ancestor of Russian nesting dolls, decorative storage and visual puzzles that adorned homes for centuries. Sally knew there should be a minimum of three boxes in a nest. She followed the same routine with the second box and was rewarded with the gift of a baby scorpion scuttling its way to freedom. Sally was on her feet in an instant, the insect crunching under her heel like a corn chip forgotten on the living room floor.

The third box was made of cherrywood, a rich red pattern in the polished grain. Both the color red and number three were considered lucky, but what was lucky for one person might be unlucky for another.

The only thing that emerged when Sally opened the lid was the smell of jasmine. She spun the box and smiled, realizing what she would find.

The sword of Tomoe Gozen was nestled in a bed of flower petals, the gently curved blade of the *nagitana* a wistful smile.

This wasn't a trap. It was a goodbye.

Sally lifted the sword reverently and rotated it to catch the light. The waves in the tempered steel made it seem alive. Just like Sally and An, it was a perfect weapon, crafted to assure victory in any battle.

An must have planted a forgery inside the museum when she stole the sword. Sally wondered if they would ever notice. She felt a stab of regret she hadn't gotten a present for An, until she realized that she had.

Sally had let her walk away.

She placed the sword carefully inside the box and noticed a simple card beneath the jasmine petals. The handwriting was meticulous. The address was in Hong Kong. An open invitation or a dare, or maybe a little of both.

A journey for another day, when Sally had time to kill.

77

"I haven't had time to kill you, which is the only reason you're still alive."

Beau loomed over Cape's hospital bed like a storm cloud. He glowered until positive that Cape was fully alert, then proceeded to stomp around the bed as if fighting an army of spiders.

Stomp—step—stomp—step.

Cape tried to follow Beau's circumlocution, but his neck protested at every turn of his head. "How long have I been out?"

"Long enough for my foot to fall asleep."

"You've been watching over me," said Cape, his voice hoarse, strange to his own ears. "That's sweet."

"Been waiting on you," said Beau. "There's a difference." He gestured at the partially open window, beige curtains rustling in the breeze. "Pretty sure Sally's been checking on you, though."

Cape started to sit up but the room shifted on its axis, so he kept his head firmly ensconced in the pillow. He had a vague memory of regaining consciousness in this bed before and wondered if it would stick this time. His side throbbed as if fire ants were throwing a rave inside his gut. Reaching for the button on the rail that controlled the bed's elevation, he noticed there was an IV in the back of his right hand.

"What did I miss?" asked Cape.

"I'll tell you what you didn't miss, Annie Oakley," said Beau. "You didn't miss the ceiling with that hand-cannon of yours. You almost turned Pier 39 into Atlantis."

"That's hearsay," said Cape.

"Only because you hear me saying it."

"Who's the tattletale?"

"Suspect from the armored car robbery that we've been looking for since, well, forever," said Beau.

"Lou?"

"Found him bobbing in the bay as the tide went out—halfway to Alcatraz before a tour boat fished him out of the water." Beau smiled at the thought. "Soon as he gets back to the pier, goes up to the first police officer he finds, and turns himself in. Says he'll tell us everything, as long as we lock him up someplace far, far away from the ocean."

"He only knows about the robbery," said Cape. "I don't think he can tell you anything about the rest of it."

"As far as SFPD is concerned, the robbery is the only thing I'm investigating."

Cape took a breath and decided to let Beau ask another question. He had questions of his own but wasn't quite ready to hear the answers.

"Why not shoot the guy who was about to shoot you?" asked Beau.

"I wanted to cause a distraction, not a tsunami," said Cape. "I didn't know the players or the teams, and there were too many guns in play."

"How many?" asked Beau. "A corpse with a spear souvenir in its chest scared the crap out of some tourists, broke the surface near the sea lions—been ID'd as the guy running the aquarium."

"Lou shot Cragg," said Cape. "In case he hasn't already confessed."

"Said it was self-defense."

"I'd call it temporary insanity," said Cape. "Or PTSD."

"He said Cragg was a co-conspirator in the heist."

"I think the pirate was playing all the angles," said Cape. "Cragg was also involved with—"

"—your client."

"I was going to say he was involved in the bigger conspir—"

"—I know what you were going to say," replied Beau. "But that's not what I said."

Cape's felt like he was caught in a whirlpool and wondered if it was vertigo or just denial. He closed his eyes and let the room spin another minute. "I was getting to that."

"Well, get to it." Beau was giving him the cop stare.

Cape started at the beginning, then jumped ahead, skipped back, drifted sideways, and finally got back on track, right up until the moment his client was pointing a gun at him. He described this penultimate betrayal with as much lurid detail as he could muster, but Beau remained impassive.

Cape ended his narrative by saying, "So in summary, I just want to thank you and Vinnie for getting me involved with her in the first place."

Beau finally blinked. "You wouldn't…"

"…hurt a friend?" Cape raised his eyebrows and spread his hands, the picture of noncommittal assurance. "How much trouble am I in?"

Beau blew out his cheeks and sat heavily in the chair, holding Cape's eyes hostage for a full minute before losing his composure and bursting into laughter. It was infectious, and Cape laughed until his ribs ached.

"You're such an asshole," said Beau.

"Is that a crime?"

"In this city, it's the secret to success." Beau rubbed his hands together. "The SFPD have what they want, a known felon linked to the armored car heist, willing to testify. You were at the scene when it all went down, but other than breaking and entering, you *could* claim you were just trying to protect your client."

It was time for Cape to ask the question he'd been avoiding. "You said Lou confessed—is Vera talking?"

"No," said Beau. "She's missing."

The news came with emotional strings attached that Cape didn't feel like pulling. There would be time for that later.

He visualized Vera landing on a mountain of stuffed animals while he crashed through a window. He guessed she'd never lost consciousness. Even with a few toes missing, she could be anywhere. "She mentioned having a place in Oregon. "

Beau shrugged. "Out of my jurisdiction, but the Feds might be interested."

"I thought this was your backyard."

"Money laundering is a federal crime."

"You said you only cared about the robbery."

"That was my job," said Beau. "But that's not me. Those printouts you gave me, the ones that looked like a Jackson Pollock painting?"

"What about them?"

"They're in the hands of a federal agent I know."

"You're full of surprises. And where did you say the printouts came from?"

"Someone left them on a table at a diner where I was having breakfast, and I picked them up." Beau grinned. "So I didn't lie. But if I got more specific, you might be cuffed to the rail of that bed."

"Thanks," said Cape. "I guess."

"Don't mention it," said Beau, "and don't mention that your felonious client was referred by the SFPD...to *anyone*."

"Deal," said Cape. "What about the others?"

"I was going to ask you," replied Beau. "Lou only knew Cragg and Vera, and the only suspects we can account for physically are Lou and Cragg."

A tentacled terror rose from the depths of Cape's memory. "I think the doctor's dead."

"What about the other two?" asked Beau. "Know anything about them?"

Cape reflected on what he knew. Russian accents, a familial resemblance, and a pair of nesting dolls that saved his life. "Can't say that I do."

Beau looked at his friend and started to say something but let it go.

Cape felt himself sinking into the bed, as if underwater once more. A concussive current ran from his head to the base of his spine and back again.

Beau stood to leave. "You'll probably forget we had this conversation."

"Have we had it before?"

"I can't remember," said Beau. "But remember when I told you how to box an octopus?"

"You said cut off its arms."

"I think you did one better," said Beau. "You tore out its heart."

78

Cape tore the IV from the back of his hand the next day, against the protestations of two nurses and the resident physician.

Cape mollified them by promising to rest at home and under no circumstances operate any heavy machinery or get behind the wheel of a car. He went straight home from the hospital, took a shower and changed into fresh clothes, then climbed behind the wheel of his convertible and started driving.

The trip to Oregon took ten hours. It would have taken eight, but Cape stopped at a diner, intending to grab lunch. He took a nap in his car instead.

The scenery was simultaneously beautiful and monotonous, rolling hills and narrow strips of highway utterly empty for long stretches, except for the occasional logging truck or family camper. The air was crisp when Cape arrived at Vera's house.

The house sat at the end of a long drive, most of the homes in this area set back from the road and apart from each other. Cape noticed a blue sedan a quarter mile before he turned off the road and wondered how long the Feds would keep up surveillance. No doubt they'd been through the house, from attic to basement.

The house was a single-floor ranch with a gable roof and a

locked front door. Cape didn't think getting inside would be much of a challenge, but he decided to walk the grounds first.

He found the graves in the backyard.

About thirty yards away from the house, two matching headstones sat under the shade of an oak tree. Both were gray stone, unadorned and two feet high.

The one on the left had a date of birth and death that made it clear this was the grave of a child. Cape ran his fingers over the letters and realized he had never asked Vera the name of her daughter. Now he knew.

Vera's name was carved into the headstone on the right, and the date of death was the same. She had died the day she buried her daughter.

Cape dragged his foot across the ground in front of Vera's headstone. It was loosely packed, soil of different textures churned and packed flat, with no grass growing. The grass in front of her daughter's headstone was thick and green.

Cape walked back to his car and popped the trunk. The folding shovel was under a tangle of jumper cables.

He broke ground in front of the headstone, careful not to disturb the stone itself. Four inches down the shovel hit something metallic, the vibrations running up his arms into his elbows.

He was filthy by the time he got his fingers under the box and pulled it free, and his side felt like a soldering iron was hidden under his shirt. The bullet had passed through, missing his kidney and anything vital, but there wasn't supposed to be a hole there and it hurt like hell.

The dispatch box was a black rectangle with a simple latch of stainless steel.

Inside was a pile of cash resting on a piece of fabric. Cape thumbed through the bills and did the math, then reflected on the number of days since he first met Vera. Based on his day rate, the total was the exact amount that she owed him, if Vera's last official day as a paying client was the day she shot him. Cape set the money aside and looked closer at the cloth underneath.

It was a red sock.

There was a jagged hole in the toe of the sock, the edge rimmed with dried blood, black against the red fabric. Cape held his hand next to the hole and estimated he could easily fit his index and middle fingers through the hole.

Cape figured they were even.

He looked at the two headstones and thought about what Vera had lost, but also what she had taken, and from whom. And what it had cost in the end.

This case had been messy from the start, with heroes and villains changing places in his mind even now. Cape sometimes felt his own moral compass spinning like a weather vane.

He took the money but placed the sock back in the box, then buried it where he had found it. As he patted the earth into place he traced the letters of Vera's name on the headstone. She might not be dead, but she was dead to him.

Cape climbed into his car and checked his moral compass one more time. Satisfied that it still pointed north, he drove south toward San Francisco as fast as he could.

79

A few days after Cape returned to San Francisco, he invited Sally to go for a walk on the pier to watch the sunset.

Sally met him by the main entrance near the hot dog stand. They strolled past the Hard Rock Café and Boudin Bakery until the aquarium loomed over them. It was still cordoned off with orange pylons and yellow tape, signs saying the aquarium was under construction and would re-open soon.

"You must be very proud," said Sally. "That's probably a personal best for property damage."

On their left, a one-story shack was being framed in two-by-fours on a newly repaired section of the pier. Blackened boards that defined the edges of the old donut shack were still visible.

"In my defense," said Cape. "I did not destroy the donut shack."

A sign proclaimed that a new donut shack would be opening next month.

"Eva's Donuts," said Sally. "They're changing the name."

"Maybe it's under new management."

"Maybe Dave retired."

"Maybe there was no Dave," said Cape.

"Then who made the donuts?"

"Another mystery," said Cape, "for another day."

"Speaking of which," said Sally, "what's happening with the judge?"

"Beau says he gave enough evidence to unleash the Feds on everybody."

"Not everybody," said Sally. "They'll never get close to the Triads, nobody does. The bank manager already got transferred back to Hong Kong."

"Maybe they won't take down the consortium," said Cape. "But they'll scare off any new investors, put a politician or two in jail if they can."

"Maybe they should lock up all politicians," said Sally. "Just to be safe."

"Now you're talking."

"Where are we going?"

"It's a surprise." Cape skirted past the T-shirt shop to the nearest stairs leading up to the second level. They walked past a jewelry store on their right and came abreast of Vera's shop.

A sign in the window: Sorry We're Closed. Most of the inventory had been cleared out, but decorations remained on the wall, playful murals evoking an idyllic childhood that never was.

Cape didn't break his stride as he passed the store, his footfalls echoes of regret. Sally glided alongside him like a stray thought on ice skates.

"I can't believe you let her seduce you," said Sally.

"How do you know I didn't seduce her?"

"Really want me to answer that?"

Cape frowned. "Turn here."

The walkway turned left then continued toward the back of the pier. Over the railing they could see the carousel, a small stage, and the banana stand. Directly ahead was a store with casement windows and a door with both English and Cyrillic writing on it. As Cape opened the door inward, a small brass bell chimed overhead.

A young woman behind the counter started to greet them, but

the words caught in her throat at seeing Cape. Standing in front of the counter was a young man who recovered more quickly. The family resemblance between the two was unmistakable. He welcomed Sally to the store and then nodded at Cape.

"I have the item you requested." Using a cane to balance his gait, the young man moved behind the register as Sally wandered around the store.

Nesting dolls stared at her from every shelf, corner, case, and table. Hundreds of rotund characters sitting in judgment, never blinking, watching to see what would happen next.

Sally returned to the counter as the man handed an item to Cape.

Cape spun it around, then presented it to Sally like a bouquet.

"I got you a present."

It was a nesting doll as tall as a mason jar with the fierce countenance of a black-clad ninja holding dual *katana* in its painted hands. Sally noticed that eyelashes had been painted on to suggest the ninja was a girl.

The man behind the counter extended a hand and Sally returned the *matryoshka*. Over a velvet cloth he proceeded to crack open the big ninja to reveal another ninja. And another. And another still. Each was painted in a different color with exceptional detail and cartoonish flair, and every oval assassin had eyelashes worthy of *My Little Pony*.

Sally nodded her appreciation to the man behind the counter and then turned a bemused expression toward Cape.

"I hate it," she said.

Cape beamed. "I knew you would." Then to the siblings behind the counter, he added, "It's perfect, thank you."

Brother and sister glanced at each other and shrugged in unison. The man wrapped the nesting doll in tissue paper and placed it in a bag.

"How much?" asked Cape.

"*Nichego takogo*," said the man. "Nothing."

Cape held the man's gaze for a moment before nodding his thanks. Taking the bag, he opened the door and let Sally exit first, looking over his shoulder as he crossed the threshold. The sister waved and called out to him.

"*Uvidimsya*, Cape."

Cape smiled. "See you around, Eva."

Sally waited until they descended the stairs before asking, "Why didn't that cost you anything?"

"Oh, it did," said Cape.

They walked in silence to the end of the pier, past shops and restaurants that blurred together, passing thousands of people trading money for memories, until the only thing in front of them was the bay.

The Golden Gate Bridge watched stoically as a container ship slipped between its legs, while Alcatraz sat brooding and impatient as always, waiting for the fog to hide its sins. Cape and Sally stared at the water until the sun was low against the horizon.

The tide was coming in.

80

The jet was flying south.

Steve glanced out the window at the California coast and wondered when they would turn west toward Boulder. Probably when they reached cruising altitude.

The corporate jet was a Gulfstream G650ER, capable of flying almost seventy-five hundred nautical miles at Mach .90 and holding up to nineteen passengers, but today it carried the six board members plus the pilot and a single steward, a man named Li.

It had been a week since Hopewell Pharmaceuticals announced the release of a breakthrough new drug in the fight against Alzheimer's. The company's stock soared on the news. FDA approval was being fast-tracked and the corporate patent would hold for at least ten years.

They were all going to be rich.

Steve looked around the cabin at his hand-selected board. George and Elaine were sitting on a leather couch, eating cheese and crackers, mimosas in hand. Pat was reclining in a leather chair that looked more like something you'd find in a living room than a plane, his eyes closed and noise-canceling headphones on. Kerry and Doris were sitting in facing chairs, having an animated conversation about shellfish poisoning.

At a cost of sixty-five million dollars, this jet was still a bargain. No customs, no airport bullshit. Traveling near the speed of sound, the Gulfstream could shave time off any trip, hours when flying to Asia. The hand-polished wood of the cabin and nubuck leather chairs made the textures of their corporate boardroom look like IKEA.

Steve recalled their last board meeting, when the Doctor hijacked their discussion and threatened each and every one of them with a Sharpie. That sociopath hadn't been seen or heard from since. *Good riddance.*

Better to enjoy the Doctor's legacy than suffer his mordant personality. The company owned the patent on his miracle drug, and with no threat from generics for at least a decade, they could charge anything and people would pay.

Who said you can't put a price on human life?

Steve smiled contently and looked at the unbroken blue of the ocean blending seamlessly with the horizon. The sun was low in the sky.

He frowned and looked down, leaning into the cabin window. He glanced beyond the wing tip, curved at the end like a bird in flight. He craned his neck to see past the tail, the twin engines partially obstructing his view.

Water, water everywhere.

Steve crossed to the port side of the cabin to get his bearings. Cerulean carpet below, azure ceiling overhead, only the gray fog of confusion ahead. He had felt the jet bank gracefully a few moments ago but couldn't remember in which direction, and they hadn't ascended much either. The jet was flying low over the ocean, headed west.

Steve started toward the front of the plane as Li emerged from the cockpit. The steward had impeccable manners and a charming British accent, but his smile was perfunctory.

"You may have noticed a slight change in course," he said.

"Slight?" asked Steve. "Boulder is southeast across the Rocky Mountains. So why are we flying west across the Pacific Ocean?"

All eyes turned toward the two men standing. George and Elaine set their drinks on the table. Pat sat up in his chair and removed his headphones. Kerry and Doris exchanged glances.

Steve pressed. "The corporate retreat—"

"I'm afraid you won't be attending," said Li.

"On whose authority?" Steve's face reddened. "We're the board of directors."

"Not anymore." Li looked dolefully around the cabin. "You've been replaced."

Elaine turned to George. "Is he threatening us?"

Li adjusted his tie. "After all the excitement on the pier, we thought it best to suspend field tests for a while. At least until the new drug is in market." As he tugged at his collar, Li inadvertently revealed a small tattoo below his hairline. It was a simple triangle, the axis aligned with his right ear.

Steve's indignation caught in his throat. After a moment he swallowed and asked, "Where are you taking us?"

"To the new research facility." Li smiled encouragingly. "In the South China Sea."

George stood and took a step forward. "Wait a min—"

"Please." Li drew a gun from inside his jacket and pointed it at George. "Don't do anything rash."

George froze and Steve took a step back, but both remained standing. Nobody else moved. The Rolls-Royce engines hummed soothingly.

"You're bluffing," said Steve uncertainly.

"He can't fire a gun inside a plane," said George. "I saw that in a Bond movie."

"Goldfinger." Li nodded. "I saw that one, too." He stroked the long barrel of his gun as if it were a pet. "But this beauty is a tranquilizer gun, low velocity darts powered by compressed air, not gunpowder." Li sighted down the barrel. "So you see, George, I can fire this wherever I want."

George took another half step and Li pulled the trigger.

A silver dart with a red tassel penetrated George's chest above the breastbone. Arms outstretched as if he'd been crucified, his lungs constricted with a dreadful wheeze, bagpipes squeezed by an invisible hand.

George fell face-first onto the plush carpeting, the only signs of life a low rasp and an occasional twitch of his left foot. The cabin pressure seemed to change as everyone released the breath they'd been holding.

All eyes were on Li as he stepped forward and, with his free hand, grabbed George by the collar and dragged him away from the group. He kept the gun raised.

"Was that really necessary?" asked Doris.

"Perhaps not," said Li. "But I wanted to make a point, Doris."

"How do you know our names?" asked Kerry.

"I know all about you." Li waved the gun to encompass the group. "Your names, your medical records, blood types, family histories—"

"—my family," said Steve. "My family is expecting me to call—"

"—mine too," said Pat.

"Pat, you don't have a family," whispered Doris.

"He doesn't know that."

"All your loved ones will be notified," said Li reassuringly. "After the search."

"Search?" asked Elaine.

"For the plane." Li pursed his lips. "Should take about a week."

"What the hell is going on?" said Kerry.

"So many questions." Li held up his free hand. "Give me a minute."

Li was standing directly in front of the door leading to the cockpit. To his left was the exit door, curved to match the shape of the bulkhead, with a release handle inset at shoulder height.

He holstered the gun with a fluidity that suggested he could draw it again just as quickly. With his left hand, Li gripped a safety strap adjacent to the door, while his right twisted the release handle on the exit door.

"You might have noticed how low we're flying." Li raised his voice against the sibilant hiss of air escaping the door seams. "Wanted to stay off radar for a while." He yanked the handle and the door swung inward. A sudden typhoon filled the cabin and everyone grabbed onto something or someone. "And depressurization at higher altitudes is so dramatic."

Still grasping the safety strap, Li wedged his right foot under George and rolled him onto his side, then bent sideways to grab him by the collar. Elaine's scream was barely audible in the maelstrom as Li dragged George sideways over the edge of the door.

One kick and the body tumbled into oblivion as if it had never been.

Li spared a glance past the engines until he saw the splash, then wrenched the door back into place. A sudden quiet fell over the cabin as the door resealed.

Drawing the gun casually, Li contemplated the remaining passengers. Five pillars of salt looked back at him with the sudden realization that their past sins were never out of sight.

Steve's face was ashen. "You killed George."

"Guess he didn't have a golden parachute after all." Li clucked his tongue. "So where does that leave us?" He reholstered the gun. "Though field tests are on hold for a spell, I think you'd agree that R&D must continue. We have a very promising cancer drug in development."

Kerry nodded woodenly. "That was mentioned in the annual report."

"Exactly," said Li. "Trials are underway at our new lab, but we need more test subjects." He glanced at his watch. "You should arrive in plenty of time."

Everyone looked nervously around the cabin, only to find their own fear reflected in the eyes of their companions.

Li continued, "Life-threatening side effects are running around twenty percent." He made a show of counting his guests on the fingers of his right hand. "So, I'd say your odds are about even."

Steve considered the odds and found himself wishing he'd left with George.

Li bowed politely and added, "Feel free to move about the cabin. Refreshments will be served in about an hour." Then he turned, opened the cockpit door, and disappeared.

Nobody said a word. The only sound was the hum of the engines.

Steve sank into his leather seat and stared out the window, but all he could see on the horizon was the setting sun.

Acknowledgments

Much like the octopus in the title, this book has a lot of moving parts, but none of them would have come together if not for some remarkable humans. Barbara Peters and Robert Rosenwald, the pioneers of Poisoned Pen Press, who defied the odds to build the best mystery imprint in publishing today, thank you for inviting me into the PPP family of authors. Diane DiBiase and the entire PPP team, thanks for getting the book that was in my head onto the page, despite my many procrastinations and mistakes along the way. Everyone at Sourcebooks, thanks for welcoming me into the fold; I'm incredible excited about the next chapter.

Kathryn Maleeny, sometimes I swear you must have eight arms and three hearts just like Oscar—and Clare, Helen, and I couldn't be luckier for it. Everyone who read an early draft, your comments and feedback turned a manuscript into a book.

And to readers old and new—and booksellers everywhere—if I had enough arms, I'd hug you all.

About the Author

Tim Maleeny is the bestselling author of the award-winning Cape Weathers mysteries and the comedic thriller *Jump*, which the *Boston Globe* called "hilarious" and *Publishers Weekly* described as "a perfectly blended cocktail of escapism." His short fiction appears in several major anthologies and has won the prestigious Macavity Award for best story of the year. A former resident of San Francisco, Tim currently lives and writes at an undisclosed location in New York City, where he is working on his next novel, a screenplay, and a book for young readers. You can contact Tim or find out more about his writing at timmaleeny.com.

Photo by Joey D'Amelio